Welc[...] [...], nestled in the f[...] [...] Bitterroot Mountains, home to the strong-willed Brody family. Life isn't always easy on the Lightning Creek, but challenges are nothing new to the men and women who live and work here.

And there's something about the ranch, something in the beauty and solitude that works a kind of magic on those in need of a second shot at life...

Dear Reader,

More often than not, when I start tossing around ideas for a book, the hero comes to me first. He's a guy with a problem, and after I coax him into the story, it's my job to make things get worse before they get better. Gabe Matthews, the hero of *To Tempt a Cowgirl*, didn't fit the mold. He *had* a problem—a chaotic childhood and a serious brush with the law—but that's been taken care of, and now he's successful and happy. How am I supposed to work with a hero like that?

I need to give him a new problem.

Gabe goes to Montana to help procure the Lightning Creek Ranch in a quiet private sale as a favor to the man who helped him get his life back on track. His plan is to get to know the owner, then broach the matter of a sale. He's good at what he does and he fully expects to succeed in his mission. What he doesn't expect is to fall for the owner of the property.

Dani Brody, owner of the Lightning Creek Ranch, has trust issues. She's been betrayed by her fiancé and has no intention of getting involved with another guy anytime soon...although her new neighbor is proving to be a bit of a temptation. The closer she and Gabe get, the more she thinks he might be a guy worth taking a chance on. And then she discovers the real reason he came to Montana.

Gabe has a problem.

I hope you enjoy reading Dani and Gabe's story. I made them work for their happy ending, but they're better off because of it.

Happy reading!

Jeannie Watt
JeannieWatt.com

JEANNIE WATT

To Tempt a Cowgirl

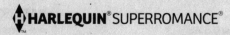

HARLEQUIN® SUPERROMANCE®

Recycling programs
for this product may
not exist in your area.

ISBN-13: 978-0-373-60916-1

To Tempt a Cowgirl

Copyright © 2015 by Jeannie Steinman

This edition published by arrangement with Harlequin Books S.A.

For questions and comments about the quality of this book,
please contact us at CustomerService@Harlequin.com.

Printed in U.S.A.

Jeannie Watt lives in the heart of a rural Nevada ranching community. When she's not at her computer writing, she collects and sews vintage clothing patterns—her latest obsession. Every now and again she and her husband slip away to San Francisco to soak up the city or run a 10K, but for the most part she enjoys living in her quiet desert setting, thinking up new ways to torture her characters before they get their happily-ever-after.

Books by Jeannie Watt

HARLEQUIN SUPERROMANCE

Other titles by this author available in ebook format.

I'd like to dedicate this book to the staff
of the Harlequin Art Department.
Thank you for all the great covers! I swear,
sometimes you guys read my mind.

CHAPTER ONE

Danica Brody stopped just inside the door of the livestock sale barn and inhaled deeply. Pine shavings, hay, damp earth and horse—heaven. Her former fiancé hadn't shared that feeling, which was why walking into this particular barn felt so damned good. She didn't have to justify her actions to a man who didn't understand her passion for horses or her need to right a wrong.

Maybe it was a good thing that Chad had been so very bad at cheating.

She bought a sale catalog, debated about coffee, then decided against it because her stomach was in a knot. Several riders circled the arena, showing off their horses' moves prior to the sale, and Dani drifted closer. Lacy J wasn't there, but she didn't expect her to be. Not unless her current owner had found someone brave enough to ride her.

"Hey, Dani!"

She turned to see her high-school friend Gina Salinas waving at her from where she stood behind a stroller a few feet away. "I'm so glad you're back," Gina said as Dani reversed course. They kept up on Facebook, but it was the first time Dani had actually seen her friend in over a year.

"I had nowhere else to go after SnowFrost closed its doors." Dani bent over the stroller to smile at the sleeping baby and was instantly charmed by his thick thatch of dark hair and amazingly long eyelashes. "He's gorgeous." Very much like his mother.

"I do good work," Gina agreed with a satisfied smile. "How long are you staying?"

Dani straightened, rolling the sale catalog in her hands. "Forever, as far as I'm concerned. Someone has to live on the ranch and feed the cows." All five of them. Sadly, the Lightning Creek was no longer a working ranch, but it was home and she was glad to be back.

"If you need a job, we'll be hiring at the café soon." Gina glanced down at her sleeping baby. "I cut back to half days to spend more time with Lucas and they're feeling the pinch."

"Thanks, but I'm going to start my own business."

Gina glanced back up. "Horse training full-time?"

"What better time that when I have a fat severance check and can live rent-free?"

"What I wouldn't give for rent-free," Gina said with a roll of her dark eyes. "But my mom just moved in with me, so I'm not complaining. Much." She smiled ruefully. "At least I have a live-in sitter and someone to share rent."

"Dani!"

She turned again, this time to find herself enveloped in a bear hug. After nearly having the breath squeezed out of her, she careful extricated herself from the blond giant's embrace. "Mac. Good to see you." She and Mac had been close friend since sharing a table in the world's most boring seventh grade science class.

Mac beamed at her before nodding a stiff hello at Gina, who smiled back tentatively.

"Hey, I'll see you later," Gina said to Dani. She smiled again at Mac, then wheeled the stroller away, disappearing into the crowd. Mac watched her go before turning his attention back to Dani. "You coming to the tavern this Friday? It's one of your last chances to see me for a while."

"Heading across the state?"

"The oil patch calls."

"If I don't, I'll make it up to you when you get back," Dani said, because she hadn't yet decided exactly what her plans were. She hadn't even planned to come to this sale until she'd heard that Lacy would be on the block. She was still unpacking and figuring out which project to tackle first on the ranch. "I assume you're here for your paint mare?"

"You aren't going to bid against me, are you?" she asked, only half-joking. Mac did love a flashy horse.

"Are you kidding? After what she did to her last owner? But I thought you might like to know that some guy has been hanging around her pen for the past half hour or so."

"Yeah?" Dani asked, her eyebrows rising as her stomach twisted a bit. "Anyone I know?"

"I don't know him." Mac gave her a dubious look. "Are you *sure* you want this mare back?"

"Yeah. I do."

She was halfway to the door leading to the holding area when he called, "You owe me a beer."

"For...?" she called back.

"General principles."

She laughed and waved, but her smile faded as soon as she started toward the pens. She was on a mission to rescue the horse she should never have sold. Her one hope was that the mare went cheaply, because the money she was about to spend should actually be going back into her business. The last thing she needed was for someone unfamiliar with the mare and her history to end up as her new owner.

GABE MATTHEWS LEANED his elbows on the round metal rails of the horse pen and surveyed the people as they walked into the holding area. So far no Danica Brody, even though he'd heard she was interested in buying the paint mare now eyeing him suspiciously across six feet of wood shavings.

Maybe he had the wrong paint mare.

Unlikely. The only other spotted horse in the entire barn was barely larger than a pony, so logic told him that the mare of interest had to be this one.

A deep voice with a distinctive country timbre came over the loudspeaker, encouraging folks to get their auction numbers if they hadn't already done so. It was close to showtime and Gabe had thought for certain that Ms. Brody would check on the mare prior to purchase. Maybe he'd gotten bad information.

He dropped his chin to study his new boots as he debated. Cut and run? Hang out a little longer?

If she didn't show, she didn't show. He wanted to meet the woman for the first time on neutral turf and this sale had seemed like the perfect opportunity, but if it didn't work out he'd figure out something else. Hell, maybe he'd buy the paint mare and Danica Brody could come to him.

"You like her?"

A feminine voice near his shoulder startled him and he turned to find himself looking into a pair of large hazel eyes set in a striking heart-shaped face.

"I do," he said, hiding his surprise in a smile. Danica Brody *had* come to him.

She gave a small shrug and placed her hands on the rail a foot or so from his, studying the horse as he, in turn, casually studied her profile. She wore a straw cowboy hat and her long wheat-colored hair was pulled back into a loose braid fastened with a silver concho.

"Are you the owner?" he asked.

"No. The owner of this particular horse should be beaten about the head and shoulders."

He laughed. "Yeah?"

She looked sideways at him, as if wondering if she should have spoken so freely. "Are you a friend of Len Olsen?"

"Can't say that I am."

"Wouldn't matter if you were, I guess," she said, looking back at the mare. "I wouldn't take back what I said." She frowned at the mare. "Do you know anything about this horse?"

"Just what's in the catalog."

"If I were you," she said, "I would steer clear of this mare. There are a lot better horses here. Horses that would suit you better."

One corner of Gabe's mouth rose in amusement. Warned off. "That's a rather bold statement, since you know nothing about me."

Danica didn't appear one bit apologetic. "I know horses and this isn't a horse I would bid on if I were you. You won't be doing anything but buying trouble. She put her last owner in the hospital."

"Is that a fact?" he asked. "Which horse would you bid on if you were I?"

She eyed him for a moment and Gabe did his best to look as if he cared about horses. Then she pulled the catalog out of her back pocket and started turning pages.

"Any of the Dunning Ranch horses are good. They have excellent foundation stock." She flipped a few more pages and pointed at a solid brown, rather boring-looking horse. "I know this gelding. He's quiet and competent."

Gabe nodded, trying not to notice just how good Danica Brody smelled as she continued to thumb through the catalog. Something spicy with a hint of floral. A nice change from the pungent smells that permeated the barn.

She looked up at him then. "Are you new to the area? Or did you drive in just for the sale?"

"New to the area," Gabe answered truthfully. "I'm at the Staley place."

"The castle?" Danica said on a laugh. "Then we're neighbors. You drive through my property to get to yours."

Gabe smiled back. "Imagine that. I'm Gabe Matthews."

"Dani," she said. "Did you buy it? The Staley place?"

"Something else I should steer clear of?"

"No. It's just that it's been empty for so long… even after it finally sold a few years ago, no one moved in and I heard a rumor it might be for sale again soon."

"Is it haunted or something?" he asked with an amused smile.

"I don't know what the deal is, but we—my sisters and I—didn't really mind when no one moved in. Less traffic across our place. More peace and quiet."

"I'm temporary," he said. "Leasing. I'm on a forced vacation and staying there for the time being."

"Forced vacation, huh?" The loudspeaker blared and Danica glanced over at the stands. "If they're clearing the arena, then I'd better get my seat." She patted the metal fence. "Good luck if you decide to bid." She almost sounded as if she meant it, but she couldn't stop herself from giving the mare one last long look.

"Same to you," Gabe said.

So why had that Gabe guy been hanging around Lacy's pen for such a long time? Mac had seen him there and he'd still been there when she arrived. And if he was on vacation, then why buy a horse?

Perhaps it was a prolonged vacation, and maybe, like Mac, he had a penchant for flashy horses. But he didn't look like a horse guy, even if he had been wearing cowboy boots. His new jeans, gray crewneck sweater and well worn leather bomber jacket had shouted *urbanite*.

Maybe he rode English.

Dani took her seat as the first horse came into the arena and when the auctioneer started his spiel, she glanced around the sea of cowboy hats to see if she could spot Gabe. She was just beginning to think she had nothing to worry about when she caught sight of him sitting a few rows down from her and to the left, a number in his hand.

Great.

If he, or anyone, bid against her today, it was only because of Lacy's color and conformation. No one would be riding the mare today, showing off her moves, because no one knew if or when she was going to explode. Thanks to Len Olsen, Lacy was a gorgeous, untrustworthy animal and Danica needed to get her back. She owed her.

"Hey, gorgeous." Mac scooted in beside her and Danica slid sideways to give him room. "I see Lacy's up fourth."

"Yes. At least it'll be over quickly." She shot a look over at Gabe, saw his number paddle shoot into the air and felt a wash of relief as he continued to bid on the palomino now spinning effortlessly on his haunches in the sale pen.

"Here to bring me luck?" Dani asked Mac.

"Why else?" But he seemed to be searching the crowd.

Dani brought her attention back to the bidding action. Gabe bid several times, then when the action got too rich, put his number back on his thigh and kept it there. Now Dani had an idea of his limit, which was unfortunately well above her own.

She closed her eyes and let out a sigh. Mac's big hand landed on the back of her neck, massaging for a moment, making her head move side to side. "It'll be okay," he said as he settled his hand back on his thigh.

But it wasn't okay. Instead of starting slowly, the bidding on Lacy took off immediately. Dani had planned to wait until the bidding slowed—not that she'd really expected it to take off—and then jump in toward the end. Instead, she sat dazed as the sale price kept rising and rising. Someone really wanted Lacy and it wasn't her new neighbor, who'd sat without moving. Dani swallowed as disappointment washed over her—she told herself that the mare would be going to a good home if someone was willing to pay that much for her. She glanced over at Gabe, saw him move his paddle, then thrust her own number high in the air. The spotter pointed at her and her competition, who sat somewhere behind her bid again. Her gut twisted.

Too rich. She just couldn't justify it. She and her sisters had just sunk a lot of money into much-needed fence repair, greatly diminishing her store of available cash. The auctioneer pointed at her questioningly as the bid stalled out. She shook her head, feeling close to tears, which was ridiculous because she didn't cry.

"Going…going…"

Mac grabbed Dani's hand and lifted it up high. Her startled gaze jerked up to his face, but he just smiled at her.

"I'm already over budget," she said, pulling her hand out of his.

"I'll loan you the rest."

The auctioneer asked for fifty dollars more. *Fifty dollars more. Now twenty-five.* He pointed over Dani's head at her competition, a questioning look on his face. No bid, but Dani still held her breath as he intoned, "G-o-ing….g-o-ing…"

Her heart was pounding. She wanted to win, but if Mac tried to force her hand up again, she was going to have to wrestle him for control or file for bankruptcy.

"Gone!"

Mac wrapped an arm around her and squeezed. "You're welcome," he murmured.

"I hope you take payments," Dani said as she got to her feet.

"And I don't even charge interest."

Dani fought a smile as they walked together to the sale office to settle the deal. Lacy J was hers once again.

FOR ONE ROTTEN MOMENT, Gabe had thought he was going to have to buy the horse. Buy it, "realize" it was too much for him and sell it at a loss to Danica Brody. She'd obviously wanted the mare badly, but had only allowed herself to go to a certain point in the bidding—at least until her friend had intervened. He lingered in his seat until he saw Danica come out of the sale office, tucking her checkbook into her jacket pocket, then followed her to the exit, where he intercepted her. Something flashed in her eyes when she saw him—recognition? Guilt? Satisfaction?

"I thought you said buying this horse is buying trouble—or was that only if I bought her," he said.

"Oh, no," she said easily. "I'm buying trouble, too. But the thing is, I know what I'm getting into."

"And you think I don't?"

"I truly doubt you know this mare like I do. We kind of grew up together."

"And then someone ruined her?"

"Something like that." She held out a hand. "No hard feelings?"

"No," he said with a half smile as he took her hand, rather enjoying the way it felt in his. Small but strong, smooth and warm. She stepped away and Gabe made his move. "Hey, since we're neighbors…I don't suppose you'd like to—"

Her expression instantly shuttered. "No," she said simply. "But thanks anyway."

DANI CROSSED THE lot to where she'd parked her truck and trailer. She'd refused to allow herself to believe she wouldn't get Lacy back, so had come prepared to haul the horse home. It would have been a lonely trip home if it hadn't been for Mac. She owed him. Owed the horse. Seemed as if she owed everyone a small debt of gratitude—even

Chad for showing his true colors before the wedding. Good of him to save her all that future heartache.

Speaking of men, her neighbor worked fast. She couldn't really blame him, though, if he was living alone in the castle. Not much to do in the isolated place and coffee with a neighbor would have probably been welcome. Of course, he might have been talking a drink or a date, but she hadn't given him a chance to offer anything. She was so not in the market right now, but he was damned good-looking with his dark hair and striking gray eyes and she'd felt a nice jolt of…something, when their fingers had touched. A corner of her mouth tilted up as she got her keys out of her pocket. Too bad Jolie wasn't here. Her sister was a sucker for smoldering hot guys. While she…she'd had enough of that for a while.

Her phone rang in her pocket and she dug it out. Allie. Her oldest sister, who'd also had enough of men for a while.

"I got her," she said as she unlocked the door to the trailer's tack room.

"For a song?"

"Uh, no. The song part didn't happen, but I got her."

"That's going to be one expensive lawn ornament, Dan."

"I—"

"Owe her. I know. And I'm looking forward to seeing her when I come for my stuff."

"Are you sure you don't want to drive over tonight? Sleep over?" Dani asked, reaching into the tack room for Lacy's old halter.

"I'd prefer not to spend the night on the ranch." Allie spoke matter-of-factly. Too matter-of-factly. Dani pressed her lips together, wishing that her sister could separate her bitterness toward her ex husband from the ranch itself.

"I understand." The silence that followed her comment stretched on just a moment too long and Dani's radar went up. "Are you okay?"

"Fine."

"What happened?" she asked flatly. She knew this tone and also knew that unless something was dreadfully wrong, Allie wouldn't share without being prodded—the burden of being the stoic older sister that their mother had depended on. "Kyle?"

"Who else? I had to threaten him with a lawyer today in order to convince him to bring back Dad's old tractor. He still insists he needs it to work around his place."

"And…"

"You know as well as I do that he doesn't need a tractor. He wants to sell it to a collector. In fact, from the way he was acting, I think he already has a buyer." Allie blew out a disgusted breath. "He actually told me that he *deserved* the tractor in return for the sweat equity he'd put into the place."

"Oh, yeah," Dani said. "He was drowning in sweat. That's why the place is falling apart."

"Exactly! I asked him why, if he'd put in so much effort, we just paid someone a boatload of money to patch up the fences and gates so the cows would stay home. He didn't have an answer to that one."

"I imagine not," Dani said.

"He is *so* pissed that he had to go back to work," Allie continued in a lower voice. "He'd never planned on working again."

Dani's former brother-in-law was openly angry that he hadn't received a share of the property in the divorce settlement, which was why he kept trying to lay claim on anything of value left on the ranch, like, say, a vintage tractor.

"Into every life," Dani said drily.

"Yeah, tell me about it," Allie said and then her voice brightened. "But, hey, I didn't call to cry on your shoulder. I called to see about Lacy. I'm glad you got her."

"She's changed," Dani said.

Allie gave a soft snort. "Haven't we all? Even Mel."

"No kidding," Dani said with a wry smile. Their ultra-driven sister had finally stopped dealing with her demons by never slowing down and had settled on a remote ranch in New Mexico with her new husband. "I need to call her, too. Tell her the news."

"That reminds me—Mom phoned late last night. They're heading off to the Great White North to fish. We shouldn't expect to hear from her for a while."

"Mom the world traveler." And she deserved it. After more than a decade of living lean in order to raise the girls on the Lightning Creek Ranch as her late husband had asked, she'd remarried and was living comfortably in Florida. "I hate to cut this short," Dani said, "but I need to load Lacy while there are still some people around to help if I have trouble."

"Be careful," Allie warned in a serious voice. "I'd like you to be in one piece when I see you tomorrow."

"Will do." Dani ended the call and dropped the phone back into her pocket. As she started for Lacy's pen, she saw someone loitering nearby, then stifled a groan as she realized just who it was. Marti Kendall. Petite, toned and tanned, dressed in slim-fitting Wranglers and a studded black T-shirt, she looked like she'd stepped out of a Western fashion ad in *Horse & Rider*.

"Hey, Marti," Dani said as she opened the gate to Lacy's pen, "was that you bidding against me?"

"No," Marti said with a light laugh, brushing back a hank of her beautifully streaked light brown hair. "I have more than enough horses to deal with. The last thing I need is a crazy one." She leaned her arms on the rails, fixing Dani with a candid look. "So is it true what I've heard?"

"Depends on just what that was," Dani said, coiling the halter rope. Marti had been a couple of years behind her in school and the undisputed queen of her class—no, make that of Eagle Valley High. The aura still clung to her, making it difficult for Dani to warm up to the woman. What made Marti so certain that she was a cut above everyone else, other than her perfect looks and amazing horse skills?

"That you've come home to start training for a living? Just like me and Dad?" she asked brightly.

"Seems like a good time to do it."

"Wow. I hope you've done your research." She spoke with a note of concern that didn't fool Dani one bit. "You know that the market is fairly saturated here."

"I'll take my chances," Dani said, trying to infuse some sweetness into her dead tone.

"I guess what I'm saying is, since you're just starting out, don't be surprised if you can't get enough work to make ends meet. Dad and I are kind of the go-to trainers in the region." She flashed her very perfect teeth. "But you know that."

"Why," Dani asked slowly, "would you care if I made ends meet?"

Marti seemed surprised by the question. "Because I'd hate to see you fail."

Yeah. Right. And I have this bridge...

"I'll be fine," Dani said. "Thanks for your concern."

"Well, good luck." Marti patted the side of Lacy's pen, the silver bangles on her arm jingling as she moved. She started for the door, then stopped and turned back. "Since you're here, can I sign you up for an Eagle Valley Days committee? We have a lot of last-minute details to work out."

"I need to work out a schedule before I commit. I may not have time."

"Oh...and Chad's family is pretty heavily involved. I understand." She sounded as if she actually did understand as she expertly delivered the Chad jab. "But if you change your mind, give a call. We're in the book."

"I'm sure I can find your number."

"Just look under 'horse training' in the Yellow Pages," Marti said with another bright smile. "I think we're the first entry."

"SHOT DOWN. HOW UNUSUAL."

Gabe smirked at his assistant, hoping the full effect came across on the FaceTime phone connection, even though Serena Anderson Widmeyer was impervious to both his charm and his temper.

"I'm not trying to date her. I'm trying to get to know her. Make friends." Then offer her a fair price for a piece of land he needed. He had it on good authority that there were stability issues on the Lightning Creek Ranch and that it had come close to being put on the market a few months ago. He planned to capitalize on that instability as soon as possible.

"Hard to do if she shuts you down," Serena said with a wicked smile that came through clearly, even though she had the airport terminal window at her back.

"You're a rotten assistant."

"That's what happens when you hire the boss's family."

"You aren't family," he muttered.

"I was at one time," she reminded him with a serene smile.

And then she'd come to her senses. She and his best friend, Neal Widmeyer, had been ridiculously unhappy in their marriage, but after the divorce, both had continued to work for Widmeyer Enterprises in different departments. Oddly, they now seemed to like each other much better than when they were married. Good thing, because Stewart Widmeyer did not take well to dissension in the ranks.

"What do you think of the place?" she asked.

"Potential. A lot of potential." Nestled against a mountain with a fishing stream running through it and within shuttle distance of a ski resort, it was a gem of a property, nicely protected from the rest of the valley by Lightning Creek Ranch acreage.

"Enough to compete with Timberline?" Timberline was the resort on the opposite side of the valley that Stewart's former partner had essentially stolen before parting ways with Widmeyer Enterprises.

"I think so. Eventually," Gabe said. But they needed more land, first to insulate the proposed resort from the possibility of encroaching housing developments and, more important, to make a world-class golf course. Timberline didn't have a golf course and had no hope of procuring the acreage at this point in the game.

That was Stewart's trump card.

He planned to make a bigger, better, more exclusive resort than Timberline, steal Timberline clientele and make his duplicitous partner, Mark Jeffries, pay. The trick was keeping the plans under wraps while Gabe investigated the possibility of buying the Lightning Creek. If anyone associated with Timberline figured out that Widmeyer Enterprises was looking at property, land prices would go up astronomically. That was where Gabe came in. Jeffries, of course, knew all the family members who worked for Widmeyer. He didn't know Gabe, who acted as an independent consultant. His name was on no company rosters—he was identified only as Process Resources, Inc. He was nameless and faceless, and was thus able to lease the Staley property with no fear of word leaking out. He'd even drummed up a few side contracts so that he had something to do while he "vacationed" in his new house.

"They just called my flight," Serena said, "which means you have to do without me for the next two weeks because I'm turning off my phone."

"Right."

"No, really. I'm doing it."

"I'll expect you to call for an update tomorrow."

Serena made a rude noise. "Won't happen. Good luck with Ms. Brody," she said. "Gotta go."

"What if I need you?" he asked, just to be a dick.

Serena made a face and then the screen went blank. Gabe smiled to himself as he set the phone down on the table.

Good luck with Ms. Brody. He was going to need it.

Temporarily moving to Montana from his home base in Bloomington, Illinois, getting to know Danica Brody and then introducing the idea of a sale had seemed a logical approach, but now that he'd met Dani, he sensed that he'd have to move carefully. Take his time, collect information. Refrain from pushing too hard and spooking her.

He could play it that way. And in the meantime...

Yes. In the meantime.

Gabe strode through the house, paused and looked out the window at the spectacular view, then walked back into the living room and unrolled a map. His side contract was a simple project designing a small park for a town in Idaho. He'd put in a low bid just to get something to work on and now he didn't feel like working on it. For the next few days, until the service providers had time to work him into their schedules, he had no internet, no TV. No company. He wasn't one for big gatherings and a lot of social interaction, but he wouldn't mind hearing the sound of a human voice, either.

When was the last time he'd been lonely? Or ever considered the possibility of being lonely?

After an hour of staring at his project and listening to music on his phone, Gabe finally walked out of the house and headed for his car. If nothing else, he'd go eat somewhere, soak up some local atmosphere.

An hour later he had to concede defeat. Atmosphere soaking had not gone well. He'd hit a small tavern that served food, ate a steak dinner by himself, then wandered into the bar for a drink. Obviously McElroy's was a very local establishment, since no one tried to make conversation with him, with the exception of the bartender, and that was duty talk.

Gabe didn't mind. He conversed with the bartender until he finished his lone beer, then tipped the guy decently and hit the road back home again. He'd learned nothing of value, but he'd made the guy laugh a few times and considered that a decent inroad.

On the drive home, he was debating about the best way to make contact with Danica Brody without getting shot down again, when he rounded a corner and something white and large—no, huge—appeared in the road in front of him. He jerked the steering wheel to the right and mud flew as the tires spun, then caught, yanking the car sideways and slamming it into the ditch. Gabe's forehead smacked the steering wheel and then he slumped back into his seat, checking his forehead for blood. His hand came away clean and he dropped it into his lap.

Well, shit.

Gabe let out a long breath, shoved the door open and got out to assess damage. In the distance, he could hear the hollow thud of hooves on the hard-packed road.

A horse.

A black-and-white horse.

And Gabe was pretty darned certain he knew where to find the owner.

CHAPTER TWO

GABE WALKED ACROSS the field toward the lights of the Lighting Creek Ranch, hunching his shoulders against the wind. The distance was deceptive and what he'd thought was at the most a ten-minute walk through the tall grass took well over twenty, but finally he climbed through the fence onto the driveway and made his way to the house.

Deep booming barks followed his knock on the front door and a few seconds later Dani glanced through the window, frowning as she realized who was on the porch. Instead of pulling the door open, she cracked it a few inches, hushing the giant dog behind her as she did so. She did not look happy at seeing him on her porch.

"I almost hit a horse with my car. I think it was the one you just bought."

The color drained from her face. "Are you sure?"

"It happened fast, but yeah."

Without another word, Dani grabbed a coat and stepped outside, shutting the door before the dog got out. She brushed past Gabe, taking the porch steps two at a time, her golden-brown braid bouncing on her back.

Gabe followed her across the driveway to the corrals attached to one side of the barn. Once there she pulled a small flashlight from her pocket and snapped it on, sweeping the light through the enclosure not once, but twice, as if she could possibly miss something as large as a horse. The corral was most definitely empty.

"How did she get out?" Gabe asked.

Dani shook her head as she reached out to rattle the closed gate. The latch held firm. "I don't know, but I have to find her before someone hits her." She hurried back across the drive, head down against the wind.

"Where's your car?" she asked.

"It's in the ditch."

Dani stopped. "Is it damaged?" she asked on a startled note.

"I don't know."

"We can use the tractor to pull it out just as soon as I find the mare."

"I'll get a tow truck."

"I can't afford a tow truck. I'm on a tight budget," she said as she once again made a beeline to the house. Gabe had to trot to keep up with her.

"I'll pay for it."

"Why would you do that when I can just pull you out?"

Gabe shook his head, then followed. Where he came from, women didn't pull cars out of

ditches with tractors. Nor did guys. They called
tow trucks, as he was going to do.

"Which way did she run?"

"I was kind of busy hitting the ditch after she
charged me, so I'm not certain."

"Think, please." She stopped again, tilting her
chin to look up at him impatiently.

Gabe reminded himself that he was here for
diplomatic reasons and couldn't afford to lose his
temper any more than he already had. "I think…
she went toward my place."

"Good. Let's go."

Gabe didn't question the "let's." He simply fell
into step and then when she jerked her head to the
passenger side of the ugliest truck he'd ever seen,
he wrenched open the door and got inside. A cloud
of dust rose from the seat cover as he sat, then he
shifted on the seat to move the deadly-looking
piece of curved metal digging into his thigh.

"Hay hook. Just toss it on the floor."

Dani put the truck in gear and it jerked forward, groaning as she shifted it into a higher gear.
She swung the wheel hard, turning the truck in a
tight U and Gabe bounced sideways in his seat,
dust rising once again. "Damn, I hope she went
your way."

So did he. He wanted Danica to recapture her
horse and he wanted his freaking car out of the
ditch. If he hadn't left his phone in the car, he'd
be seeing about it right now.

THIS WAS A NIGHTMARE, plain and simple. She'd just gotten Lacy back and now she was gone again. More than that, if the mare hadn't gone to Gabe's place, she was a menace to traffic. She could easily lose her horse and get sued in one fell swoop.

"We'll find her," Gabe said from beside her, keying in on her thoughts. It'd be pretty hard not to know what she was thinking, hunched over the steering wheel like a crazed woman.

She turned down the drive to the castle, slowing as they passed his car, which was a good five feet off the road. It looked very expensive—the kind that needed parts special-ordered—but she wasn't going to worry about that now.

"I see tracks," Gabe said, pointing at the road.

Sure enough, there were U-shaped divots that the horse had brought up out of the road as she'd cantered toward his place. Great. Now all she had to do was hope that the mare was still at his place and hadn't taken off cross-country.

"This horse means a lot to you," Gabe commented.

"She was my 4-H project. I raised her, trained her with my dad's help, won a lot of money on her, then sold her to help pay for college. All part of the plan I'd made with my dad before he died. The ass-hat that bought her abused her with big bits and spurs."

"That stinks."

"It hurt. Lacy trusted me. She was a fantastic

roping horse. Before…" Dani spoke without looking at Gabe, then slowed the truck to a stop and got out. Gabe followed and as soon as the truck door banged shut, they stood together in the darkness, looking, listening.

"There she is."

Dani turned in the direction Gabe was pointing and saw the pale outline of the mare standing in the shadows behind the large stone, cedar and glass house. "Stay here," she said. "Block the gate if she tries to leave."

"Sure thing," Gabe said.

"Easy, baby," Danica said, slowly approaching the shaking horse. Lacy snorted and stomped a foot. Dani stopped instantly and took a step back. The horse rolled her eyes, but stayed put.

"Easy," she cooed as she slowly approached the horse, stopping and taking a half step back whenever the mare looked as if she was going to bolt. Finally she reached out and rubbed the mare's lower neck, then slipped the rope around it. As soon as the rope touched her, the mare stilled.

Dani bit her lip and eased the halter over the mare's nose. Lacy's head jerked up but Dani held tight to the rope, tried again once her nose came down and this time managed to fasten the halter. Her shoulders sagged with relief and she sent Gabe a weary look that she doubted he saw through the darkness.

"Well done," he said.

"Yeah." She continued to stroke the mare's neck, crooning at her under her breath. "You don't have a lot of light around here," she commented, wanting to check the mare for injuries.

"Apparently the yard lights are all dead. I'll have to see about getting the bulbs replaced. I've only been here a couple of nights and haven't had time to call a service guy about it."

"Service guy?"

"I don't seem to have a ladder that tall," he said.

"I'll lend you one," she said, patting the mare soothingly. "And we'll see about getting your car back on the road."

"I'll get a tow truck." He seemed to mean it.

"Suit yourself," she said.

"Nothing personal. It's just that my insurance will cover a tow. It probably won't cover you ripping my rear axle off with a tractor."

Dani didn't know whether to laugh or be insulted. Regardless, she was responsible for whatever happed with his vehicle and told him so.

"Let's cross that bridge when we come to it. Right now we need to focus on getting the horse home. Do you want me to help you get your trailer?"

She shook her head. "I'll just lead her home."

"Home is a good mile away."

She shrugged.

"It's dark."

"I have a flashlight."

"How about I come with you?"

Again she shook her head. "I've put you through enough tonight. I'll be back in the morning for the truck if you don't mind if I leave it here."

"Why would I mind?" he asked innocently.

DANI ARRIVED AT Gabe Matthews's driveway early the next morning just as a tow truck pulled out, a sports car attached to the towline. How much was this going to cost her? It'd looked as if the car had simply ended up in the grassy ditch last night when she'd walked by leading Lacy, but knowing her luck, the frame was now bent, or some chunk of special German-made chrome needed to be replaced.

Well, such was life.

But why was life always this way when money was tight? When she was trying to live on a shoe-string budget as she started her dream business... the one that Marti Kendall had pretty much told her was doomed.

Yeah, we'll see about that, Marti.

Jingling the keys in her sweatshirt pocket, she continued down the driveway. Worrying didn't do a lick of good. All she could do was focus on the positives, and there were positives. She had a place to start her business; a place where she could live rent-free.

After she and Jolie had talked Allie and Mel out of instantly selling the ranch following Allie's divorce, the sisters had agreed that as long as one of them wanted to live on the place, they would keep it. If Dani and Jolie didn't want to live on the place, they would revisit the idea of a sale. Dani didn't see that happening. Her father had once told her that he didn't regret not having a lot of money because he had something better—a life that made him glad to get up in the morning. That was what Dani wanted. In a way she was lucky that her company had folded when it did. It gave her the kick in the butt she needed to start living a life that made her glad to get up in the morning.

She walked over the cattle guard at the Staley gate and paused for a moment, studying the house. It'd literally been years since she'd been close to the house, but it looked better than ever. Even though no had lived in it for the past year or so, the windows sparkled in the early-morning sun, the cedar appeared freshly oiled and the lawn was green and manicured. The Staleys had paid a pretty penny to keep the place they'd grown tired of maintained as they'd waited—and waited—for a buyer. Apparently they still hadn't found one if Gabe's company was only leasing.

She'd decided against checking in with Gabe before leaving in the truck. It was early—barely after sunrise—and she imagined a guy on vacation would want to sleep in. She'd just started for her beat-up vehicle when a voice behind her made her jump.

She turned to see Gabe standing on the porch, wearing jeans and a gray-and-black plaid shirt, half-buttoned, with the tails hanging out. His dark hair was still rumpled from sleep, his feet were bare and he wore glasses. Dark horn-rimmed glasses that made him look like a sexy scientist. "You're here early," he said, running a hand over the back of his head.

"My sister is coming later this morning."

"She could have given you a ride." He walked down the damp stone steps. Dani pulled her eyes away from his bare feet and fixed them back onto his face.

"I like walking."

"I noticed. How's the mare?"

"I put her in a stall in the barn. As far as I know, she's still there." She took a few steps closer, turning the keys over in her hands. "I saw your car... leave."

"It's a company car, so I figured it'd be best to have it checked out."

"What company?"

"I doubt you've heard of it," he said with a half smile. "I'm a consultant for a company that designs parks and gardens for towns and universities."

"Does the company have a name?"

One of his eyebrows lifted slightly at the question. "Gabe Matthews, Consultant, LLC."

"You're forcing *yourself* into a vacation?"

"It was either that or a heart attack."

"Do you have other employees?"

"I contract my help for the most part."

Which only brought more questions to mind, but Dani forced herself to step back. Her neighbor's business had nothing to do with her. "Well, let me know what the damages to your car are."

"Danica, I don't quite know how to break this to you, but you're not paying."

"I'm not?" The words came out on a note of challenge.

"That's what insurance is for."

"What about the deductible?"

"My company has a top-notch insurance policy. Low deductible." He stepped onto the purplish flagstones. "I'll tell you what you can do."

"What's that?" she asked, her eyes never leaving his. They were the most amazing stormy gray, and looked even grayer because of the shirt he was wearing.

"You can give me a ride to town when I get the call to pick it up."

"I could do that," Dani agreed. "And maybe even buy you lunch." It seemed the least she could do. Then maybe she could get answers to the questions she probably shouldn't be wondering about in the first place.

"Or dinner. My treat," Gabe said.

"That isn't exactly me buying you lunch."

"You can buy a drink later."

Dani shook her head. "Lunch."

"I'm not hitting on you," he said on a note of amused exasperation.

"You're not?" she asked, cocking an eyebrow.

He smiled crookedly. "Maybe a little, but in a neighborly sort of way."

And maybe that was a bit flattering, but Dani shifted into retreat mode. She still had some Chad issues to work through before diving back into the dating—or even the quick-drink—pool. "I don't know you and I don't go out with guys I don't know."

"How do we get to know each other?"

"I guess we go to lunch." Because that was as far as she'd let things go, even if he was the best-looking guy she'd seen in forever.

"Lunch it is."

Okay. Dani Brody truly was skittish. He had to take care not to appear to be hitting on her, but he had to admit, it was a bit difficult when everything in him reacted to her in a positive way. A very positive way. It didn't help that she looked pretty damned delectable wearing jeans she probably hadn't expected to be seen in since she'd arrived so damned early. Form-fitting, well-worn, frayed holes at the knees…he blew out a short breath, shaking his head as he watched her ass while she stepped up into the truck. Yeah, the woman could wear jeans.

She started the engine and with a quick wave swung the vehicle into a circle and drove past him. The old truck groaned as she shifted gears, and not because she was bad with a clutch. No, this was more of a transmission-on-its-last-legs groan. Well, when she sold the ranch to Widmeyer, she'd have plenty of money for transmissions. She could buy property elsewhere and set herself up in style. New house, new truck. Big barn. Just without quite as much acreage as she had now.

He went back into the house and almost turned around and went back out again. He'd been rattling around alone inside of the elegant box for three days and now, without the car, he had no means of escape. Granted, he had work to do, but he preferred to work in the evenings, losing himself in his plans until somewhere along the line he realized it was early morning and he needed to go to bed. That was what had happened last night and it'd only been a fluke that he'd woken up and glanced out the huge window next to his bed to see Dani walking down the drive.

He reached into his pocket and pulled out his phone. When his friend Neal Widmeyer answered he said simply, "I'm going to need more to work on while I'm here to keep from going stir-crazy. Have anything you can send my way?"

"Not at the moment," his friend said. "Go mingle with the locals."

"I have no wheels." Briefly he gave a rundown of what had happened and then Neal laughed.

"Sounds like you have your pretty neighbor right where you want her—beholden to you for not suing."

"True," Gabe said. "But she's not very friendly." Actually that wasn't totally true. She was friendly, but only superficially so. She had barriers that Gabe was going to have to work around.

"I know charm is not your strong suit, but you'll have to see what you can do. Push the envelope."

"What are you talking about? I'm charming." Gabe settled his hip against the black granite countertop, staring across the room at the state-of-the-art stainless-steel range and cooktop. Maybe he could take up cooking.

"No. You have money. There's a difference."

"You're saying woman only like me because of my money?"

"Pretty much."

"Bullshit. They like me because of my… Never mind."

"Dream on," Neal laughed. "Anyway, I'm glad you're getting to know Ms. Brody. I've never seen Dad so determined to bring in a project."

"Probably because he's never been bent over and so thoroughly screwed by someone he trusted." Gabe crossed to the front door and stepped outside to look out across the fields at the Lightning

Creek Ranch. He could just see the rooftops of the two barns between the tall poplar trees. "Let him know that I'm doing my best to help him rectify matters."

"Can you hurry?" Neal was only half-kidding.

Gabe gave a soft snort. "I don't think this is a hurrying situation." And even though Stewart was showing uncharacteristic signs of impatience, Gabe intended to approach the matter methodically, just as Stewart had taught him.

"You're right. Best not to hurry and screw things up further." He cleared his throat, then asked, "Did you hear from Serena?"

"Off on her vacation and she swears she won't check in."

"Right. Well, when she doesn't check in, will you have her call me?"

"Uh, sure." Gabe wondered why Neal didn't simply call her himself, but decided against asking questions. At least not at this point in time.

"Thanks. If I find any work, I'll send it, and in the meantime I know Dad's fine with you picking up contracts."

"Easier said than done."

"Not with your charm."

Gabe hung up and smiled. When he and Neal had first met, neither had seen their friendship lasting so long. Why would they have? They'd had nothing in common except for being forced to work at the same youth center during the summer before their freshman year. Neal had been there because his father had wanted him to see how the other half lived and Gabe because his youth probation officer had thought it was a good idea. Meanwhile, Gabe's best friend, Sam Cody, had been enjoying all summer had to offer. Gabe had been pissed and Neal had been doing his best to rebel against Stewart—while still showing up for work on time.

Gabe's lips twisted on the memory. Oh, yeah, Neal had been quite the rebel.

At first Gabe had tolerated Neal hanging with him—the kid had money and money was handy—but eventually he'd come to trust Neal as much as he was able to trust anyone. Considered him as much of a friend as Sam, even though he never let the two of them hook up for any length of time. Sam didn't understand Neal. Sam wanted to work him, exploit the rich kid. Gabe hadn't allowed that to happen. He felt protective of Neal and, in a weird way, he'd learned something about life from the kid. Living with a foster family more concerned with getting a monthly stipend than actually parenting the moody teenage boy in their care, Gabe had done whatever he pleased in his off hours, while Neal had curfews and responsibilities. He couldn't stay out all night. He had to study. He had dreams and aspirations that seemed

very exotic and out of reach to Gabe. College.
Grad school. A retirement plan.

Things Gabe never thought he'd have, but did,
thanks to Stewart Widmeyer.

CHAPTER THREE

"I HAVE NO idea how Lacy got out," Dani said as she helped Allie fold her winter clothes and put them in a plastic bin to haul off to school in Idaho. "Unless she dropped to her belly and crawled out under the bottom rail. The gate was latched. There wasn't enough room to get a running start to jump. I'm mystified."

"You're just lucky she went to the neighbor's instead of heading for the county road." Allie held up a sweater, grimaced and put it back down again. "I can't face this one. Want it?"

"No. And I'm aware I'm lucky," Dani said drily. The donation pile was about five times larger than the folded clothing in the plastic bin.

"Do you think someone let her out?" Allie asked just a little casually as she folded a sweat-shirt and put it into the bin.

"*Why* would someone let her out?" Dani asked, shocked at the question.

"No idea. It seems about as realistic as her crawling under the fence or jumping over it from a standstill."

"Gus did go a little nuts just before I got into the shower yesterday." The Pyrenees-border-collie mix raised his black-and-white head at the sound of his name, then laid it back down on his paws with a heavy sigh. Gus wasn't exactly a ball of energy unless he was chasing a bunny, his chosen prey.

Allie stopped folding. "I don't like this."

"You aren't talking about the sweatshirt, are you?"

"No."

"Did you have trouble with…intruders when you lived here?" Dani asked reasonably, shaking open a black plastic bag.

"I had trouble named Kyle," her sister retorted bitterly.

It took Dani a second to realize what her sister was getting at. "You think Kyle let the mare out?"

"Last time we talked he was pretty angry."

"Why would he do something like that?"

"Because I taunted him about the fences and gates?"

Dani let out a sigh. "Kyle isn't responsible for everything bad that happens here."

"But he is responsible for a lot of it and if we sold the place, we wouldn't have to put up with him." Allie sat down on the edge of the bed, her expression intense as she said, "You shouldn't have to deal with him alone while I'm at school."

"I don't think I'll be dealing with him once he brings that tractor back." Which he'd grudgingly promised to do the next day.

Dani sat down next to Allie, bunching the T-shirt she held into a loose ball. "I don't want to sell."

"Dad died here."

"And sometimes I feel like he's here with me," Dani said as she started stuffing clothing into the bag.

Allie simply pressed her lips together and shook her head. "You don't remember the bad times like I do."

"Yeah. I do. But they affected me differently. I see them as something we got through."

"And then I started them all over again by bringing my husband here."

"You know...we all liked Kyle. A lot." Allie glared at her. "In the beginning," Dani amended. "What I'm trying to say is that we were all taken in by him."

"Yeah." Allie popped the lid onto the box. "But you didn't spend as much time with him as I did. I dated him for two years and still didn't see the real guy. I believed in him. Made excuses for him while he ran this place into the ground."

"Would selling it honestly make you feel better? Or just make it so that you never had to come back here and be reminded of the past."

"Does it really matter which?"

"I wish the place didn't make you so unhappy."

"I made a mistake moving back here. We should have gotten our own place. Then we could have sold, I could have paid the bastard off and he'd have left us all alone." Allie gave Dani a weary look as they walked downstairs together, Allie carrying the box and Dani dragging the heavy bag. "I won't make noise about selling the Lightning Creek as long as you and Jolie are happy here, but the instant things start to go sour, I say we slap this place on the market."

"Jolie and I are in total agreement. We just want a chance to make a go of it."

"And I don't begrudge you that." Allie opened the back hatch of the Subaru Forester and shoved her box in before turning to reach for the bag.

"I can take it to the donation box if you want," Dani offered.

"No. I want the satisfaction of kissing my old life goodbye." She hefted the bag and shoved it into the crowded cargo space, jamming it on top of the boxes.

"Have at it."

Allie hugged her with one arm before heading to the driver's side of the car. "Who knows," she called over her shoulder, "maybe the ranch will treat you better than it treated me."

"Mel did okay here."

"She was only here for a short time."

"Don't make me feel guilty about loving the place," Dani said with a hint of frustration. She hated having this wedge between them.

Allie raised a hand. "You're absolved from

guilt. I'm off to make a new life in Idaho. But—"
her voice became stern as she said "—if you suspect Kyle is doing anything, anything at all—"

"I'll call the authorities."

"Promise."

"Scout's honor." Although she was pretty certain that this wasn't a promise she'd have to keep.

A few moments later, Dani watched her sister drive away. Maybe after a semester of college, Allie would start to feel more in control of her life and better about the ranch. Maybe Kyle would back off.

Regardless, Dani would not allow herself to feel guilty about insisting that they keep the Lightning Creek. In a way, she felt as if she was helping Allie dodge a bullet. Cash was good. But land was forever.

THE CALL FROM the garage came sooner than Gabe expected, just after noon, when he was thinking about taking a run to work off some of his nervous energy. The car was fine with the exception of the cracked headlight, now fixed. If he wanted, they could send someone out to pick him up.

"No. I have a ride."

Gabe hung up and proceeded to call his ride, who answered her phone almost instantly. Gabe found himself smiling at her husky *hello*. Damn, but he was beginning to love this woman's voice. It resonated, stirring something deep inside of him. Something that made him halfway wish he could get to know her for real—and how long had it been since he'd felt like that?

Too long, probably.

"I've just gotten a call from the garage."

"And?" He could hear instant stress in her voice.

"No problems."

"Not one?" she asked suspiciously.

"Cracked headlight, but it was cracked before the accident." A white lie wouldn't hurt. "They offered me a ride, but I wanted to take you up on your lunch offer. If you'd rather not, I'll call them back."

"No. I owe you lunch."

"And I'm taking you up on it." When she didn't say anything, he added, "It's not easy being the new kid on the block."

"And not working while on vacation?"

"Uh...yes. Exactly," he said, surprised.

"I'll be right over."

"No hurry."

"Now is good," she said in a tone that made him think she wanted to get this over with as soon as possible. That wasn't exactly the way he'd hoped she'd approach lunch together, but he'd work with it, see what kind of foundation he could lay.

He dragged off the comfy long-sleeved T-shirt over his head and pulled an ironed shirt out of the closet before changing into his clean jeans.

There'd once been a time when all he'd owned were T-shirts and ratty jeans and he'd been okay with that—until he figured out that people judged you by what you wore and treated you accordingly.

Dani showed up fifteen minutes later and he was glad to see she was driving the newer truck she'd had hitched to the horse trailer at the sale, rather than the one that threatened dust poisoning.

"Do you want to eat first, before we pick up my car?" he asked as he got into the passenger seat.

"That'd probably be easiest," Dani agreed without looking at him.

Gabe settled back into his seat, telling himself that all things took time. He couldn't risk pushing matters.

"Any ideas where to eat?" he asked.

"That all depends if you prefer Mexican or burgers."

"If I prefer burgers are you taking me to a drive-in?"

"No. A café with booths," she said. "Red vinyl."

"It doesn't get any better than that."

She smiled politely and started the truck. Ten minutes later she parked in front of a building that had obviously once been a gas station. He held the door for her and a woman in a classic pink waitress's uniform pointed them to a booth in the corner. The menus were waiting at the table, but Dani made no move to look at hers.

"There's only one thing to get here—The Works."

"I always make it a point of trusting those that know," he said, stashing the menu back behind the napkin holder.

"An excellent practice," she said, sipping her water. The waitress started toward them but stopped when Dani held up two fingers. "I hope you don't mind Coke," she said. "It's either that or orange soda."

"Coke is fine," he said reaching for his own water. "Quite the ordering system you have here."

"Saves time."

"Looking to get away fast?" he couldn't help asking.

"Oh, no," Dani replied, looking vaguely guilty. "It's just that…" She fought with herself for a moment, then one corner of her mouth twisted a little before she said, "To be honest, I was engaged to be married until a little over a month ago. I'm not looking for, well…anything."

"Not even friendship?"

She frowned as she studied him, as if debating whether or not that was possible. "Friendship is fine," she finally said. "But I make friends slowly."

"Warning me off again?"

"I'm a believer in full disclosure," she said, her hazel gaze meeting his candidly. "I like to know where I stand and I assume other people are the same."

"I agree."

Dani leaned back as the waitress set two Cokes on the table, waiting until the woman walked away before saying, "Please understand that I'm not saying we won't become friends. It's just—"

"Full disclosure. I get it."

"Thanks." She pushed the napkin-wrapped flatware aside so that she could rest her elbows on the table. "How is it that you came to vacation at the Staley house?"

He gave a casual shrug. "I wanted to...disappear, I guess—somewhere in Montana—and I found the place through a private company that specializes in leasing executive homes."

"Oh." She gave a considering nod. "I always thought of the Staley house as more of a big-ass mansion than an executive home."

Gabe smiled. "It is huge. I rattle around in it, but the windows are big and the light is great."

"You'll have to give me a tour before you leave. I've lived next door, endured their traffic while growing up, but have never been in the place."

"Sure," Gabe said, pleased that she was talking about seeing him again sometime in the future. "Does the traffic across your place bother you?"

She shook her head. "Not recently, because no one has lived there, but when the Staleys were in residence, yeah. The road is just a little too close to the house. Dad used to cuss out Granddad for granting the original owners access across our property, but there wasn't much he could do about it."

"Shame," he said, sipping his Coke. And interesting. He waited until the food came before he asked her what she did for a living.

"Until recently I worked in marketing at a winter equipment wholesaler, but they went out of business, so I decided to move home and try my luck at training horses."

"You can make a living training horses?" Gabe asked.

"I'm going to try. It's the perfect time. I have a little severance pay to invest in my business and we own the ranch outright."

"Those are good circumstances," he agreed.

"My sister Jolie might join me after she gets done with graduate school. She's doing an internship right now at a big experimental farm in southern Idaho."

"She trains, too?" This was looking worse and worse, but the more he knew, the more he could plan how to approach this matter.

"She's a barrel racer. She puts on clinics, but I prefer working with horses to people."

"Why?"

She smiled. "Horses," she said, tapping her spoon on the table, "are logical. People are not."

"I'm logical." A characteristic he'd ignored until he started college and discovered that there was comfort and security in step-by-step processes—

a welcome change from his former scattershot approach to life and the resulting chaos. He'd reached the point where he couldn't imagine operating any other way…or perhaps he was afraid to, afraid he'd lose everything he'd worked for if he went back to shooting from the hip.

"To a point. But if a horse does something, it's the result of a stimulus, either current or remembered. The right stimulus will produce the right result. Progress may be slow, but if you take your time—" she shrugged her shoulders "—you're usually successful. People, on the other hand… people have agendas."

He shifted slightly. "Are you saying all horses behave logically?"

"Oh, no. Sometime horses are too traumatized to overcome their flight responses. They short-circuit."

"And are no longer logical." He wondered if she was talking about the paint mare she'd just bought.

"They would be if they could overcome the fear factor."

"Maybe people are the same."

"They are," she agreed in a halfhearted way that made him wonder if she was thinking about her own recent past.

"Do you prefer horses to people, Dani Brody?"

She gave a slow considering nod. "Yes. A lot of the time I do."

THERE WAS SOMETHING about Gabe Matthews that drew in Dani, made her want to know him better. Perhaps even trust him. Maybe it was that behind his easy charm, she sensed that he was as guarded as she was. That he had his secrets and his vulnerabilities, just as she did.

Once upon a time she hadn't been guarded, or even all that vulnerable, despite the knocks life had sent her way. Nor had Allie—at least not in the way she was now. But look at the two of them today, ready to believe that anyone who was friendly or showed the slightest inclination toward pursuing an acquaintanceship had an agenda. She wasn't as bad as Allie, but she now had barriers where there hadn't been any prior to her experience with Chad the Liar.

Was this how she wanted to live?

A small voice told her that this was the way she had to live until she got a handle on what Chad had done to her. He'd betrayed her, made her feel stupid for trusting him, made her lose faith in her own judgment. She hated that.

After dropping off Gabe, Dani stopped at the mailbox, then turned into the driveway leading to the house. She was almost to the cattle guard when she stepped on the brake and leaned forward over the steering wheel to peer out the windshield.

"What the hell?" she muttered as she got out of the idling truck and walked over to the edge of a huge stream of water flowing from the edge of the lawn across the driveway to the barn. The white plastic standpipe had been snapped at the base. Dani bit back another curse as she saw a second river flowing behind the barn.

"Son of a bitch," she said, as she approached river number two. That standpipe was also snapped. What had happened and, more important, where was the water main?

She hadn't a clue and had no idea where to start looking.

A few minutes later she stalked back to her idling truck, pausing for a moment before she got in to check the driveway for tire tracks and footprints. Nothing.

A fluke. This had to be a fluke.

She put the truck in gear and parked it a few yards from the water flow before heading to the house, where Gus was barking, demanding to be let out. He galloped out, heading straight to the flowing water when she opened the door. Dani followed, taking her phone out of her pocket and holding it for a moment as she debated. She had to call Allie and if she didn't know where the water main was located, then she had to get Kyle's number. No way around that, even though she was going to get another earful about bad ranch karma. Not to be helped. She punched her sister's number into the phone, got the out-of-range recording.

Great. She pressed her lips together for a moment. Mac was working halfway across the state, Gina had babies to tend to. With a sigh, she called her sister again, left a message telling her she needed Kyle's cell number, then, after ending the call, she hit the number of the closest able-bodied guy in the area. Gabe.

"Hey, this is Dani Brody," she said when he answered. "Are you busy?"

"Not really."

"Are you handy with plumbing tools?"

There was the briefest hesitation before he said, "I don't think I have any lying around."

"I have the tools. I just need some muscle and know-how."

"Be right over."

WATER WAS FLOWING across the driveway when Gabe drove in.

"We need to shut off the main," he said as soon as he got out of his car.

Dani gave him a frazzled look. "I'd love to do that, but I have no idea where this one is. I turned off the two I know about, but no luck, so I called Allie and she's calling her ex-husband, and I should have an answer—"

The phone buzzed in her hand and she turned her back to Gabe as she answered.

"Thank goodness…yes, I'm sure he was happy you had to call him…" Dani started walking

"Right…yeah, I know…he's where? Well, at least that's good to know."

Gabe followed as she walked around the barn and kicked dirt off a round cover with one foot. He lifted it, revealing a couple of faucets a good arm's length down the hole.

"I guess if we turn off both of them, it should handle everything," Dani said to him, then into the phone she said, "My neighbor. Everyone I know is at work…of course it makes sense."

Gabe lowered himself to the ground and shoved his hand into the pipe, gritting his teeth as he worked to turn the stubborn handles with little more than the tips of his fingers.

"Is there a key?" Dani asked into the phone. "Thanks. I'll look." Dani disappeared into the barn and came out with a long metal fork that she bent down to give him. "Use this."

Gabe pushed himself to a sitting position, took the fork and shoved it down the hole, using the tines to twist off the faucet. The flow from the closest broken standpipe slowed to a trickle within a matter of seconds.

"Yes, it worked," Dani said. "Thanks, Al. I know this wasn't easy…yeah. I will. Promise. Drive safe."

Dani clicked the phone off and dropped it into her pocket. "Thanks. I kind of panicked when I couldn't find the main and Allie was out of cell range."

"Sure thing," he said, brushing the loose dirt off his side. "Let's take a look at the problem."

The problem was that the two standpipes had been snapped off at ground level.

"This is strange," he muttered.

"Yeah," Dani agreed.

"I'll need a shovel."

"You don't have to fix them," she said. "I just needed help shutting the damned water off."

"And I don't have a whole lot to do right now." He gave her a long look and Dani finally nodded.

"I'll get a shovel."

A few minutes later he'd dug around the pipe to the point that they had something to work with. "Are all your standpipes PVC?" he asked.

"Only the ones that Kyle, my ex-brother-in-law, put in. He was all about saving a buck."

Gabe surveyed the place for a moment, taking in the run-down appearance despite the fact that everything had been recently painted. It also appeared that Kyle wasn't too deeply into working hard, either. No wonder rumor had it that he'd wanted to sell before Dani's sister had filed for divorce. It was easier than maintaining the place. Now if he could just convince Dani that the property was better off in other hands…but no. Instead of doing that, he was helping her fix the place.

Neal would love it if he could see this. Gabe was going to keep this bit of information to himself.

The pipe hadn't cracked below the surface as

Gabe had feared. It was a somewhat clean break, one that could be sawed off and coupled to the original stand.

"All you need is an inch-and-a-half coupling, some PVC cement and a hacksaw."

"I have a hacksaw and I'm pretty sure the hardware guy can talk me through the rest."

And he was pretty certain he was going to do what he could to help her out—if she would let him. But there were things about his situation that bothered him. "I have to ask," he said, leaning on the shovel, "is this the way your life always goes? Crisis to crisis?"

"Pretty much," she said with a faint smile. "I think it's my personality."

"But this doesn't seem like an accident. Not unless you have some pretty damned big gophers around here."

An odd look crossed her face as she tilted up her chin. "It had to be. I mean…what else could it be?"

"Two snapped standpipes?"

He stabbed the shovel into the ground and crossed the distance between them, stopping short when her gaze shot up warily. "Maybe you should report this to the authorities. The mare, the standpipes—it just seems odd."

"Yeah. Maybe so."

"No maybes, Dani. It's odd."

"This isn't exactly something I want to report to the authorities."

"Why not?"

"Because Kyle is a deputy sheriff."

"All the more reason to report it. Especially if you think he might be involved."

"He's on vacation right now."

"But where was he when these pipes got snapped? Call."

She held his eyes for a moment, her troubled hazel gaze meeting his no-nonsense expression dead-on. Then she said, "You're right. You want to come in while I look up the number?"

A break. She trusted him—at least enough to let him in her house.

CHAPTER FOUR

GABE FOLLOWED DANI through the front gate and up the walk to the two-story house. It was sturdily built, with classic Victorian lines, and he wondered if it would be possible to move it to a different location on the property. In the rough plans he'd drawn up, the main lodge would stand where the house was now. The fields beyond would become the golf course. The barns, fences and outbuildings would have to go.

Dani opened the door and then glanced back over her shoulder at him before walking inside. Her footsteps echoed, rousing the big dog enough for him to raise his head.

"You, uh, seem to be lacking furniture." There was a recliner with a small folding table at one side, a ladder-back chair pushed against the wall with horse tack hanging from it and not much else. From what he could see, the dining room was empty except for a large carved armoire.

She looked around. "Yes."

He frowned at her as she walked to the armoire and pulled open a drawer. After digging out a phone book, she riffled through it then punched the number into her phone. Tipping the receiver away from her mouth, she said, "The divorce wasn't pretty. The only furniture that stayed are the things that Jolie and I—" She suddenly brought the phone back to her mouth and said, "Yes, hi, this is Dani Brody. I need to report an… incident, I guess."

Gabe listened as she described what happened, idly surveying the tangle of leather straps hanging from the ladder-back. He doubted that the authorities were going to take her report too seriously, because the tone of Dani's voice made it clear that she wasn't convinced it was anything to worry about. But having her call the sheriff made him feel better. She was pretty damned isolated, living alone, and if someone wanted to screw with her, all she had for protection was that giant mutt, who appeared to be semi-narcoleptic now that he'd given Gabe the canine all-clear.

Dani hung up the phone and turned back to him with a small shrug. "They told me to report anything else suspicious."

"Good. Now they have a record."

"Yeah," she said. For a moment they stood on opposite sides of the room. The awkwardness was becoming palpable and Gabe realized that she didn't know what to do with him now that he was in her house. That deal about making friends slowly, no doubt. The last thing he wanted was her to feel self-conscious around him, so he smiled and said, "I'm glad you called. If everything's okay now, I'd better get back to what I was doing. I have a deadline."

"You need to work on your vacation skills."

"I'll make a note."

"With an alert?" she asked mildly. "Practice vacation skills from nine a.m. to ten a.m.?"

"Something like that." He paused at the door, debating for a split second before he said, "Call if you have other issues, okay?" When her expression started to close off, as if he was getting too familiar too fast, he added, "I'd jump at any chance to procrastinate from my project."

He reached for the doorknob and her features relaxed—because of what he said, or because he was almost out the door?—and she took a few slow steps toward him as he walked out onto the porch. She stopped at the door, putting a hand on the frame. "I appreciate you coming. Sorry if my hostess skills are rusty." She gave a soft snort, then smiled at him. "Who am I kidding? I was never a good hostess. That was for my sisters to handle."

"Well, I've never been a big fan of anything fancy."

"Your car says otherwise."

His eyebrows lifted. "Touché. But there's no getting around the needs of the Y chromosome."

She laughed at that, a dimple appearing in one cheek close to the edge of her mouth, charming the hell out him. And making him very aware that he needed to get out of there a winner. "Good night, Dani Brody," he said in a low voice before forcing himself to step outside. He needed to leave because it would have been too easy to stay and he was not going to blow this by overstaying his welcome—even if she had called him.

"Good night." The door was closed before he looked back, but he'd definitely heard a husky note in her voice.

All in all he'd made some decent progress... but truthfully, he was glad she'd called for other reasons. The standpipes and the horse concerned him.

DANI STOOD BY the door, waiting until she heard the fancy car roar to life. Then she wrapped her arms around herself and took a few slow paces through her empty living room as the low rumbling purr disappeared into the distance. She shook her head. *Dani, Dani, Dani. Get a grip.*

This was the time to focus her energy on building and establishing her business, not being distracted by the hot vacationing guy next door.

You called him.

Indeed. And he'd been nice enough to come over and lend a hand. And that was where it stopped. A little neighborly help.

She still had mixed feelings about calling dispatch. Maybe this did need to be reported, but now Kyle would know something was up. Kyle,

who had nothing to gain by sabotaging the place.
So if it wasn't Kyle, the only person who had anything even resembling a reason to vandalize the
place, then...

Then it had to be a fluke.

She just wished she could still the small voice
echoing what Gabe had said—*two* snapped standpipes?

EARLY THE NEXT MORNING, Dani went to Lacy's
pen, feeling ridiculously relieved to find the gate
closed and the horse still there. During the long
night, she'd let paranoia get the better of her, wondering if someone *was* sneaking around her place
causing mischief, but now, standing in the warm
sunshine, her fears felt overblown.

Lacy stood stock-still while Dani approached
and crooned soft words as she moved closer, but
when she raised her hand to pet the mare, the
horse jerked her head back.

"It's okay," Dani murmured, leaving her arm
outstretched until Lacy finally moved forward
to touch the back of Dani's hand with her nose.
When she thought of what a trusting, confident
animal Lacy had once been when she sold her, it
was difficult to tamp down the anger. People like
Len Olsen shouldn't be allowed to own animals.
But they did and there was nothing she could do
about it, except try to rescue Lacy, bring her back
to where she'd been.

"Ah, Dad," she muttered. It would have hurt him as much as it did her, to see the only offspring of his favorite mare in this condition.

"I MADE CONTACT," Gabe told Stewart during their first touch-base call early the morning after Dani had called him about the standpipes.

"It went well?"

"Yeah." Not entirely according to plan, but he wasn't going to argue with success. He also wasn't going to tell Stewart that his car had almost gotten totaled by a horse or that he was making repairs on the Lightning Creek Ranch.

"What's your read?"

"That this will take time."

"How much time?"

"If I act too soon, my gut tells me the deal isn't going to fly. Ms. Brody is…not quick to trust." To put it mildly. "I can't slap money on the table and be assured the Brodys will take it." And if he made his move too soon, there was a good possibility that he wouldn't get a second chance.

"I want this done soon," Stewart said before coughing and then clearing his throat for the second time in their short conversation. "I need it done soon."

Which concerned Gabe. He'd worked with Stewart for several years and had never seen the man impatient, which in turn made him feel edgy.

"I'm confident that I can bring Ms. Brody around to our point of view."

"The sooner you do, the sooner I'll sleep at night." A rare admission from a guy who made it a point to never show weakness. "But no pressure," he added in a way that made Gabe feel like the vise had just been cranked another notch.

"Right," Gabe said drily. "I'll be in touch."

No pressure. Gabe ended the call, then walked to the window and clasped his hands at the back of his neck as he stared out across the fields at his target.

Were the standpipes still standing? The horses in their pens?

Was Dani all right?

She was playing at the edge of his thoughts in ways that weren't associated with property procurement. She was attractive and he sensed she'd be fun once she let her guard down. He liked her and that made him want to make certain that she felt as if she was making the right move when she decided to sell to him. He had no doubt it was the right move. Granted, she currently had a property she could live on rent-free while she started her business, however, that place needed a lot of work. If she sold, she could buy a smaller, nicer property with her share of the proceeds. A place that didn't need work and would allow her to funnel all of her money toward her business and herself. Hell, she could probably even afford some furniture.

And he'd told Stewart he could get the property.

All he needed was a logical reason to keep in contact with Dani, to get to know her better—to get her to trust him. A legitimate, motive-will-not-be-questioned reason.

There was only one solution he could think of, although it had a few inherent flaws he'd have to work around, like not having ridden a horse in twenty years. But maybe riding a horse was like riding a bike. Maybe you never forgot.

Hoping that was indeed the case, Gabe went to his computer and brought up the Montana Craigslist and started shopping for horses.

DANI LEFT THE house through the back door so that she could set a bucket of compost on the pile next to Allie's neglected garden. Every year her sister had poured all of her energy into tending flowers, tomatoes, vegetables, the same way she'd attempted to tend her marriage. After the first year, the marriage had done about as well as the garden was doing now—struggling along without much hope of growth.

Everyone had liked Kyle when Allie first brought him home. He was caring and protective of Allie, charming and easy to talk to, but as time passed, it became apparent that he also had a huge sense of entitlement that kept him from engaging in such mundane things as daily chores and responsibilities. He dreamed big dreams, starting projects he never finished, forging ahead with half-baked ideas, then cut corners to get them done fast. When Allie had tried to discuss matters, he'd accused her of having no faith in him. If anyone had had faith in him, it was Allie, but even she had been worn down. And then bitter.

Dani snorted softly as she emptied the bucket then left it next to the compost pile. Not that long ago, she'd been thankful that Chad wasn't like Kyle, that they worked on all aspects of their shared lives as partners, except for the Megan Branson aspect. Chad worked on that all by himself.

"Hey," she called softly as she approached the three mares standing in adjoining pens. Lacy ambled closer to the fence, then stopped a few feet away as always. Gus wandered into the pen and Lacy approached him slowly, sniffed at his coat, then nudged him with her nose as she used to nudge Dani for treats. Gus touched her nose with his and then moved on to the next pen.

Dani was a little surprised at the contact, since Gus generally ignored horses and cows, preferring bunnies and deer, which he charged after even though there was no possibility of catching them. It was like a canine duty thing, which always left Dani smiling.

She tossed hay into Lacy's feeder, then moved on to the next pen, where two young mares, her first contract, stood side by side. Both three-year-olds, they'd been raised together and barely touched beyond being halterbroken. As near as Dani could tell, the owner, a recent transplant from Seattle, wanted them gentled into kids' horses ASAP. Dani had patiently explained that thirty days would give them the basics and sixty days would get them to the point that a person who knew how to ride would have a well-trained, confident mount, but achieving kids'-horse status took a few years and a certain temperament.

The woman had simply beamed at Dani, as if she thought Dani was being modest about her abilities, and said she was certain Roxie and Rosie would surprise her. They were so gentle. They ate treats out of her pocket and came when she called. Dani didn't have the heart to tell her that the treats were probably a large part of the reason for their affection.

She fed the mares and then leaned on the fence, soaking up a few minutes of early-morning sun before heading out to feed the cows. This contract would pay for two months of living expenses if she was frugal, and allow her to put ten percent into savings. The furniture would have to wait until she had a few more horses on contract, but she didn't care about that. It wasn't as if she was entertaining or anything. She needed enough money to make a down payment on a canvas-covered arena, allowing her to train year-round, and that wasn't going to happen if she blew her money on furniture. Like Kyle, she was dreaming big, but unlike her ex-brother-in-law, she was also making a plan.

The phone buzzed in her pocket and Dani pulled it out as she headed to the cow pasture to check the water tank with the sticky valve. "Hey, Kelly," she said.

"I might be a few minutes late. My brother went to town and Corrie needs me to help her load some hay, but as soon as we're done, I'll head over."

"Not a problem. See you soon."

Dani pocketed the phone again. Living alone was one thing. Training alone was another. It was so easy to get hurt and if no one was around, who would render first aid? So she'd arranged the equivalent of a babysitter until Jolie moved home. Her friend Corrie's young sister-in-law was studying for the SATs, so Dani had arranged for her to study at the house during her training time. She'd have to come up with something else once school started, but for now, this worked. When Jolie came back home, as she promised to do when her internship ended, the problem would be solved.

As she walked back to the house, she saw Gabe's low-slung car cruise by her house. She was surprised he was awake this early, since as near as she could tell, he didn't sleep at night. For the past few nights—since the standpipe incident—she'd woken up every few hours on alert, despite the fact that Gus hadn't stirred. Every time she'd awoken, the lights across the field had burned brightly. City guy.

Well, until recently she'd been a city girl, although she had a feeling that Gabe would not consider Missoula a real city. She didn't know his background, but his demeanor didn't cry out rural. Rural guys didn't wear ironed button-down shirts with their jeans. Not that he didn't look great in those shirts. And not that she was looking. Much.

BUYING A HORSE that needed training was more of an ordeal than Gabe anticipated. His goal was to find an animal that needed work, but not one that was so ill-tempered that it would be a danger to Dani. And then there was the matter of him actually riding it…he hadn't been on a horse in two decades and he had a feeling that Dani might notice a small detail such as that.

As he walked to his car from his fourth unsuccessful attempt to buy a suitable mount, his phone rang. He pulled it out of his pocket, noted the name on the screen and smiled wryly as he brought the phone to his ear. "Serena, I thought you weren't going to call."

She gave a small sniff before saying, "I'm just checking on you as a friend, not as a business associate."

"Ah. In that case, I can tell you that living alone

in a rural area is trying my patience. I need to find a hobby."

"What about the park you're designing?"

"Done."

"Design another."

"I'm working on a spec project." It was a design he doubted he'd be able to use, but just in case Stewart was amenable to moving Dani's house, he was trying to come up with suitable surroundings. It seemed a logical way to fill downtime.

"I see."

"So, how's vacation?"

"Good. Good."

"Great." A healthy stretch of silence followed, which Serena finally broke by saying, "If I had called about business, what would you have said to me?"

"I would have said that getting to know Dani is slow going. I don't really have a reason to hang out with her."

"After getting shot down."

"Yes. Twist the knife, Serena. You know how much I like that."

She laughed softly. "I'm sorry. It's just that getting shot down does limit your options a bit, unless you two join the same club or something." She paused for a thoughtful moment before going on to say, "How did you originally plan to make and keep contact?"

"I planned to wing it." He figured if he could

dig up some information on her, he could decide how to proceed. It had seemed to work the first few days—the horse sale, her call to come and help her with the standpipes. Even the horse escaping had been fortuitous. But since calling her to make certain that everything was okay on her property—nothing. Not one bit of contact and Stewart's call had only served to remind him that the days were slipping away.

"And now?"

"I'm buying a horse."

"Great idea. Do you know which end to feed?"

"Yes. One of the few things I do know."

"So…you're going to buy a horse and have her train it."

"Yes."

"And somehow not let her know you don't ride."

"I've ridden." In fact, some of the happiest days of his life had revolved around a big brown gelding of uncertain breeding, owned by the only foster family who'd treated him like one of their own kids.

Serena made a disparaging noise. "When?"

"A long time ago. Okay?"

"So what are you going to do? Ask her to give you brush-up lessons?"

"She prefers horses to people."

"And therein lies your problem," Serena said on a note of amusement.

"Maybe I could flip the horse." The idea struck

him out of nowhere, which was why he needed to talk to actual human beings sometimes. "Then my rusty riding ability won't be an issue."

"Is horse flipping like cow tipping?"

Gabe frowned, wondering what the hell she was talking about. "It's like flipping houses. I could buy a young horse, have Dani train it and then sell it at a profit."

"Not a bad idea," Serena said slowly. "Except I kind of wonder how cost effective that would be. And flipping horses might sound kind of mercenary to a horse lover."

"Okay, forget flipping. Maybe I had a traumatic horse incident as a child that I want to get over." And maybe he needed to be careful not to stack up too many lies. Or any lies for that matter, other than those made by omission, which really weren't lies in this case. Stewart needed the land. Dani and her sisters had once been on the brink of selling. Timberline personnel couldn't find out about the prospective purchase. Given all those factors, omission was the only sane course of action.

"From what I hear from Neal, your entire childhood was a traumatic incident."

"I overcame," he said darkly, and then he smiled as the perfect answer struck him. "I'm going to give the horse to you."

"No, you're not."

"Yes. I am. You can keep it here. Sell it. Whatever. That way I can have it trained and not have to ride it."

"Well, this has been a great hypothetical conversation. Would you keep me posted so I don't have to call and *not* ask about business?"

"You bet, Serena. Enjoy the rest of your time off."

"I hope I can," she said softly. "Bye, Gabe."

"Bye."

Gabe pocketed his phone and started the car, waving at the horse owner, who'd started toward him and was possibly wondering if Gabe had changed his mind about the nasty beast he'd advertised as being the perfect mount for the right person. The right person apparently needed to be able to mount a horse that skittered sideways and reached back to try to bite the rider's knee. Granted, the owner had been suitably embarrassed by the animal's performance, but Gabe had no doubt that the guy would sell to anyone just to get rid of the horse.

He turned onto the main highway and started following the GPS directions to the final place on his list. Now that he had a plan, as in giving Serena a horse whether she wanted it or not, he felt better. More confident.

More honest.

He didn't like lying to people and now he wouldn't be lying to Dani. He just wouldn't be

telling her the entire truth. And if he didn't owe
Stewart a debt of gratitude, he didn't know that
he'd be doing any of this.

CHAPTER FIVE

DANI HAD THOUGHT it would take time to grow her business, but less than a week after putting out her advertisement, she booked her last training slot. Feeling a deep sense of satisfaction, she finished the notes she'd made while talking to her client, then shoved her feet into her boots and headed for the door. Later that evening she'd make up an official work schedule, and in the future she'd have to stagger her clientele. She was okay right now because she had four thirty-day clients, three sixty-day clients and one that wanted a two-week tune-up. That filled eight hours a day and when she added on care and feeding…yes. Full schedule. And the best part was that she wouldn't need to touch her severance pay for living expenses. If things continued like this, she could probably take on a few more horses and hire a part-time assistant until Jolie moved back home to join the business.

Marti Kendall wasn't going to like this one bit. Oh, well. As far as Dani was concerned, she was due. She'd always had to work pretty damned hard for everything she'd ever gotten and even then she had a way of catching things at the tail end of success. SnowFrost was an excellent example.

It had been a thriving business when she'd first been hired, but the owners were slow to change and the market had passed them by. Other more nimble companies had filled the available niches and left SnowFrost in the dust, which was a lesson in itself. She needed to pay attention to the business end. Sudden success could evaporate at any time, leaving her struggling to make ends meet.

Jolie would have smacked her for thinking like Allie, but Dani couldn't help herself and Jolie didn't need to know.

The day was hot and sweat was trickling down her back between her shoulder blades when she finally brushed down the piebald filly, her last horse of the day. All in all, she was satisfied. Exhausted, but satisfied. She tossed hay and scared a few mice out of the grain barrel. They practically ran over Gus's feet and the dog watched them go by with a bemused expression. Small rabbits, perhaps? Dani made a mental note to check the Humane Society for cats, then closed the barn door. She was halfway across the drive when she heard a vehicle pull into the drive and stopped dead in her tracks.

Kyle.

Great.

Calling Gus close, she waited under the poplars that edged the front yard until Kyle pulled to a stop and got out of his vehicle. Gus pushed his big body closer to Dani's legs and lifted his head, zeroing in on the man crossing the drive. He made no sound, but there was no mistaking the fact that he was in full protection mode. Kyle, smart man that he was, stopped a few yards away.

"How's it going?" he asked casually, glancing around as if looking for changes before bringing his attention back to Dani. He still had his golden-boy good looks, but they were somewhat marred by the grim set of his mouth.

"Going well," she said noncommittally. Now that he was here, she couldn't help but flash on the standpipes. The horse escape.

"Good." He attempted a smile, but it didn't reach his eyes. "Hear from Allie lately?"

"I have," she said, the same noncommittal note in her voice.

"Is she doing okay?"

"Starting school is an adjustment, but yes. I'd say she's doing okay." She and Kyle had gotten along just fine until Allie had become so unhappy with her marriage. After that, things had gotten awkward. And now that she was wondering if he'd been vandalizing the ranch out of spite, she wanted him off her property. Now.

"She did say that you were bringing the tractor back soon," Dani said, pushing back a few strands of windblown hair as she tipped her chin up at him.

His face started to go pink as it always did when he was confronted on an issue. "I'll bring it back this weekend. I've been on vacation at the Washington coast." He spoke with an edge of challenge in his voice, making her wonder if he expected her to question his whereabouts. It also made her wonder if she was in for more retribution via property vandalism if she crossed him. "I heard you made a call to Dispatch while I was off."

"A week ago."

"Today was my first day back and when I heard, I thought I'd stop by and check out the situation."

The fact that he was doing that made her wonder when exactly he'd left and if he'd stopped by the Lighting Creek on his way out of town to stomp a few standpipes, let a few animals go. It'd be a passive-aggressive way to give Allie grief… or maybe to take out his frustrations on the ranch he wasn't going to get a piece of.

"Nothing to check out," Dani said. "A neighbor helped me with the problem and he was the one who suggested that I make a report."

"A neighbor?"

"Yeah." She turned to point across the field. "A guy who designs parks is renting the Staley house for a vacation." As if Kyle wouldn't already know this. Sheriff's office personnel knew everything in this county. "Long story, but we'd met a couple of times and when I found the standpipes broken off, I called to see if he could help me find the water main."

Kyle frowned in the direction of the house for a few thoughtful seconds before turning his gaze back to Dani. "You don't think that's a little suspicious?"

"What?"

"He moves into the place next door, then strange things start happening here?"

Dani frowned back. "No. I don't find it suspicious because I don't think he had anything to do with it." Yes, he could have let out Lacy, because she didn't know his whereabouts when that happened, but she knew exactly where Gabe was when the standpipes were snapped—with her.

Kyle didn't look convinced and Dani had to bite her lip to keep from saying, "Nice try, Kyle, but I think I know who's responsible for doing those things…and so do you." He'd only deny it and right now her objective was to get him off the property.

"I heard Jolie is moving back," he said as if she hadn't spoken.

Dani smiled, wondering when her ex-brother-in-law was going to get the hint that he wasn't going to get a lot of family information from her. She didn't want to burn any bridges, but she wasn't going to open up to him, either.

Kyle glanced down at his dusty boots, his eyebrows drawn together in a thoughtful frown, then back across the field at the Staley house. "I might just see what this guy's about," he said.

"He's not about anything," Dani said, earning herself a sharp cop look.

"You don't know that."

She let out a barely audible sigh. "No, I don't. But I haven't seen him in a week."

"And nothing's happened in a week."

"Are you trying to make me nervous?" she asked.

"I'm trying to keep you safe. Allie and I might have split the sheets, but that doesn't mean I can shut off feeling protective just like that."

Dani had never noticed a lot of protectiveness before the divorce, but she wasn't fool enough to say that when all she wanted was to get rid of him. "Look. I just want to be a good neighbor. I don't feel threatened. Would you mind holding off on seeing what the guy is about until something else happens?" Which she was pretty damned certain wouldn't.

Kyle studied her for a moment and Dani did her best to look unconcerned. "If you have anything strange happen, you call me," he said, pointing his index finger at her.

"I will."

He nodded. "All right." Another awkward face-off and then he headed to his SUV.

Dani walked toward the house, even though she still had outside chores. She needed a drink. Or maybe just to splash cold water on her warm face. What she didn't need was for Kyle to harass her next-door neighbor. She'd just as soon stay off the guy's radar, because frankly, she didn't like how easily she could conjure up that mental picture of him standing on his porch when she'd gone to collect her truck, looking all rumpled and sexy. Or the way she'd found herself leaning across the table toward him when they went to lunch. Oh, yeah, she was attracted. Like a magnet. She knew nothing about the guy, had been recently burned in the worst way, yet her primal instincts were saying, "Oh, yes. We must have some of this."

Not. Going. To. Happen.

Of course it wasn't. She hadn't seen Gabe in a week. He'd made a duty call after the standpipe incident and after that, nothing. For all she knew, Gina, who'd made no secret about finding him supersexy, was having her way with him and he'd never given her another thought... No, she *would* know that, because Gina wasn't quiet about her conquests. But that didn't change the fact that he was keeping his distance and that was exactly the way she wanted things.

She glanced over her shoulder at the Staley house before pulling open the door. Off the radar. That was where she wanted to be.

"She's a real nice little horse," the older man leaning against the fence said as they watched the dark brown mare with the white legs trot around the round pen. "What exactly are you looking for?"

Gabe shot him a look and the man said, "A trail horse? Arena horse? Cutting? Roping?"

"Ah. Well, to tell you the truth, I'm looking for a horse with no bad habits and I figure if I get one that hasn't been used and have it trained, then I might just get that."

The old guy smiled broadly. "You're on the right track there." He gestured to the round pen, where a woman with golden-brown hair that fell almost to her waist was putting a horse through its paces. She looked a lot like Dani, only smaller, her hair a shade darker. "Marti is one of the best trainers in the area. If she wasn't, then she wouldn't work here…even if she is my daughter."

Gabe gave a polite nod, watching as the daughter stopped the horse, then walked over to pet its neck and slip a halter onto its head. "We have a partnership," Paul said, bringing Gabe's attention back to him. "I raise horses, Marti trains. She brings in outside horses, but she also trains my youngsters for their new owners. Gets them off to a good start, like you were talking about."

Gabe gave a tight smile and turned his attention back to the mare. He liked her looks. She was quiet and trusting and when he'd scratched her ears, she'd bobbed her head appreciatively. A far cry from the nervous, anxious, skittish and just plain mean horses he'd looked at over the past few days. He knew next to nothing about buying a horse, but even to his unpracticed eye, this mare looked well put together and the price was right because, as the man had explained, the cost of hay had tripled recently due to severe drought, so horses were going cheap.

The bottom falling out of the horse market put a damper on his resale plans, since Serena made it clear that she was not accepting a gift horse, but he'd figure out how to get the mare a good home later—even if it was at a loss. Right now the connection with Dani was more important than money lost or gained.

"She's been started under saddle, but she's still green. What's your riding level?"

"I haven't ridden in a while. I want to get back into it while I'm here," Gabe said without hesitation.

"With a young horse? That's a wreck waiting to happen."

A soft laugh came from behind them. "Not necessarily."

Gabe turned to see Paul's daughter standing behind them. "Hi. I'm Marti," she said, running an eye over Gabe as if he was himself a piece of horseflesh. "You look athletic."

Gabe shrugged. "I run and bike. Swim a little."

"Triathlete," she said with a smile. "You have balance then. And stamina." He almost smiled at the way she said *stamina.* "Tell you what," she said, crossing her arms. "You buy Molly from Paul, I'll train her and throw in a couple weeks of riding lessons. We'll start you on a finished horse, then shift you over to Molly once I'm confident she's ready."

Damn, damn, damn. Gabe forced a smile. "Very generous of you."

"It's one way of building repeat clientele."

Gabe looked over at Paul. "Tell you what—give me a day to think about it. I have another horse to look at later today, then I'll call and let you know."

Paul pushed off from the fence where he was leaning. "All right. I'll hold her until tomorrow for you. After that…" He shrugged.

"I understand. Thanks." Gabe started for his car and Marti fell in step. "My offer stands even if you don't buy Molly. I have a few open slots in my schedule and I'd be happy to work with both you and your new horse."

Gabe stopped at the car. "I appreciate the offer. Thank you."

"Anytime." She patted the top of his car, then stepped back as he got inside. Gabe drove away thinking it was too bad he couldn't take her up on her offer. He had a feeling that Marti could teach a guy a lot.

"I'M FULL UP." Dani felt a ridiculous pang of regret as she said the words, but facts were facts. "Eight horses, eight hours in the workday." She smiled a little. "Not counting all the other things I have to do."

"I understand." Gabe spoke matter-of-factly, but she'd caught the flash of disappointment in his expression. Well, one thing was for certain—if Kyle had indeed stopped by to "check him out," Gabe didn't hold a grudge. "I can give you the names of other trainers in the area."

"I'd appreciate that."

"What kind of horse did you buy?"

"A dark brown horse."

"Breed?"

"Quarter horse?"

"Gender?"

"Female."

"What do you know about horses, Gabe?"

"Not a lot." He smiled disarmingly. "I want to learn."

"Do you ride?"

"I don't have a lot of experience, but I have ridden."

She studied him askance for a moment. "Do you plan on learning to ride better?"

"That's the next step."

She couldn't help smiling. "Do you have a checklist?"

"A mental one." He shrugged one shoulder. "I can't help the checklist. It's the way I'm wired. And I like horses, but never got a chance to learn to ride well. It's not easy for a guy my age to get back into it." He smiled a little. "Since we have a small amount of history, I thought of you."

Something about the way he said the last words made Dani very aware of, well, him. His effect on her, which wasn't the effect she was looking for right now. "If I had one less horse…"

"Again, Dani. Not a problem."

"Do you want me to get you those names?"

"I already have one. Marti? She offered to train the horse and give me lessons at the same time."

"You've met?"

"At the place I bought the mare."

Dani forced a smile, said nothing. Gabe smiled back and she realized he was truly disappointed. It was all she could do not to say, "Sure. Another horse. Why not?" But she couldn't. She was too busy.

It wasn't until he'd driven away and the rooster tail of dust had settled that she admitted the truth to herself. It wasn't all about being too busy. When you started a new business, you made sacrifices. It was something about Gabe Matthews himself and the gut-level attraction she felt toward him. That and a sense that he was showing one side of himself in order to protect another. A sense that he had trust issues as deep as hers.

A sense that he was a guy with deep secrets.

The last thing she needed in her life was a guy with secrets, but she couldn't deny the fact that she was drawn to him.

Moth to flame. No good ever came from that.

"MARTI'S NOT EVIL. She'd just hard to be around."
Dani took a sip of her coffee, Gina's treat, since
Dani was sharing her break with her after the
morning rush at the café.

"No. She's evil," Gina countered.

"How so?"

"I was at a meeting last night of the Eagle Valley Days fund-raising committee chairmen—"

"You're a chairman?"

"I'm in charge of the silent auction, thanks to
my mom." She made a face that indicated that
she hadn't exactly volunteered. "I need some help
and someone mentioned that you were back in
town and might be interested. One thing led to
another, someone said you were starting a training
business and then Marti announced in this snotty
voice that anyone could bill themselves as trainers, but that doesn't mean they knew what they're
doing. She said there should be a licensing board."

Dani stared at her for a moment, feeling her
blood pressure start to inch up. "Indicating that I
don't know what I'm doing."

"I'd say that was the message loud and clear."

"Was Mitzi Thorensen there?"

"Yes. She's in charge of the ice cream social.
Why?"

"Because she called this morning and told
me she's decided to wait a month or two before

starting her filly. I was supposed to start working her tomorrow."

"Probably *not* a coincidence," Gina said, leaning back against the booth cushion.

Dani flexed her fingers, telling herself to stay calm. Marti had never before caused her trouble, but Dani had never before gotten in her way. With Marti it was easier to just step aside and let the queen pass by, but that wasn't possible in this circumstance, when the woman was messing with Dani's potential income and reputation.

"Hey," Gina said, bringing Dani's attention back to her. "Do you want me to start a rumor… like that Marti's training facility is infected with some dreaded horse disease?"

"Tempting," Dani said. "But I think instead that Marti and I will have a chat."

"I'd like to see that." Gina tilted her head, raising her eyebrows inquiringly. "Any chance…?"

Dani shook her head regretfully. "I think we'll have a private talk."

"Fine." Gina placed her palms on the table in front of her. "And on to another topic before smoke starts coming out of your ears. Any chance you could give the chairman of the silent auction a little help?"

"I don't have a lot of time right now," Dani said. "What would it involve?"

"Pretty much soliciting more donations, help setting up, monitoring the room. I had two other volunteers, but one moved and the other has quit answering my calls."

"Do I have to attend any meetings?"

"None that Chad's family will be attending."

"Not that I'm chicken, but if I don't have to see them, I don't want to." She and Chad's family had never really clicked, even after their engagement. It wasn't that they didn't like her; it was just that they'd hoped Chad would marry "up," as he'd once told her when he was describing how it was impossible to please his family.

At the time Dani hadn't been all that insulted. She'd been well aware that the Andersons were conscious of social status and Chad had made it clear that he thought their mind-set was ridiculous. But now she couldn't help but wonder if Chad hadn't shared their feelings on a deeper level, since the woman he'd cheated with was an honest-to-goodness business heiress.

"Hey. I get it," Gina said. "I don't like seeing Mark's family, but I have to because of the baby. I just need someone I can count on in a pinch."

Dani reached across the table and patted Gina's hand. "I'll help as much as I can."

"And I'll try to find other warm bodies, but it's good to know I have you if I need you."

Dani rolled her shoulders and glanced out the window.

"Hot to have that chat with Marti?"

Dani smiled grimly at her friend. "Yeah. I am."

"Well," Gina said, sliding out of the booth, "I won't keep you, but you have to call and tell me how it goes."

WHEN DANI PULLED into the Kendall Ranch, there were horses in all three round pens and one tied to the learning line, where young horses became accustomed to being tied up. Dani got out of her car, hoping that Marti saw her before Paul did. She had no problem with Paul—not yet anyway—but she had a big problem with Marti.

Why the attack? Looking at the number of horses they had, it seemed like, well, sour grapes. They couldn't handle all he horses in the area, but Marti didn't want anyone else to train.

Thankfully, it was Marti who glanced over as Dani parked. She did a double take, then stopped her horse and patted it, letting it wander off across the pen as she headed for the gate.

"Hey," she said as she approached. "Are you here looking for some tips?"

"No," Dani said, making an effort not to match Marti's teasing tone. "I'm here to give one."

"You are?" Marti wrinkled her brow.

"Yes. Do not trash-talk me in the community."

"I——" Marti abruptly cut off the sentence as she pressed a hand to her chest in an I'm-innocent gesture, then a look of understanding crossed her face. "I think I might have been misquoted."

"No. I think you made it clear that you don't think I know what I'm doing."

"That isn't what I said."

"Licensing board?"

Pink stained Marti's cheeks. "How long have you been training?" she said, going on the offensive. "Did you grow up in the business like I did?"

"I interned under some pretty decent trainers when I was at U of M."

"Interned." Marti gave her a look of a disparagement. "I was training horses for clients in high school under the tutelage of my father, who, *as you know*, is one of the best trainers in the country."

"So what?" Dani pointed her finger at her. "That doesn't mean I'm not an excellent trainer."

It was clear from Marti's expression that she didn't think so. It was also clear that Dani wasn't going to win this battle, but that hadn't been her intention.

"No more trash talk," Dani said. "It comes off as unprofessional." She gave a small smirk as she spoke. "*That's* my tip to you."

"Telling the truth isn't trash talk. If people ask my opinion, I'll tell them."

"Did Mitzi Thorensen ask your opinion, or did you just offer it?"

Marti narrowed her eyes, but didn't answer.

"Yeah. I thought so." Dani gave her head a disgusted shake, then turned and headed back to her truck.

CHAPTER SIX

THE PHONE RANG just as Gabe shoved a pencil behind his ear and stood back to view his newest drawing. He crossed the room to pick up the landline, straightening his posture slightly when his hello was answered by "Hi. This is Dani."

"Is everything okay?"

"It is." She hesitated for a fraction of a second before diving in. "Have you found a trainer?"

"Still working on it."

"I'm calling because I've reconsidered...if you're still in the market. I have a slot open."

"You do?"

"A cancellation. So I can work your horse into the schedule." She cleared her throat. "Are you still interested?"

"Yeah. I am."

"Well, if you want to stop by later and take a look at the contract, I'm free after five."

His first impulse was to ask if she wanted to discuss it over dinner, but he already knew the answer to that. "I could stop by at five-thirty."

"Why don't I come over there? I can meet your horse. Assess."

"I'll see you then."

She hung up without a goodbye, leaving Gabe holding the phone and wondering just what had prompted her change of heart. Not that it mattered. He now had a legitimate reason to get to know Dani better. He set the phone aside and went to the plans he'd been drafting when she called. If Stewart was amendable, he'd come up with an excellent site to resituate the house and then use it as their most private corporate getaway. It was intimate, yet large enough to allow people to have their own space. He wasn't certain of the exact floor plan, but he had an idea of what was possible from the small amount of the interior he'd seen the night he'd been with Dani when she'd called the sheriff's office.

He'd planned a landscape with an enclosed backyard, a pond surrounded by flagstones, a fire pit and a modified outdoor kitchen that could be shut down during inclement weather—which, from what he gathered, could happen at any time. He liked the idea of saving the house. Using it. Of course, Stewart may not be in agreement, since it would take a sizable investment to get the place renovated, but Gabe would present it to him and outline how long it would take to earn back the money.

Gabe stifled a yawn as he headed for the back door. He'd been unable to sleep and had gotten out of bed at 2:00 a.m. to finish the plans and now it was catching up with him. Or maybe he

was just bored, since lack of sleep had never bothered him prior to moving to Montana. His mind
hadn't wandered so much, either. Not since high
school anyway.

His new mare was pastured next to the house.
He'd been concerned about lack of shelter, but
Paul had assured him that the horse would be
fine—even in the winter—as long as it had a
windbreak. Gabe was fairly certain that his mare
would have a new home by the time the snow
flew.

She came to meet him as he let himself in the
gate, positioning herself so that he could easily
rub her neck and ears. He smiled to himself. It'd
been so damned long since he touched a horse—at
least twenty years. Make that twenty-three. He'd
been almost nine when he'd moved in with the
Carothers family. He'd spent eighteen months with
them before his mother decided she wanted to try
being a family again. Oh, yeah. That had worked
out well...

He crossed to the shed next to the pasture and
took out a new brush. The youngest Carothers
girl, Jenny, was seventeen when he'd moved in
and she'd been horse obsessed. From her he'd
learned what little he did know about horses—
how to feed them, groom them, clean their feet.
He'd been a veritable stable boy to Jenny and had
actually grown to appreciate horses. She'd put him
on her horse, Dozer, when she wasn't using him

herself, which was rare, but he could still recall the exhilaration he'd felt the first time he'd viewed the world from the back of her gelding.

Funny how he hadn't thought about that most excellent feeling in a long, long time. He moved the brush over the horse's coat, the scent stirring memories long forgotten. Horses smelled good in an odd sort of way. He smiled reminiscently as he moved around the back of the horse and started brushing the other side. That probably wasn't information he'd share with Neal or Serena.

AT ALMOST EXACTLY five-thirty Dani pulled up her old truck next to his car and parked. Gabe had been watching for her and came out of the house, sliding his arms into a jacket. The day had started out almost too warm, then the wind had come up, blowing in dark clouds that now hung low over the mountains behind Dani's house.

She stopped halfway across the drive and waited for him to approach.

"Hey," she said with a touch of self-consciousness. She gestured toward the pasture. "I know that filly."

"Do you?"

"One of Paul's, right?"

"Right."

"He has nice horses. Good temperaments."

"He said she'd been saddled but is still green."

"Just the way I like them," Dani said. "That

way I don't have to waste time undoing stuff other people have done." She cocked her head. "Marti must have started her if you got her from Paul."

"As I understand it, yes."

She nodded as if things were falling into place. "Shall we?" she asked.

Gabe led the way to the pasture gate, opening it for her. The mare met Dani halfway, just as he had a few minutes earlier. "Oh, she's nice," Dani said as she rubbed the mare's ears, then walked around her, examining the horse with a critical eye. Gabe couldn't help but wonder what she saw that he didn't, but he didn't ask. He'd let Dani take the lead here; after all, she was the expert.

"You shouldn't leave a halter on her."

"I shouldn't?"

She shook her head. "It's dangerous for the horse."

"I didn't know."

"Halters can get hung up on fence posts or other objects and if the horse goes down, it'll strangle them."

Gabe grimaced and reached for the buckle on the halter. "So noted." He removed the halter and then rubbed the horse's nose where the band had been.

She looked up at him, a serious expression in her eyes. "What's going to happen to her when you leave?"

Gabe simply stared at her for a moment. "I may be here for a while."

"What happened to the forced vacation?"

"I've been working from here and you know what?" He smiled a little. "Must be the lack of distractions, but I've been getting more done here than I do in my home office."

"So you're staying."

"For a while. Longer than I expected."

"Open-ended return."

"That pretty much sums it up," he agreed.

"But what then?"

So Dani didn't get easily sidetracked. All right. "She's going to a good home…nothing like what happened to your mare."

Dani nodded. "I'm used to people making more of a commitment, rather than buying a horse because they're on vacation and want to ride."

"It's more than that," he said quietly, and realized that what he said was true. He felt like he was touching a part of his past that he'd buried deep, maybe because it hurt to think about it. Not that he hadn't already dealt with all the shit that was his past, but apparently there were still things he needed to contend with. Outliers.

It struck him then that Jenny Carothers's horse had looked a lot like Molly. A gelding rather than a mare, but he'd been dark brown with white legs and a kindly expression in his deep brown eyes. The corners of Gabe's mouth lifted at the memory.

"What?" Dani asked and he glanced over at her.

"Just thinking about a horse I used to know."

"Known many?"

"Only one." A blast of wind hit them and Dani turned her back to it, wrapping her coat around herself more tightly. "Damn, that's cold," he said, pushing his hands deep into his pockets. "I feel bad that she doesn't have a shelter yet, even though Paul assured me that horses have lived outside through most of their evolutionary history."

"She'll have shelter soon." Dani glanced over at her place. "Do you want to start tomorrow? I can bring the trailer to pick her up."

"I'll walk her over."

Dani's lips twisted into a wry smile as she hunched her shoulders against the cold, making him wonder if he should take a chance and invite her inside. "It's a good mile."

"I think I can manage." He smiled at her again.

"I'm curious," she said. "Why didn't you book Marti?"

"I was hoping you'd change your mind." He regarded her candidly. "I didn't think you would, but thought I'd give it a day or two just in case."

"Because I'm close?"

"That's part of it." For a moment their gazes held and he could see that she was working over possible interpretations of his words. He decided to clarify. "I trust you because you went out of your way to rescue that paint mare. You care about horses." The words came out on a low note.

"I see," she said in a way that made him wonder if she saw more than he intended. She cleared her throat then, tearing her gaze from his. "I'd better get back. I still have evening chores to do. You can either walk your mare over tonight or tomorrow morning. I start working the horses at five."

"That's about what time I go to bed."

"I know." She flashed him a quick look, as if realizing what she'd just said and how it could be misinterpreted. "Your lights…I can't help but notice."

"I figured."

"I'm not keeping tabs on you or anything."

"You don't look like the tab-keeping type," he agreed easily.

Dani shifted her weight. "What I meant to say was I see your lights when I can't sleep."

"Why don't you sleep, Dani?"

"I do, usually, but I worry about things sometimes. Think too much. Then I get up and wander the house a bit. I see your lights. Wonder what you're doing."

She shrugged casually, but color had risen in her cheeks, as if she wasn't comfortable having him know that she thought about him. He wondered how she'd take it if he told her that he liked being in her thoughts. A brief second later she huffed out a short breath, and her voice was all business as she said, "So will you bring the mare tonight or tomorrow morning?"

"The morning."

"See you then." She quickly covered the distance to the gate and let herself out. Gabe stayed where he was with one hand on the horse's neck. Dani Brody was skittish. She found him interesting, but whatever had happened to her recently had made her one gun-shy woman. Well, that was all right, because all he wanted to do was to get to know her better and discover what her thoughts were on selling the family ranch.

SHE'D BLUSHED! DANI smacked the steering wheel with her palm as she drove through the gate on her way up the drive. She'd blushed like a junior high kid. Son of a bitch.

It was his fault. If he wasn't so damned hot and so very off-limits, well…

Dani pushed her hair back from her forehead. He didn't need to be off-limits. She was making him that way, but she had good reason. The problem was that she was thinking about him way too much for a woman who wasn't interested in getting involved with someone. Even a gorgeous landscape architect.

But what about some no-strings-attached sex?

The thought edged into her brain and Dani considered for a moment, very much aware of the curls of warmth unfurling deep inside as possibilities tumbled through her mind.

So not her style, yet…so tempting.

Chad had done a number on her. She needed a confidence builder that wouldn't turn around and dump on her emotionally. From what she'd seen so far, Gabe seemed to be a good guy. Not a user. But she wasn't totally certain on that front and wasn't yet willing to take that risk. The no-strings sex would have to wait until she was certain. And even if she became certain, there was no guarantee he would be interested.

Really? Have you noticed the way he looks at you?

Okay, he'd probably be game, which was all the more reason to take small steps rather than tumble in over her head.

Unless tumbling was the way to go… She needed a sister talk.

Dani drove home, made herself a cup of tea, curled up in her chair and started dialing. Mel was out of cell phone range as always. She spoke to Allie for almost thirty seconds—long enough to discover that her oldest sister was studying for her first quiz and, being the overachiever she'd always been, was totally on edge. Dani knew that side of Allie all too well, wished her good luck and punched in Jolie's number. As soon as the call connected she could hear the sounds of a raucous party on the other end and her sister trying to shout over the noise.

"Let me get to a quiet place!" she yelled.

"Where are you?"

"What?"

"Where. Are. You?"

The sound muffled and Jolie said, "I didn't hear you. I'm at a rodeo dance."

"Sounds like a free-for-all."

"Show me a rodeo dance that isn't— Hey!"

"Hey, me?"

"No, hey to the guy who's pounding on the door."

"Where are you?"

"Bathroom. I'm beginning to think it's the men's."

"Maybe I better let you go."

"I'll call you tomorrow."

"Make it after five. No, make that six."

"At night?"

"Yes." As if Jolie would see 6:00 a.m., unless of course she wasn't yet in bed by that time. "Talk to you soon. Have fun."

Another given. There was rarely a time when Jolie didn't have fun. Just for kicks, she punched in Mel's number and reached the out-of-service recording.

So, given the circumstances of her isolated sister, her party sister and her cranky academic sister, Dani was pretty much on her own. Not that she would have divulged many details…or even discussed the fact that the guy next door was making her squirm. She just needed to feel as though she wasn't alone.

"Just you and me, big guy," she said to Gus as she set down the phone. She walked over to the window and pushed the curtain aside. Light filled the large windows of the Staley house. Would it be that way all night, like usual? Or would Gabe get some sleep before walking the horse over?

Dani pulled the curtains shut and promised herself that tonight she wouldn't check. Or care.

GABE SHOWED UP with his mare close to eight o'clock the next morning. Dani was already working her second horse of the day, a former barrel horse that needed to learn a few manners. The horse was making progress, although Dani had concerns about the new owner's ability to remain consistent with the animal. Sometimes it was as much of a matter of training the owner as the horse.

As was the situation with Gabe.

If he really hadn't ridden since he was eight or nine…well, that was an issue. Especially since he'd bought a young horse.

None of your concern. If he wanted to follow a dream, so be it, and at least the animal would be well started for him. And if she had to spend a few hours bringing him up to speed…well, so be that, too.

"Morning," she called from the round pen where she'd been working.

"Yeah," Gabe said gruffly, running a hand over his dark hair, grimacing as his hand hit a cowlick that refused to stay down. "Morning."

Dani couldn't help smiling. "I would have driven over with the trailer."

"It's not the walk. It's the hour."

"So I guessed." She hadn't gotten a lot of sleep herself. She'd gone to bed at the usual time, but unresolved matters, such as how to handle her attraction to her neighbor, had made sleep impossible. Finally she got out of bed, stopped at the window and stared at the Staley place. Wondered what Gabe was doing.

She wasn't ready to be attracted to anyone, but when she'd stood at that cold window, her fluffy robe wrapped tightly around her against the chill of the night air, she'd realized that while she hadn't gone looking for an attraction, she needed to stop feeling threatened by it. It wasn't as if she was going to lose her head and do something she regretted. She needed to trust herself, her ability to deal—just as she had before Chad.

Dani reached out for the horse's lead rope and when her fingers brushed against Gabe's and she felt that warm rush of awareness, she simply smiled at him. She could control these feelings. Oh, yes, she could. "I'll take her. I have a stall all ready for her."

Gabe followed her as she led the mare into the barn. She shot him a look as she opened the door. "What's her name?"

"Molly."

"That fits." She led the horse inside and opened the last stall door. The mare walked inside and Dani reached up to take off the halter, which she hung on the hook outside the door.

"I have some paperwork in the house you'll need to read and sign." Her lips twisted a little as she added, "I have coffee, too, and frankly you look like you could use a cup."

CHAPTER SEVEN

"I ALMOST FEEL obligated to give you a ride home," Dani said, looking back over her shoulder at Gabe before she opened the front door.

"I look that bad?"

The last thing he looked was bad, but Dani wasn't going to confess that, so instead she smiled. "More like exhausted."

"Deadlines. I've never been able to move past the up-all-night work schedule." He smiled with a hint of weary amusement. "But you already know that."

And she wasn't touching that one. Wasn't going to let him know she'd been at it again the previous night. "Must make it hard to have a day job."

"I think that's why I contract. I can work on my own strange schedule." He followed her into the house and it struck her that she'd lived there for several weeks, and other than Allie and Kelly, Gabe was the only person who'd set foot in the house with her. She should probably see about getting a social life, but who had time? Of course, if Marti had her way, she'd probably have plenty of time since she'd have no horses to train.

"I see you haven't made any headway on the furniture front."

Dani waved a hand. "As long as I have a bed and a place to sit, I'm good. There are things I need more than furniture, not that I won't eventually get some." They entered the kitchen, Gabe pausing just inside the door as she crossed to the cupboard and opened it, pulling out one of the two remaining cups. When she had all her dishes washed and put away, she had four cups, all with tractors on them since she'd bought them at the feed store when she'd realized she owned no cups. She really did have a Spartan kitchen. "I'm waiting for my sister to move home before I invest. No sense in bearing the brunt of the cost myself."

"Is she moving home soon?" Gabe asked.

"That's the plan. Her internship ends soon and she's been saving her money…I hope. We're going to invest in an indoor arena so we can train year-round." She smiled over her shoulder at him. "We have a ways to go, but we'll get there."

Gabe leaned against the doorjamb. "So you can't train in the winters without an indoor arena?"

"I could if I was a fan of frostbite." Dani poured coffee into a cup with a John Deere tractor emblazoned on the side. "I'll probably train until November, then get a job to tide me through the winter."

"It's that easy to get a job?"

"The schools are always looking for substitute

teachers and I can probably waitress at the café. I need something I can walk away from in the spring when I start training again."

"What is your degree in?"

"Animal science with a minor in business accounting." Smiling wryly, she asked, "Guess which one has gotten me more work so far?"

"I'm guessing the business."

"You've guessed right."

Setting the coffee on the table, she waved him to a seat, then went to the huge carved-oak armoire just inside the dining room and dug out the manila folder with the contracts. When she came back into the kitchen, he was staring into his coffee, but he looked up as she approached, a half smile lifting one corner of his mouth. It was all she could do not to swallow drily, he looked so damned good. A sexy guy with slightly rumpled hair, sitting at her kitchen table, playing hell with her hormones. He was wearing his usual oxford shirt, but like his hair, it was slightly rumpled, making her wonder if he'd crawled out of bed and put on yesterday's shirt. She had no problem with that.

And if she wasn't careful she would soon be fanning herself.

She tried to recall the last time she'd had such a strong reaction to a man...and couldn't. Not even Chad. This was new territory, but as long as she kept her wits about her she'd be okay—if she could get the parts of her body south of her brain to agree.

"It's good. The coffee." He held up the cup in a small salute.

"I do love my coffee. Keeps me going during long days."

"Same here."

"Only for you it's long nights, right?" she asked, sitting across the small table from him.

"No. The days. I come awake at night."

"How vampiresque." She slid a contract in front of him, trying not to notice the way amusement lit his eyes at her offhand comment. Or the way her body was reacting to the warmth in his expression. "Please read through it so you know exactly what you're getting into. The short version is that I guarantee thirty hours of training for this price. You release me from indemnity if your horse hurts another horse and vice versa as long as I keep your horse segregated from all other animals. There's more…"

Gabe took a sip of his coffee and then pulled the contract closer. He read it quickly, gave a nod and reached for the pen. Dani did not ask again if he understood all the clauses because being a contractor, the guy dealt in contracts. "Looks good," he said.

"Are you going to be here for thirty hours' worth of training? I only train six days a week."

"Only six."

"Look who's talking," she said. "The guy who forces himself to take a vacation and then works anyway?" She gave a dismissive sniff. "Besides, sometimes I only work a half day on Saturday."

"And another half day on Sunday to make up for it?"

She shot him a look. "Maybe." Her mouth twisted as she regarded the contract for a split second, then she asked, "How many days a week do you take off?"

He gave her a touché smile and shook his head.

"As I thought. However, you never answered my original question—will you still be here when I finish?"

"Yes."

Her heart really shouldn't have jumped at that. "Thinking of making the move permanent?" Because she wasn't certain how she felt about him staying—although he probably wouldn't be living at the Staley house if he remained in the area. That lease had to cost a bundle. Even if he wasn't her neighbor, she wasn't sure having him in the area on a permanent basis would be all that great for her peace of mind.

"I don't know what I'm going to do," he said.

"Must be nice to have that kind of freedom."

"Double-edged sword," he said. "Contracting can be feast or famine. When the economy tanks, there isn't a lot of call for landscape architecture. That said, I can design from anywhere."

"You have to make site visits."

"That's why I have a fast car."

Dani laughed and then pulled the contract toward her and put it into the folder. "I'll have a copy of this for you by tomorrow."

"No hurry." He drained his coffee, then took the cup to the sink and rinsed it. Dani watched him with a small frown. Really? A great-looking guy who cleaned up after himself? This could only mean that when she found his fatal flaw, it would be a big one. Maybe he was bad in bed…

Her throat went a little dry as he turned back toward her and wiped his hands on the sides of his jeans. No, that would be too cruel…for someone who wasn't her.

"Everything all right?" he asked curiously.

"Fine," she said briskly. "I just need to get to work." Kelly would show up within the hour and until then she was only doing groundwork with a young filly. "But I will give you a ride home."

She had to make the offer, but she felt a whisper of relief when he said, "I'll walk. Thanks."

"And I'll be in contact about Molly."

He stopped on the porch. "Would it be all right if I came by to watch you work her? Not every day, of course, but since I'm close…"

He shrugged and Dani heard herself say, "Sure. I'm all right with that. But give me a couple days, okay?" That would give her time to get acquainted with the mare.

"Great. Thanks."

He started down the path, but Dani stopped him by calling his name. When he turned back, she said, "Just what are your plans for Molly? You never told me."

"I'm giving her to a friend as a present."

"Must be some friend."

"Oh, she is." He smiled, raised his hand in a brief salute, then headed down the driveway, leaving Dani with something to think about. Maybe it didn't matter if he became a permanent resident. And she was glad about that.

Regardless of how her stomach had twisted at the word *she*.

GABE WANTED NOTHING more than to conk out for a while, but he forced himself to stay awake. He really needed to break this late-night habit if he was going to keep normal hours, watch Dani train his horse, live like a normal person. But it was killing him. His ability to live on two hours of sleep for days at a time seemed to be slipping away.

Stewart had sent another small job his way—redesigning the entrance area of an older getaway hotel that he was refurbishing—and Gabe was determined to take his time instead of blasting out the entire project in a few marathon sessions.

He wandered outside and sat on the front terrace with his sketch pad. He'd barely touched his pencil to paper when a rooster tail of dust at the far end of his driveway caught his attention.

Dani?

She had his number and would call first.

A salesman? A neighbor coming to greet him? A package delivery?

No—it was law enforcement.

Gabe got to his feet as the white sheriff's SUV came to a halt at the end of the path leading to the house. The guy that got out was tall and lean, wearing a cop face.

"What can I do for you?" Gabe called as he walked down the path, thinking he'd rather be on the offensive than the defensive. It'd been well over a decade since he'd had any kind of trouble with the law, but old habits and knee-jerk reactions were hard to shake.

The deputy tipped back his hat, his expression shifting toward friendly as he held out a hand. "I just wanted to stop by and thank you for helping my sister-in-law the other night. I'm Kyle Randolph."

So this is the brother-in-law.

"Gabe Matthews." Gabe automatically shook hands, wondering what the real purpose of this visit was, because the message he'd gotten from Dani the other night was that Kyle wasn't particularly concerned about the welfare of either her or the ranch.

"Not a problem."

Kyle glanced around the property, assessing, then brought his attention back to Gabe. "I'm just glad someone was close by. I read the report and, frankly, it's probably just a string of coincidences—kids getting their kicks—but you never know."

"That's why she made the report," Gabe replied. "Just in case it wasn't." He shifted his weight slightly before saying, "You used to live there. On the ranch."

"Yeah."

"She mentioned that she'd tried to call you to find out where the water main was."

"I was out of town on my first ever vacation, so I didn't get the call." He smiled ruefully. "And don't think her sister didn't give me an earful over that."

"If you didn't get the call, I don't know how you can be blamed," Gabe said smoothly.

"Exactly." Kyle smiled distantly. "I still care about Allie and her sisters, even if we couldn't make things work. You can't just shut off feelings like that."

"No doubt."

"So…I hear you're leasing this place. Are you considering buying?"

Gabe shook his head. "It's not that kind of lease. It's a vacation deal…and I'm not thinking that far ahead. I just needed some time away from the day job and this seemed like a good place to do that."

"Not many people can do that," Kyle said. "Just…take an unlimited amount of time from the day job."

"I'm an independent contractor, so I'm still working, actually."

"I see." But Gabe didn't think he did. In fact, he couldn't quite figure why the guy was there. It wasn't to thank him for looking out for Dani. So…

Whatever the deal was, Gabe didn't want to alienate the guy. Not right now anyway. Unless he messed with Dani a little too much.

The thought startled him. Not only was Dani probably more than capable of fighting her own battles, but her affairs were also none of his business. He found her attractive, yes, but in the end, he was moving on and she was getting a new ranch. He needed to remember that.

"What exactly do you do?"

"I design parks and landscapes. A lot of my business is a matter of drafting up plans after site visits. I can do that here. I also consult."

"You own your own business."

Gabe thought he'd just said that, but since Kyle seemed to need reiteration, he smiled and nodded. "Yes. Which makes it possible to make my return open-ended."

"Return to where?"

"The Midwest." He wasn't about to say the Chicago area, on the off chance that Kyle or anyone else put two and two together. He was being paranoid, but since Widmeyer was located in Chicago, he wasn't going to make any mention of the city. Hell, he didn't think he was even going to return to the city. The solitude here certainly made it easier to work without distractions. Not that he planned to stay in this particular area, but he was seriously considering moving to a less urban, lower-rent locale.

"No mountains there."

"You've been?"

"I went to Des Moines for SWAT team training." This guy was on the SWAT team? Somehow that seemed wrong. Then Kyle made things better by saying, "I'm not actually on the team, but went in case there was an opening."

"We may not have mountains, but we have lots of mosquitoes," Gabe said.

Kyle laughed. "We have a few of those here, too." His expression sobered and Gabe wondered if the half-ass interrogation was almost over, because he had stuff to do. "Well, I gotta get going. I just wanted to stop and say thank you. Like I said, just because Allie and I couldn't make things work, that doesn't mean I've stopped watching out for the Brodys."

"I don't know Dani that well, but I'm sure she appreciates it."

Nothing like lying through your teeth with law enforcement. Kyle smiled as if he was pulling something over on Gabe.

"If you hear of anything else happening, would you let me know? Dani tends to try to handle things on her own, which makes me surprised that she called Dispatch, which in turn makes me think she had to be spooked pretty badly."

"Or maybe I told her to call."

Kyle's expression shifted, but Gabe couldn't quite read where it had gone. "That was a wise thing to do. Thank you."

"You bet." Gabe took a step back, indicating that he was done chatting, and Kyle took the hint, touching his hat before he started back for his vehicle. "Nice talking to you."

"Same here," Gabe said and Kyle gave a quick satisfied smile, looking as if he truly believed he was the one in control of the situation.

Which told Gabe that he hadn't lost his touch.

ONE OF THE laws of nature was that people needed to eat, and early Saturday morning Dani come to the conclusion that she'd better go shopping or she was going to be pretty damned hungry for the remainder of the day.

The cupboards were empty—and not because it was hard to afford groceries, but because it was hard to find the time to go to town. Today was the day, and after she'd worked her horses, she showered, put on her last clean pair of jeans—laundry would commence the next day—and drove to the local supermarket.

Her needs were simple—coffee, bread, butter, cold cuts, cereal, milk, a bunch of fruit, a bunch of salad stuff and a big stack of frozen dinners. After tossing a family-size container of Oreo cookies on top of her load, she headed for the checkout only to stop as Marti wheeled a cart around the corner. *Great.*

The aisle had a column in the center, which meant that one of them had to wait while the other wheeled past it. Dani did the honors, hoping Marti would walk on by. No such luck.

"Hey, I just wanted to say sorry about our last meeting," Marti said after rolling to a stop.

"Well, it's over and we can just move on."

"That's what I'd like." She smiled a little. "Have you seen Chad yet?"

Dani frowned at her. "What are you talking about?"

Marti looked genuinely surprised. "You don't know?"

"Know what?"

"Chad just took the job as branch manager of the local US Western bank."

"Oh." Somehow her lips stretched into something that might have been a smile. "I didn't know." And all she could think was thank goodness US Western wasn't her bank, although that was a small consolation.

Marti gave a little shrug. "He and his new wife

just bought that house on the corner of Barnes and Fifth Street. You know the one?"

Oh, yeah. She knew that house—more of a mansion, really—but the part that had caught her attention was the reference to his *wife*. Chad had married Megan Branson?

The day just kept getting better.

Dani forced a mock sweet smile, very similar to the one Marti was now wearing. She was going to be civil, take the high road, then go home and have a stiff belt.

"I really need to go. Nice talking with you." With that, she wheeled the heavy cart down the aisle and past the column, toward the checkout stand and freedom.

Chad. Back.

Mental note—stay away from the US Western bank. She was so not ready to bump into her ex. This truly sucked. She'd come back to the Eagle Valley to start fresh, remove herself from Chad's sphere, and now he was here, too. With his new *wife*.

That was a slap in the face she didn't need. They'd been engaged for over a year and now he'd married the woman he'd cheated with less than two months after they'd broken up?

That sucked. Pure and simple.

Saturday was officially Dani's half day and even though she'd already worked the horses scheduled for that day, she went out to the corrals after returning home from the grocery store and caught Johnny, her first horse scheduled for Sunday. She worked him on the ground for well over an hour before turning him loose, then she did the same thing with Sarge, a rangy palomino gelding that she'd developed a soft spot for. He was a grudging performer, but loved his daily grooming sessions, stretching his neck and sticking out his lip when she hit the itchy spots.

He did a lot of neck stretching that day, since Dani brushed him for twice as long as usual, doing her best to distract herself from obsessing about Chad's return.

She was not successful.

No matter how many times she assured herself that she didn't care if he was in town, that what he did was none of her business, the sad fact was that she did care. She'd never been a person who spent much time worrying about what people thought of her, even as a teen, but now she felt as if everyone would be watching her, commenting on her broken relationship.

Self-centered? Yes. Paranoid? Probably.

But the town was small and it was a certainty that she would bump into him and the new missus—which was totally unfair, given the amount of times he'd mentioned how much he liked living in Missoula, how he'd never move back to the Eagle Valley. Now here he was. Back in her territory. When they did meet, there would no doubt be witnesses and it would not doubt be uncomfortable, since the last time she'd seen him had been the day she'd kicked him out of her apartment after throwing his girlfriend's panties at him.

And if this is your biggest problem in life—that your ex married his girlfriend and moved back to town, your life is pretty damned good.

Dani rolled her stiff shoulders after she finished grooming the big horse and then turned him into his pen.

That was true, but she still wished Chad had kept his ass up north.

Dani heard the landline ringing as she mounted the porch steps. Only one person called the landline—her mother, Anne. And if Dani didn't answer, then she'd call until she did.

"Hey, Mom," Dani said, forcing a smile and hoping that made her sound upbeat when she was actually feeling beat down. "How are you?"

"I was about to give up on you," Anne said. "This is my third call."

"I was just finishing up on the last horse."

"It's a little late for that, isn't it?"

"I went to town today, so had to play catch-up. How was fishing?" There was a brief pause as if her mother sensed she was being sidetracked, so Dani added, "Did you get a chance to use the new tackle we got you for Christmas?"

"I did and it brought me better luck than Richard had with his lucky lures."

"Excellent," Dani said. "When's the next trip?"

"We haven't decided," her mother said before abruptly saying, "I heard a rumor that Chad moved to the Eagle Valley."

So much for sidetracking. "I take it Gloria called." Her mother's husband, Richard, had a snowbird sister who spent part of the year in the Eagle Valley. Unfortunately, she hadn't yet flown south for the winter.

"She did."

"Apparently that rumor is true."

"And..."

"That's life, Mom. I'm pretty sure he didn't move back here to make me feel bad. He probably doesn't want to see me any more than I want to see him."

"Just checking."

"I'm fine."

"Nothing odd going on at the ranch?"

Damn. Gloria had been a busy little bee. "Odd?" Dani asked smoothly, hoping she didn't trigger mother radar. "A plumbing emergency and a horse got out, but, no, nothing odd. Just ranch stuff, you know? The kind of stuff Allie used to deal with on a daily basis."

"I handled a few of those issues myself," her mother said with a touch of wryness that made the tense muscles in Dani's neck start to relax. Her mother had put in enough worry time trying to raise the four of them on a ranch that was slowly sinking into the red during hard economic times. The sisters had tried to convince her innumerable times that they were as capable as she was, that she taught them well and she didn't need to worry about them, but once a mother, always a mother. So she and her sisters did whatever was necessary to keep their mother from worrying.

"That you did. Remember the time the cows got out during that blizzard?"

"Which time?" her mother asked drily. "Why do you think I signed the ranch over to you girls? So I never had to deal with that stuff again."

"Do you miss the ranch?" Dani asked. The sisters had debated that subject more than once. Had their mother signed over the ranch because she never wanted to see it again? Or was it because Richard had invested well and she didn't need the income, so she'd given her daughters their inheritance early?

"I do," she said slowly. "During the summers anyway." There was a brief silence before she continued. "The ranch wasn't easy—"

Dani gave a soft snort at the understatement and her mom laughed lowly.

"Okay, there were times when the ranch was brutal, back when we had all the cows and the hay contract fell through." In other words, back when it was a working ranch that they depended on to pay their bills, not the fallow operation it was now.

"But I always felt as if I could draw strength from the land, you know what I mean?"

"I do," Dani said softly. Because she felt exactly the same.

"So, yes. I miss it, but that part of my life is over. I don't care what you girls do with the place as long as you're happy with your decision."

"I'm happy living here," Dani said. "I'm glad that I'm back and I don't care if Chad is back, too. I'm tough enough to deal with it."

"I know you are," Anne said. "I just sometimes need to hear that."

IT SEEMED THAT Gabe had barely put his head on the pillow when his buzzing phone jerked him awake again. Neal...who worked normal hours.

"Yeah?" he grumbled into the phone, fully expecting some kind of bad news.

"I didn't realize you'd be in bed," Neal said.

"Did you consider the time difference?" Gabe asked as he flopped onto his back.

"Since it's nine o'clock there, no...but it is Sunday, so I'll cut you some slack."

Nine? Gabe squinted at the clock. "I got going on something last night and didn't think to stop until four a.m."

"I hope it wasn't work." Neal was altogether too chipper and Gabe was about to tell him so when he said, "I'm calling because I heard from Sam yesterday."

Gabe propped himself up on his elbow. "What did he want?" He and Sam had parted ways shortly after Sam had gotten out of prison the first time, having served fifteen months of a three-year sentence for burglary. He'd wanted a place to live, help getting back on his feet. Gabe had complied and things had gone well for almost a month. Until Sam had needed more money than he was earning at his crappy job.

Gabe had told him he was tapped out, and he was. So Sam robbed the apartment. Not that he ever confessed, but Gabe wasn't stupid, and shortly after that, Sam robbed a Pizza Hut and back into the slammer he went. Now apparently he was out again, only this time he'd contacted Neal for help instead of Gabe.

"Don't give him any money," Gabe growled.

"I don't need to. He's going back in. Third strike. He'd only been out for a month when he got arrested again and the conviction just came down."

Gabe's stomach knotted. "I had no idea."

"Me, either."

Third strike meant Sam wouldn't see the light of day. Not for a long time anyway. "He brought it on himself," Gabe muttered more to himself than to Neal.

"Agreed. He called because he wanted me to make sure his dog got a home. He didn't trust his girlfriend."

Gabe closed his eyes. That was the Sam he'd grown up with. The Sam who'd been his friend before drugs and street life had changed his priorities.

"I feel for him," Neal said softly.

"Yeah." Gabe swallowed. "Does the dog still need a home?"

"No. He's going to one of the IT guys here. I just…I don't know."

Gabe knew.

After Neal hung up, Gabe got out of bed and wandered into the kitchen, where he turned on the coffeemaker. Then he turned it off again. The last thing he needed in his stomach was more acid.

You are not Sam's keeper.

But they'd been like brothers once and Gabe wondered, as he always did, what would have happened to him if Stewart had not tossed him that lifeline the night he'd gotten into trouble. Would he be like Sam? In and out of prison? Looking for the easy bucks because he lacked the training to earn a decent living legitimately? His decisions and Sam's hadn't differed all that much until the night he'd been arrested for selling weed just days after his eighteenth birthday. Seeing no other choice, he'd called Neal to beg for bail money. Instead Stewart had showed up at the jail.

Gabe could still recall the utter shock he'd felt when he'd come face-to-face with Neal's grim-faced father. Shock, anger, shame at getting caught when he should have been better than that. He'd expected threats, but instead of warning him away from his son, Stewart had offered a second chance.

Why? Gabe still had no idea. And no matter how many times he told himself he would have eventually pulled his head out of his ass even without Stewart's help, he didn't know that for a fact.

Gabe pushed off the counter and paced through the house, then went into the bedroom and shoved his legs into his jeans.

He needed to move. Clear his head. Get out of this stone-and-glass box.

ON SUNDAY, DANI woke to a cloudless sky, and after toast and coffee worked the two horses remaining on her schedule. Once that was done, she went back to the house and, having nothing better to do, cleaned the floors before putting in a few hours on her marketing and business plan. She researched canvas-covered arenas, made a casserole for dinner, then went back out to the corrals to give Lacy some one-on-one.

She'd promised both Allie and Kelly that she wouldn't get on the mare unless someone was there, but she hadn't promised not to saddle her. She caught the mare and tied her to the hitching rail, then disappeared into the tack room. The mare's ears went back as soon as Dani reappeared in her vision with the saddle in one hand, the pad in the other.

Dani stopped, waiting for Lacy to relax, and then when the horse's ears went forward again, she approached the mare. There was a slight quiver when she placed the pad on the horse's back, a bunching of muscles when she settled the saddle, not out of the ordinary for the first tack-up—but nothing to prepare her for the explosion that occurred when the cinch touched the horse's belly.

Lacy threw herself backward while twisting sideways, lost her footing and landed on her side as Dani scrambled out of the way. For a moment she lay there, the saddle half under her, nose in the air, held in place by the taut halter rope. Dani dashed forward and yanked the rope, tied in a quick release knot that had nevertheless tightened when the mare fell. She yanked again and the rope came free, allowing Lacy control of her head. The mare let out a groan, then heaved herself up to her feet. Dani caught the rope before Lacy took off, and for a moment they stood facing one another. Both of them were shaking. Gus hovered nearby, whining his distress until Dani shushed him.

She took a slow step forward and Lacy snorted and tossed her head. Dani stopped and waited for the mare to lower her head again. Lacy had reacted, as horses would, to a stimulus, but now she needed reassurance, so Dani moved forward to slowly touch the lower part of the mare's neck.

Lacy quivered but stayed put, allowing Dani to stroke her. Dani continued to rub the mare's body, working her way over the taut muscles, still holding the lead rope in one hand, not wanting to risk tying her up again.

After fifteen minutes of slow massage, Dani released Lacy, who shook her head and started toward the water trough, Gus ambling along by her side as if offering his own brand of reassurance. Dani leaned her forearms on the fence, then slowly lowered her forehead to rest on her arms. She didn't know what to do. As a trainer, she was facing a problem that should be dealt with. As the guilty owner of a horse that wouldn't have been abused if she hadn't sold her, part of her just wanted to let the mare live in peace.

She'd bought Lacy to give her a home, not to ride her, although a small part of her had hoped that would be possible, despite what had happened to the last owner. What was the best thing to do here? Attempt to rehabilitate a fifteen-year-old mare, or just let her live out her life grazing with the other horses and playing field tag with Gus? If she chose to let the mare be, she had to commit to keeping her forever—but that had been her plan anyway.

What a week. Chad, Marti, Lacy—by themselves not all that significant, but added together… yeah.

Dani raised her head, staring out over the field,

thinking it was time to count her blessings instead of her crosses. The problem with living alone was that there was no one to distract her from the things weighing on her mind. No one to unload a few problems of their own, make her feel as if she wasn't the only one carrying a bit of a burden.

No one to keep her from noticing Gabe striding purposefully along the path that led from his house, across her property, to the river. She climbed down off the fence and went back into the house, paced a few times, then decided it was a great time to tackle the upstairs floors. But instead of sweeping she stopped at her bedroom window, broom in hand, and stared out toward the river, where Gabe had disappeared in the willows.

"Gus," she called a few minutes later as she trotted downstairs. The big dog lifted his head then slowly hefted himself to his feet as she said, "Let's go for a walk."

Time for a little distraction.

CHAPTER EIGHT

GABE HAD KNOWN that something was coming through the brush long before Dani emerged from the thick willows that edged the river. He'd hoped it was a deer or cow and not a bear. Having that something turn out to be Dani was a pleasant surprise.

"You found the swimming hole," she said as she walked toward him, dressed in cutoff jeans and a loose tank top that seemed to emphasize her breasts rather than conceal them.

"I guess so." He smiled at her, noticing that there were faint circles under her eyes and her mouth tipped down at the corners. Stress? Exhaustion? "I followed the path from the house across your fields. It's kind of narrow, but well used."

"It's a deer and coyote path," she said moving a few steps closer. "I don't think the Staleys ever used the swimming hole. They weren't swimming-hole kind of people."

"I've seen the deer," he said. "But no coyotes."

"They're a little shyer, but they're around."

"Guess I'll take your word for that." He nodded at the towel she held. "You really are going swimming."

"I'm thinking about it." She shrugged. "Or it might have just been an excuse to have someone to talk to. I saw you walking this way."

"Spying on me?" His tone took on an amused note—he knew she was probably the last person who'd take up spying on him.

She shrugged again. "I was sitting on the fence and saw you head toward the river. I decided I'd see if you found the swimming hole or were just wandering the banks."

"I might wander later." He sat down on a bleached log, but Dani remained standing where she was.

"Rough day?" he finally asked.

She shrugged carelessly. "I've had better." She glanced over at the opposite bank, then back at him. "I had kind of an incident with Lacy. I decided to saddle her and, well, it didn't go well."

"What happened?"

"She exploded when the cinch touched her belly. She was tied to the rail and went down and I was lucky to get the rope loose before she choked herself." She rubbed her fingers over her forehead. "I shouldn't have had her tied when I saddled. I just hadn't expected…" She exhaled "But I guess I should have, knowing she'd been abused."

"How close did you come to being hurt?" he asked gruffly.

She looked at him as if surprised that was a concern. "I was out of range when it happened."

"Out of range." Now it was his turn to let out a long breath. "What now?"

"That's what I've been wondering. Do I rehabilitate or just let her be?"

"Keep her as a pet?"

"Yeah."

"Kind of an expensive pet."

She cocked her head and her hair spilled over her shoulder. "Not logical?" she asked in an I-dare-you-to-say-yes voice.

"I'm not touching that one."

She gave a small snort. "Don't worry. My sister Allie agrees with you."

"Why'd you sell her in the first place?"

Dani sighed. "It was part of the pay-for-college plan. My dad was a fantastic rope horse trainer. Lacy was out of his favorite mare. We planned to train her, sell her, help pay for college."

"A rope horse brings that much money?"

"A good one. One of Dad's friends used her for a year on the rodeo circuit, won some good money on her. I used her in high school the one year we could afford to rodeo." Dani leaned back and looked up at the sky. "I sold her because it was part of the plan my dad and I made before he died. He said rope horses of her caliber only went to people who cared for them." She continued to stare up at the sky for another moment, then dropped her chin. "It was a good fairy tale."

An awkward silence followed, which Gabe

eventually filled by asking, "How's Molly coming along?"

Dani glanced at him with a half smile, as if glad he'd offered up a friendlier subject. "She's smart and quiet. She'll be a good present for whomever she's going to."

"My best friend's ex-wife."

Dani gave him an uncertain smile. "I probably won't ask any more questions."

Gabe laughed. "She's also my assistant, but at the moment she's on vacation. Or she's supposed to be. She's as good at vacations as I am."

"A horse seems like a very generous present."

"You have no idea how much she does for me." Another dubious look and he added, "She's my right-hand woman. I depend on her when she's not on vacation."

"Will she be joining you here in Montana?"

"I guess I should have said she's more of a virtual assistant."

"Ah."

"And she and my best friend are still friendly. They just had trouble being married."

Dani finally sat down on the other end of the log, her smooth legs stretched out in front of her. "I wish things were friendly between my sister and her ex, but no."

"Divorces tend to be that way in the beginning."

"Have you been divorced?" He shook his head. "Are you married?"

"Nope."

"You never know," Dani said, looking off into the distance.

"Been hit on by a lot of married men?"

"Not many, but I've seen it happen," she said without looking at him.

"And you wanted to make sure I wasn't one of them."

"Like I said…" She gave an eloquent shrug.

"The deputy came to see me."

Dani sent him a sharp look. "He didn't hassle you, did he?"

"Thanked me for looking out for you."

She gave a small snort. "He said he was going to check you out, as if you might be a suspect in the standpipe assault. I told him not to. Of course he did as he damn well pleased. As always." Her mouth tightened before she said, "He couldn't care less if you looked out for me."

"And I imagine you don't particularly like being looked after?"

"I don't mind an ally, of my choosing."

He smiled and gazed into her eyes. "Well, you know where to find me if you need me."

Look away.

But it was so damned hard not to stare at those amazing gray eyes. Closer to the color of storm clouds than steel, with flecks of pale gray and white, yet somehow conveying a sense of warmth.

No, make that heat. Dani cleared her throat. "Would you let me know if he stops by again?"

"Sure." Gabe picked up a weathered stick and idly drew a line in the sand near his feet. "Is he territorial or something?"

"He's still getting over losing the ranch. He thought he was going to get a piece of it in the divorce settlement. When that didn't happen, he got—" her mouth curved wryly as she met those gray eyes again "—cranky?"

Gabe gave a soft laugh. "Very tactfully put."

"He took one of Dad's old tractors. We're still waiting for him to bring it back."

"Think he will?"

"Allie just contacted the lawyer, so, yes. Eventually."

Dani decided against telling him that she and Allie were fairly certain that Kyle had been behind the broken standpipes. She didn't think he was a danger—just a man prone to tantrums. She liked Gabe, but she didn't know him. Didn't know if he was any good at keeping a secret—although instinct told her he was.

"But you two got along all right?"

Dani smiled a little. "He always treated me like I was twelve. Or stupid. I could never decide which. He acted as if I needed the guidance of someone older and wiser. He treated Allie the same way. For a long time we viewed his behavior as protectiveness, but eventually we all realized he was a control freak. And a lazy one at that."

"Probably didn't do the marriage a lot of good."

"No," Dani agreed softly. It was time to change the subject. Her sister's failed marriage wasn't something she needed to discuss. She let out a breath and tossed a small pebble in the water a few feet away, watching the ripples.

"I can leave if you want to swim, although it's not good to swim alone."

She laughed as she said, "Yes. This river is almost four feet deep in places."

"You might get a leg cramp."

"And need to be rescued?" she asked wryly. He shrugged a shoulder, his eyes holding hers in a way that told her he was game for a good rescue. A low, slow burn started deep inside her, telling her that she was just as game.

"You could go swimming, too." She couldn't believe she just said that—or maybe she couldn't believe the tone she'd just said it in.

"I don't have anything to wear."

If he thought she was going to ask him to skinny-dip with her, he was about to be disappointed, because Dani was making a Herculean effort to get herself back under control. Not that she would have minded seeing him naked, but it would only complicate matters right now. She couldn't, on one hand, say that she wasn't interested in getting friendlier than they already were, and then on the other to invite him to swim in the nude.

But maybe if she turned her back until he got into the water…

Dani gave herself a mental shake. "Next time come prepared," she said.

"I will, now that I know this place exists." He looked at her, standing next to the water and feeling more awkward by the second, then glanced over his shoulder at the house. "I do have work to do. Got a new project."

"I bet that's a relief for a workaholic."

"You can't begin to imagine." He hesitated for one more long second, then said, "Be careful."

Dani couldn't help laughing. "I've been swimming here for over two decades. It's safe. And if it wasn't Gus will rescue me."

The big dog lifted his head at the sound of his name, as if to assure Gabe that he wasn't unconscious and was up to lifeguarding.

"See you around, Dani."

"Yeah, see you," she echoed. She stood where she was at the water's edge until he disappeared from sight and only then did she shuck out of her shorts and shirt. Slowly she waded into the water, letting it cool her overheated skin. And since it wasn't a particularly hot day, she had no illusions as to why she was warm.

DANI WAS AN ATHLETE. The muscles of her legs and arms were long and smooth, her backside well toned, as was to be expected from someone who rode horses for a living. What he hadn't expected was his inability to stop thinking about how good she'd looked in cutoff jeans, with her hair hanging loose around her shoulders instead of in a braid down her back.

She'd sought him out at the river, brought along a towel as a prop, yet had openly admitted she'd followed him there. However, she couldn't bring herself to swim until he'd left.

Mixed messages. She didn't know what she wanted and right now, neither did he. He had a job to do: he needed to broach the subject of a sale. In his head, before meeting her, he'd thought that he'd get to know her in some capacity, find out what had tipped the scales, kept the sisters from selling before, then address that issue.

So far he hadn't even managed to discover why they had been on the brink of selling and then backed off. And it wasn't all because Dani was cautious and he didn't want to spook her. It was because...

Honestly, he didn't know.

And that bothered the hell out of him.

The phone rang about an hour after he'd returned from the river, while he was staring blankly at his project, waiting for some kind of inspiration.

"How's it going?" Stewart asked without a hello.

"Slowly."

"Not the answer I was expecting."

"I need time to lay more groundwork."

"I thought that was what you're doing."

"I am. Danica is not a very trusting person and I don't want to send her running in the opposite direction by making the suggestion of a sale too soon."

"Serena says she's training a horse for you."

"It provides a good reason for contact." Although he was beginning to see that he didn't really need a reason. He was well on his way to seeing her simply because he wanted to, because it made him feel good to be around her.

"And that you're threatening Serena with that same horse."

"Hey, everyone needs a pet."

Stewart laughed, but it turned into a cough. "Just…get this done. All right? I don't mean to push you, but I want this deal settled before fall."

"You know I'm going to give this everything I've got." Because it was important to the old man, it was important to him.

But after Gabe hung up, he found it impossible to shake the dark, rather guilty feeling enveloping him. He wasn't being totally honest with Dani, but she needn't ever know. It wasn't as if he was doing her harm. In fact, until a couple months ago, she'd wanted to sell. He just needed her to come around

to that way of thinking again—to understand that
selling would give her a better life. She and her
sister could afford that arena, they wouldn't have
the property tax bill that had to be eating them
alive and they'd be able to afford furniture.

If she agreed to this sale, everyone would come
out a winner. And that was the thought he was
going to hold on to.

GABE SHOWED UP at the Lightning Creek Ranch at
four o'clock the next day, the time Dani said she'd
be working Molly. Sure enough, she was leading
the mare into a round corral just as he drove up.
She unsnapped the lead rope, leaving the horse
alone, and crossed the gravel to meet him halfway.

"Properly dressed, I see," she said, smiling
down at his new cowboy boots, the ones he'd
bought for the horse sale where he'd "bumped
into" Dani for the first time.

"When in Rome…"

She flashed a smile at him and a jolt of gut-
level attraction shot through him. Oh, yeah. This
was good…if he wanted to let Stewart down. If he
could just settle this damned deal, then he could
move on to other matters with no conflict of interest. Yeah.

"I used to work her first thing, but I shifted her
in the rotation so she goes last." The dimple appeared next to her mouth as she said, "So you can
get some sleep before you come over."

"I appreciate that." Gabe fell into step with her as she headed back to the pen. "I'll have you know, though, that I fell asleep at midnight last night."

"And got up at...?"

"Eight."

She gave a soft snort. "I'd already worked two horses by then."

"You know, I do have a regular schedule when I'm back home. Here, though, I just fell back into the old pattern."

"Don't you get bored over there, living alone?"

"I could ask the same question."

She cut a quick look his way as she opened the gate. "I have the horses. And Gus."

"And you prefer horses to people."

"Most people," she said, picking up a longish stick that had been lying on the ground at the center of the arena. She clucked to the mare and the horse obediently started moving around the pen.

Conversation was over, but the last comment stuck in Gabe's brain. It probably shouldn't have made him feel as good as it did. She may have been referring to anyone. But she wasn't. It was pretty damned clear that she'd been referring to him.

As Gabe watched, standing a few feet back from the corral, Dani moved Molly in both directions at a walk, trot and canter, sometimes letting her stop. A couple of times she dropped the whip on the ground and approached the horse, who met her halfway for soft words and scratches behind the ear.

After the warm-up, Dani saddled the mare and repeated the process. At the very end of the lesson, she mounted and rode her around the pen using only the halter.

"I did the ground exercises before you got here," she said as she led the mare back to the gate. Gabe opened it and she brought Molly out. "If you come earlier sometime, you can see those, too."

"Yeah. That'd be interesting."

"Hey, Dani!"

Gabe and Dani turned in unison to see a short teenage girl open the door of a white car. "I'm out of here. See you tomorrow."

"Bye."

Gabe turned back to Dani. "You're not so alone after all."

"That's Kelly. She's my babysitter." Gabe lifted a questioning eyebrow and she explained, "A person can get hurt working horses, so it's not safe working them alone. Kelly comes over around noon and stays until four studying."

"What about the morning?"

"I figure at the very least she'll find me."

"Not a pretty picture."

"I send a text before and after each ride to my sister." She pushed her hair back from her forehead. "Sounds overboard, I know, but we knew someone who got seriously injured working a horse and it left a mark."

"As well it should."

DANI WISHED SHE hadn't told Gabe about her friend who had gotten hurt while working a horse alone during her college internship. It might have been the obvious concern on his face, or maybe the fact that for a minute it felt as if he was going to reach out and touch her. Whichever it was, she needed to step back. She wasn't ready to get touched yet... was she?

"So," she said as she led Molly to the hitching rail and tied her. "That's what a lesson looks like." She hooked the stirrup over the saddle horn and began loosening the cinch, superaware of the guy standing a few feet away, silently watching. Emphasis on silent. What was he thinking? Dani pulled off the saddle, balanced it on her thigh, then pulled the blanket off with her free hand. She held it out to Gabe.

"Do you mind?"

"Not at all."

Together they walked to the shed she used as a tack room and Gabe opened the door. Dani stepped into the small space, hefted the saddle onto the rack, then reached out for the blanket, thankful that he didn't follow her inside. When she reemerged, Gabe shut and latched the door.

"You know, if you ever need an emergency sitter, I'm available."

More time with Gabe? More time to feel torn between looking and acting? Dani met his eyes directly as she coolly said, "Thanks for the offer."

"But no thanks?"

"Kelly is very dependable."

"No doubt," he said with an easy no-pressure smile that made the backed-into-a-corner feeling start to evaporate. "Like I said, in an emergency."

"Thanks," she said. "I need to turn out Molly. I've been thinking about putting her in with Lacy. They made friends over the fence and Lacy has a larger area."

"I don't mind," he said in a surprised tone.

"It's in the contract that I won't put horses together."

"Why?"

"They bite and kick when they play and can take the hide off each other."

"They play rough."

Dani laughed. "Yes. For us. Not for them."

"If you think they'd do well together, I don't care."

"Horses are herd animals. They like to love on each other, scratch each other's itches."

"I'm kind of like that, too."

"Aren't we all," she said lightly as she opened the gate and led Molly inside. Lacy started across the field, trotting when she realized she was about to have a friend with her. Dani slipped off the halter and stepped back outside the gate, which Gabe shut and latched.

The mares approached each other, touched noses, snorted, then Lacy started to run, circling the pasture, with Molly at her shoulder.

"Good. No kicking."

"They like being together."

"Horses aren't meant to be alone."

"Neither are people," Gabe said in such a low voice that Dani wondered if she'd heard him right.

GABE STAYED AT Dani's place while she worked another horse. She had an appointment in town the next day and wanted to free up an hour, so he'd stayed. And she'd let him, which was an excellent step in the direction he wanted their relationship to go—toward trust.

When she was done and had released the horse, she asked him if he wanted a beer, but he declined. "I have a few things to get done."

"I understand." She smiled at him—he caught a hint of the dimple next to her mouth and thought to himself that this had been a well-spent afternoon. In many ways.

As she walked with him to his car, he said, "Before I ask, I want you to know that this isn't a come-on. It's just a question…what do you do with your evenings, Dani?"

Dani regarded him for a moment, her head

slightly tilted. "Well, on Saturdays if I'm not unconscious by six o'clock, I might head out to a
friend's bar—McElroy's—although I've only gone
once since coming back." Because Gina had only
been able to talk her mother into sitting once and
Dani did not go to bars alone—even those belong-
ing to people she grew up with.

"Nice place?"

"Familiar place. It's owned by the brother of
one of my friends. Mac. The guy who helped me
buy Lacy."

"I remember him," Gabe said. "About fourteen
feet tall? Solidly built?"

"That's him. His brother, Jim, looks the same."

"I know the place," he said. "Although I haven't
seen any giants in there. I did get a locals-only
feeling in the place." And he was damned glad he
hadn't asked questions about Dani if the brother of
the blond giant who'd helped Dani win the horse
at the auction was the owner. From the vibe he'd
gotten that day, if he asked anything about Dani,
the owner of the place would want to know who
was asking and why.

"That's kind of what it is."

"Anyplace else?"

She thought for a moment. "There's the Timberline. That new resort on the other side of the
valley. I hear it's really nice in an escargot kind
of way."

Gabe laughed. "A snail way?"

"A fancy schmancy snail way."

"Ah. Have you been there?"

"I haven't been back in town long enough to check it out. My friend Gina and I have talked about it. You know Gina—she works at the café?"

It was hard not to know Gina. She was, in a word, friendly. And if he wanted to use another word, it would be *sexy*. Friendly and sexy were a nice combination, but it also offered up complications he didn't need, as did his gut-level attraction to Dani.

"I might check it out sometime," he said. "But I like places that are smaller, more intimate. More, I don't know…normal?"

Dani laughed. "I think I know what you mean. You can go to a fancy place and have someone park the car and take your coat and make you sniff a cork—"

"Force fancy snails upon you."

"Yes!" Dani pointed at him as if he'd just made a profound statement. "But it doesn't feel as good as a night out at the local steak house."

"That," Gabe said with a smile that threatened to become heartfelt, "is exactly what I mean. I love a good steak in an underwhelming environment. Bells and whistles put me off."

"Then I guess you're a cheap date."

His eyebrows lifted a little. "I'm not going to ask you if you'd like to find out."

"Because you know the answer?"

"Pretty much."

Dani glanced down at the graveled path momentarily, then her eyes came back up. "The way things are—the way I am—it's not because I don't like you. I do." A delicate rose color stained her cheeks, but her expression was very serious as she said, "And that's kind of a problem."

"How so?" He asked the question, then held himself very still, not wanting to put her under any kind of pressure to answer before she was ready.

She dropped the hand that had been resting casually on the side mirror of his car and met his eyes, her expression candid as she said, "I've been burned recently. In a bad way."

"Is there any other way to get burned?" he asked.

"There are degrees."

"Agreed." He shoved his hands in his back pockets, met her honesty with some of his own. "I want to be friends, Dani."

"*Just* friends?" she asked with an arch of her eyebrows.

"For now."

"For now." She glanced down at the ground again, scraped a pebble aside with her shoe.

"I'm not going to lie and say that there's no possibility of anything else, ever. Not when…" His words trailed off before he stated the obvious—not when there was such a healthy buzz of awareness between them.

One corner of her mouth quirked up, telling him that she knew exactly what he'd been about to say. "Well, I appreciate the no-lying part, given my recent past." Once again she took hold of the mirror. "I have things to work through and I want to be fair. To both of us."

"Don't worry about me."

"If I didn't, then I wouldn't be a very nice person, would I?"

He moved closer, but resisted the urge to reach out and touch her, trace his fingers over the smooth curve of her cheek. "I won't burn you," he said in a low voice.

"I won't give you a chance."

"Then we should be fine."

"Agreed," she said, matching his tone, but she still had a wary look about her.

Don't push things.

He pushed. "Now that we understand each other, I'm going to take a chance and ask if you want to come over to my place tonight when you get done with all your horse stuff. Because if I spend another evening alone, my head is going to explode."

Dani's lips twitched, which he took as a good sign. "I'll barbecue steaks. You can bring your giant blond friend if you want, or Gina, or both…"

"I'll be fine on my own," she said drily. "Since we understand each other."

"You'll come?"

"I will, but I have plans for tonight, so how about tomorrow?"

"Maybe the night after?" He had a conference call lined up with Stewart and Neal in the late afternoon about an unrelated project and had no idea how long it would last.

"Sounds good. Should I bring something?"

"No. I'll be happy just to have some company."

CHAPTER NINE

CONVERSATION. BARBECUED STEAKS. Just friends. For now. She'd made that clear. He'd agreed.

Then why did it feel kind of like a first-date thing?

Because she wanted him. She felt the urge to engage, touch, move closer. Yet, she was afraid, thanks to that asshole Chad.

Dani closed the tack-room door and whistled for Gus, who was out romping with Lacy, before letting herself through the pasture gate. Chad had turned out to be a cheating jerk. That didn't mean there weren't a lot of guys out there who had integrity, believed in honesty. The only problem was that she'd thought Chad had integrity, which meant that her integrity radar wasn't the best and that was the source of her concern.

Dani started across the pasture toward the river with Gus trotting along behind her, heading to the swimming hole. Her thinking place. Now that she had the house to herself, having a dedicated getaway was unnecessary, but there was something about flowing water that calmed the soul, put out small fires that threatened to burst into flames.

Was she getting to close to a flame by going to

Gabe's place the next night? Probably. And maybe a few flames wouldn't be a bad thing. She could ease back into social waters with a guy who had no agenda. A guy who was going to go back to his real life. He might have extended his stay, but he was admittedly lonely and Dani couldn't see him lasting in the Eagle Valley for any length of time…and she wanted to know more about him. She'd risk being burned—she just wouldn't get so close to the flames that she got incinerated.

On the way to the river they encountered a couple of rabbits who had the audacity to eat clover in Gus's field. The big dog let out a low booming bark and the chase was on—kind of. The rabbits disappeared into the brush by the river long before Gus got anywhere near them and that was when Dani noticed that Lacy had followed them more than halfway across the field, stopping at the point where Gus had taken off after the rabbits. As Dani watched, the mare turned around and ambled back toward the other horses.

By the time Dani reached the river, Gus had eased into the slow current and was paddling across the broad stretch of not very deep water, his nose held high. He reached the other side and shook. Dani hesitated for a moment, then slipped out of her shirt and shorts and waded up to her thighs. Heavenly. She pushed off into the water and swam over to where Gus was pawing at a stick at the edge of the shore. Brushing her hair back from her eyes, she sat on the warm rocks and tilted her chin up to the sky…and thought about Gabe.

It was nearly dark when Dani returned home. She checked the horses, checked the standpipes, because she always did that now, made certain that the tack shed was locked. Once upon a time that hadn't been necessary, but with the price of saddles rising and the possibility of someone meaning her mischief, she wasn't taking chances.

Gabe's lights were on, but instead of the large windows being lit up, there was one lone light shining through the darkness. Maybe he really was giving up his late-night working hours. In preparation for returning to his old life?

Dani idly ran a hand over her arm as she studied the light. Maybe that was all the more reason to take advantage of this opportunity to get to know him better. They were talking to one another. Laying things out. Being honest. He wasn't a guy who would promise to stay by her and then make a fool of her, because he wasn't going to get the chance to make any promises.

So maybe there was no harm in enjoying each other's company.

Maybe she was ready to loosen up and see how things played out. Risk a small burn. As long as it was on her terms.

DANI STARTED WORKING horses an hour earlier than usual on the day she was slated to have dinner with Gabe, so that she could be free to attend the Eagle Valley Days fund-raising meeting with Gina that afternoon—a meeting Gina assured her didn't involve Chad's family. As it turned out, however, it did involve Chad.

She'd barely parked in front of the café, where the meeting was being held in the banquet room, when a very familiar Lexus pulled into the lot and parked a few spaces away. Chad got out of the car without even glancing her way and swaggered into the café. Moments later Dani watched through the oversize picture windows that made up the front of the building as he shook hands and slapped back.

The hero returns.

And she wasn't going in there.

For a moment, Dani simply sat and tried to draw the courage to get out of her car and walk inside. She wasn't one to back down—never had been. When she encountered trouble she faced it head-on, but she couldn't face this. Not yet. The pain was still too damned raw, and how awkward was it going to be for everyone in the meeting to have to sit with the formerly engaged couple pointedly ignoring each other? Because right now Dani couldn't fake friendliness. Not after what he'd done.

Reaching down and turning the key in the ignition, starting the car and thus giving in to cowardliness made her feel like crap, but some primitive emotional survival instinct had kicked in and Dani didn't fight it. She put the car in gear, drove out of the lot, then stopped a few blocks away and sent Gina a text that simply said, Sorry, can't make it to meeting. Her friend would understand. She'd probably think Dani needed to suck it up, as did Dani herself, but she'd understand.

You're going to have to meet him sooner or later.

But it didn't have to be in front of an audience.

On the way home she debated about how she wanted to handle this Chad situation. She wasn't going to spend her life avoiding her ex-fiancé. It wasn't worth the effort, so maybe she should go to the bank where he worked, have a talk, get the first "bump into" over with.

She hated that idea.

On second thought, maybe she should keep her wits about her and avoid him and his wife as much as possible.

All she wanted—really, really wanted—was to feel like her old self again. To go after what she desired without fear of being hurt. Walk around her hometown without worrying about who she was going to run across. Was that too much to ask?

After returning home, Dani fed the cattle, then went in the house to shower and see what she had that was both clean and acceptable to wear to a neighborly barbecue. She had no idea how this was going to play out, but after the events of the day, a distraction was in order and Gabe could distract her like no other.

Finally, dressed in a simple blue scoop-neck T-shirt and her jeans with the bling on the back pockets, she slipped her feet into sandals, slapped on a couple of silver bangles and headed out the door. This was just going be an evening of shared conversation and food. Nothing else, so there was no need for butterflies.

The butterflies weren't listening—probably because she was lying to herself. This was not about just food and conversation. This was about two people deciding what their next move would be—and the fluttering intensified as she parked her car, then crossed the neat lawn to the redwood deck, where Gabe was tending the coals in a barbecue.

"Hey," he said with an easy smile. He was wearing his glasses and instead of the dark jeans and oxford shirt with the rolled-up sleeves, he had on well-worn jeans that hugged the muscles in his thighs and a charcoal-gray T-shirt. He looked comfortable, laid-back—pretty much the exact opposite of how she felt.

"Hey yourself," she replied, smiling as if she was as relaxed as he. "I didn't think about it until

I was driving over, but I should have brought beer or wine or something."

"I have plenty."

"Glad to hear it," Dani replied with more feeling than she intended.

Gabe cocked an eyebrow. "Bad day?"

A breeze swirled by and she brushed the hair back from her face. "Long day." She wasn't going to broach the matter of Chad and the reunion, mainly because she was disgusted with herself. "Yesterday—that was a bad day."

Gabe motioned to the wood-framed glass door leading into the house and Dani followed. "What happened yesterday?" he asked as he held the door open for her. "It didn't involve Lacy, did it?"

"No. I had a run-in with a client," Dani said as she stepped inside. The interior was almost as empty as that of her house, except that it was much more opulent. Black granite counters, stainless-steel appliances, a vaulted ceiling. Built-in bookshelves and cabinets lined two walls while the south wall, which faced her ranch, was entirely glassed-in, giving him a tremendous view.

She turned back as Gabe set a glass on the counter and Dani realized that even though he was there temporarily, he had nicer wineglasses than she did. Perhaps because hers had been free with the purchase of a bottle of Christmas chardonnay.

"What happened with your client?" he asked over his shoulder.

"I was too candid. Bad habit of mine. I think I'm being tactful, but sometimes I just say things."

"When one works with the public, candid isn't always the best option."

"You sound like someone who knows."

"No. I'm someone who doesn't work with the public for that very reason. That's why I have Serena. She fronts for me."

"Perhaps I should get Kelly to front for me."

"What happened?" Gabe asked again as he handed her the glass.

"The short version is that I told a client that she was a beginner and that the horse she'd purchased wasn't a beginner's horse. She said she'd thought that it was my job to turn the mare into a beginner's horse." Dani rolled her shoulders as she recalled the uncomfortable discussion where she had to walk the thin line between truth and smoothing the client's ruffled feathers. "Then I said that was my job, but that I needed to work with her, too, so that she knew the same cues the horse did. For some reason she thought I was telling her that she was a poor rider rather than a beginning rider, which wasn't my intention, and..." She lifted the wine in a salute.

"Are you certain you want to make this your chosen profession?"

"Oh, yes." She spoke with certainty. If there was one thing she was sure of, it was her chosen profession. "This is part of the game. I did manage to convey what I was really saying. Finally. The woman apologized for misunderstanding, but it was kind of stressful. I wasn't unhappy to see her get into her car and drive away."

Gabe smiled at her from across the counter, where he was rubbing olive oil on two steaks. "Sounds like you did all right."

"Funny how much more important these encounters are when you're running your own business. One person bad-mouthing you can cause considerable damage."

"Yeah. I know."

Dani cocked her head at him. "How long have you been in business for yourself?"

"Five years. I interned while in college with some pretty big firms, then was fortunate enough to get a start-up loan from the father of a friend, who also threw some contacts my way." One corner of his mouth tightened wryly. "One of the few times in my life things went according to plan."

"You've hit a few bumps in the road?"

"You could say that," he answered smoothly, lifting the plate with the T-bones. "How do you like your steak?"

"Medium."

"I'm no grill master, but I'll do my best."

Not a grill master indeed. He had a station set up next to the barbecue kettle that would have done a surgeon proud, all the implements lined up in a neat row—tongs, spatula, fork—and the seasonings in another. He allowed the palm of one hand to hover over the charcoal for a few seconds, gave a satisfied nod and carefully set the first steak on the hot grill, lifting it, then resettling it so the meat wouldn't adhere, then repeated with the other steak.

"Done this before, have you?"

"I'm a guy. I like cooking dangerously."

"All you need is a Kiss the Cook apron and the picture would be complete."

"I wouldn't mind that," he said as he shifted one steak a fraction of an inch.

"An apron?"

He slowly shook his head. "No."

Dani felt a smile start to play on her lips as she caught his drift. "I thought we agreed to a friends-only evening?"

"Hey," he said with an innocent shrug. "Kissing the cook is a time-honored tradition and totally innocuous. Like kissing a maiden aunt."

"I think kissing you would be nothing like kissing a maiden aunt," she said drily.

"Want to find out?" he asked with a waggle of his eyebrows that made her smile finally break through, despite the unsettling low, slow tumble deep in her abdomen. She was edging closer to that flame and rather enjoying the flicker of heat.

She stepped back. "Maybe I'll wait until you put on your apron."

He set down his tongs with a clatter. "I'll just be a minute…"

Dani laughed, but even though he gave the appearance of kidding, he wasn't. He wanted to kiss her. She could see it in the way his eyes kept drifting to her lips and realized that she was going to have to make a decision here. Fish or cut bait.

"Can't blame a guy for trying…in a friendly way." He picked up the tongs and turned his attention back to the steaks and Dani drew in a breath. She had no doubts now that they were heading in the same direction, despite the friends-only talk. Her question was how far did she want to go?

She sat on the edge of the redwood deck and watched Gabe's profile while he tended the grill. He might not be married, but he had to be involved with someone. Guys like this didn't just walk around unencumbered—not unless there was some kind of chink in the armor.

"What?" Gabe asked and Dani realized just how intently she'd been studying him.

"Just wondering what your fatal flaw is."

"Too many to count," he replied easily, returning his focus to the steaks.

"I guess that's why you're single."

He turned an amused gaze toward her. "Probably," he agreed. "You do have a gift for being candid."

"I'm nothing compared to my sister Jolie."

"She's the one moving in with you in a few months."

"Yes. She's the reason we still have the ranch. My older sisters, Mel and Allie, wanted to sell after Allie and Kyle decided to split up. I agreed to sell, too, even though I love the place, because I thought I was going to be with SnowFrost for a long time." She took a sip of wine. "Then the bad thing happened."

"Company went under?"

"Oh, yeah. And it was a surprise. The owners had done a superb job of making us believe that everything was going well—not to fool us, but because they were hoping it would eventually be true. That things would turn around. They didn't." Gabe pulled the first steak off the grill and set it on a plate. "At first I was devastated. I knew I could find another job, but working at Snow-Frost… It was small and intimate. I loved my job. And it was gone."

"Stinks."

Dani smiled. "But then I realized that although SnowFrost had failed, at least the owners had taken a shot, and maybe it was time that I also took a shot—while we still owned the Lightning Creek. It was the perfect place to set up the business I dreamed of, but honestly never really planned to embark on because it wasn't secure. Well, neither was my nine-to-five job in the end."

"Did it bother you to think about selling? Back when you'd thought you wanted to?" Dani shot him a questioning look and he said, "You mentioned that your older sister never liked the ranch much, even though she settled on it. I was wondering how you felt."

"Like I said, I love the ranch, but felt for Allie. She was so unhappy, and Mel, who worked in real estate, seemed to think selling was the best bet." Dani shrugged. "So I went along with it. Sometimes you have to cut ties with things you love in order to move forward."

Gabe's gaze seemed to sharpen as he slowly nodded. "Good point."

"How about you? Do you have any deep emotional ties to a place?"

"I traveled too much as a kid."

"Military brat?"

"Foster child. Juvenile delinquent."

Dani felt her mouth start to drop open and managed to shut it again. "I had no idea."

Gabe shrugged and brought the plates to the table, where he'd already laid out a simple green salad, a loaf of French bread and butter. "It's just the way things were," he said before smiling at her. "I hope you don't mind simple."

"Me? The queen of the frozen entrée? I think not." But she was still working on that foster-child thing. It was one thing to have one pair of foster parents, but to be moved around a lot—that didn't sound good at all.

Gabe sat across from her, picked up a steak knife and carved out his first bite. Dani did the same, missing the easy camaraderie that had been there seconds before. Gabe concentrated on his meal for a few long moments, then looked up and addressed the issue with a few quick sentences. "I was a foster child because my mother was unstable. Living in someone else's house wasn't that bad."

"Because yours was."

"Yeah." He spoke matter-of-factly, without a trace of self-pity, and Dani began to relax as his acceptance of his past became evident. "I was removed from the home the first time when I was seven, after my grandmother died. Mom wanted me back when I was eleven. That lasted almost a year, then I was put back in the system and stayed there."

"You've made a success of your life."

An odd look crossed his face, then vanished. "Because someone eventually hammered into me the point that I was the only person in charge of my life. I may not have been able to choose the life I lived as a child, but I could choose my future."

"You appear to have chosen well."

Gabe lifted his wine, gave a small salute before he drank. "Honestly? I have no complaints."

"Neither do I," Dani said. "Well, if I had a do-over, I would have my dad live. But other than that, I have no complaints."

"He died young?"

Dani set down her fork and dabbed at her mouth with the napkin. There was half a steak left, but she was done for now. "In his late forties. An out-of-the-blue heart attack."

"Must have been hard on your mother, having four kids and no husband."

But at least she *had* a mother who wanted her. A mother who had worked her ass off trying to hold on to the ranch so that she and her sisters could grow up there, as their father had wanted.

"She's tough. We all are."

"I noticed," he said, smiling his crooked smile at her and making her pulse bump up again. She was beginning to enjoy the sensation rather than feel threatened by it. Gabe wasn't Chad. "Does she still live in the area? Your mother," he added when she looked at him blankly.

Dani smiled. "After Jolie graduated high school, she had a wild fling with the school principal, whom she'd fought with on and off throughout all of our academic careers. They married and retired to Florida."

"So the story had a happy ending?"

"And we're trying to keep it that way. We kind of…edit our lives a bit when we talk to Mom. Otherwise she'd fly home, kick butt and take names."

"Probably a good thing for Kyle you do that."

"The Kyle situation is hard to finesse, but Allie does her best to make things appear more amicable than they are. We all fly down to Orlando once a year to have mother-daughter time, so…" She lifted her eyebrows and raised one shoulder in an eloquent shrug.

"You're handling your own problems rather than letting her take them on."

"That sounds so much better than saying that we're kind of lying to our mom."

He laughed at that and then the conversation shifted to other less personal areas, such as the community and whether Montana winters were any worse than Midwest winters—safe subjects that allowed Dani to stop measuring her words. Gabe was easy to talk to and Dani had found herself discussing matters she generally didn't—like her family life. And she was enjoying the vibe between them, the subtle hum of attraction that neither was acknowledging at the moment although they both were more than aware of it.

If he had a fatal flaw, did it matter? Would she let herself get close enough that it did matter?

Not without a whole lot of forethought and caution.

But there were other ways to get close—ships-that-pass-in-the-night ways. She could do that. In fact, the thought of doing it made her feel deliciously in control—to the point that when Gabe finally walked her to her truck as twilight fell, she turned and took his face in her hands and rose up on her toes to gently kiss him good-night.

That was the plan, anyway, but as his lips parted beneath hers, she couldn't help but explore a little farther. He tasted so damned good—his lips were firm and warm and wonderful, and she sensed that while he was holding back, he could be easily pushed over the line. She was tempted to give him that nudge, but instead stepped back. Dropped her hands from his face, even though she really, really wanted to pull his lips back to hers and see exactly what he had to offer.

There was a clear question in his eyes as she put a little space between them and slowly she shook her head.

"I just had to know," she said matter-of-factly, ignoring the way her heart was hitting her ribs. "For the record, Gabe, that was nothing like kissing my maiden aunt."

GABE STARTED TOWARD the house after Dani turned her truck around and headed down the drive, shifting himself so that he could walk more comfortably. She'd barely kissed him and he'd become instantly hard. It'd been so damned difficult to keep from touching her, but he was fairly certain if he had, she would have backed off—even though she'd been the one to initiate. He hadn't touched, she hadn't backed off and they'd parted on good terms. The only problem was that he was now fully aware he wanted Dani in a way that didn't fit into his plans. Not yet anyway. Later...

He'd think about later, well, later. Right now he had a goal and he felt that he'd made some decent headway on getting to know her and gaining her trust. She had talked rather openly about her family and for the first time since...maybe ever... he'd told someone besides Neal about his mom. Not much, but a little.

Why?

To get Dani to open up, of course. But it had felt like more than that. It was one thing to tell her he'd been in foster care, another to give her details. He didn't give details of his life, because the next thing you know, all the sordid truth would come out. He didn't think he should still be doing penance for teenage mistakes, but he also didn't want to be judged on those mistakes, and if life had taught him one thing, it was that people judged first.

He turned before opening his door and watched the old pickup kick up dust as it thundered down the driveway to Dani's house. Yeah, he'd made headway, but it didn't feel right.

She'd wanted to sell the ranch before she'd lost her job. That was what he needed to focus on.

Sometimes you cut ties with things you love in order to move on.

Something else he needed to focus on. She'd verbalized exactly what he wanted her to see—

that she and her sister would be better off moving on. They'd get paid handsomely and the older sister would no longer be reminded of a painful past. Plus Deputy Kyle wouldn't have any reason to mess with them any longer. Win, win, win. And another win if he counted Stewart.

Gabe walked back into the house and booted up his laptop to see what he could find about Jolie Brody—particularly who she worked for.

CHAPTER TEN

WHAT WAS SLEEP?

Something that had eluded Dani after she returned home from her "friends-only" evening with Gabe, leaving her yawning the next morning and doing her chores in a haze. Apparently sleep had eluded Gabe, too, because every time Dani rolled over in bed to face the window, she could see his lights. Nothing new, because he was a night guy, despite his insistence that he was changing, but she couldn't help but wonder if he was thinking of her. She sure as hell couldn't stop thinking about him.

How crazy had it been to give in to temptation and kiss him?

A little crazy, but nothing she wouldn't have done pre-Chad. She'd kissed Gabe because he was attractive and she wanted to reassure herself that she was still in control, that she didn't need to be emotionally paralyzed by what Chad had done to her. And she had been in control—right up until her lips had touched his and a primal urge for *more* had slammed into her. Even now the memory of the brief kiss, the way her hands had automatically tightened on his shoulders as she pulled herself closer to him, made her grow warm. She'd been lucky to have walked away as easily as she had, without losing face or ending up in his bed.

In his bed.

She gave her head a small shake to clear it as she cranked on the water trough faucet. Some nice imagery there, but not what she needed just now…

Or maybe it was exactly what she needed to wipe Chad out of her head once and for all and restore her confidence.

Warmth pooled deep within her at the thought, making her wonder if she should indulge in a hot session of confidence restoration. Logically she knew Chad's cheating was a reflection on him, but a small part of her still occasionally whispered that maybe she hadn't been enough and that was why he'd cheated.

"Bull," Dani muttered to herself as she adjusted the flow with a sharp twist of her wrist. She didn't need to sleep with Gabe to restore confidence when her only shortcoming had been in believing Chad. Trusting him too much.

She leaned down to scoop out a couple of soggy leaves that had swirled to the top of the icy trough water, then wiped her hand on her jeans. Nothing like getting the figurative punch to the gut to make her realize past errors in judgment. In retrospect, she should have figured out something was going on long before she had. The signs had been there, but she had chosen not to see them. It was Chad, after all. The love of her life.

Dani moved the hose from the first trough to the next, splattering her pant legs as the water splashed onto the dry ground.

The love of one's life didn't screw other women.

She wouldn't be that careless again.

She filled all the troughs and then dove into pen cleaning, resolutely turning her thoughts away from Gabe and toward her plans for the horses that occupied those pens. She'd just finished mucking out the last area when the phone rang in her pocket. If it hadn't been Allie, she would have ignored the call.

"What's up?" she asked, hoping that her sisterly radar was wrong; that this was just a touch base call. It wasn't.

"Kyle." There was a moment of silence, as if she was calming herself before continuing on. "He'll bring the tractor back this weekend, but now he wants the armoire. The same one he told me to stuff when we had a fight over who got what." She exhaled, then said, "He never liked it and never seemed to care what it was worth. But now he wants it."

"Let him have it," Dani said.

"I don't want to. It was mine in the settlement and I gave it to you."

"Let him take it."

"It'll set a precedent."

"Of what? Do you have anything else he can demand?" No, because Allie had sold almost everything she'd gotten in the settlement to pay for college and to get the stuff out of her life. Even the dishes had gone. Only the tractor and the armoire remained, and the armoire was there because Dani had asked Allie to leave it, planning to buy it from her at a later date, as in when her business was solidly in the black.

"I hate doing this."

"Do it. Give him the armoire and maybe he'll go away."

"It doesn't feel like he's ever going to go away. He's dead set on making me pay for making him feel like a loser. Nope. He's not going away."

Dani gave a small, brittle laugh. "We're a pair, Al."

"How so?"

"Chad's not going away, either. He's branch manager of the local US Western."

"Get out."

"It's true. And when I went to meet Gina at the Eagle Valley Days meeting, there he was, working the crowd."

"Aw, Dani. That stinks."

"I agree. I came here to get away from him." And the moral was that maybe running didn't solve anything, but she wasn't saying that out loud to Allie just yet. Not when her sister was still so raw from everything that had happened with Kyle.

"You can cope. I know you can."

"So do I."

"What happened at the meeting?"

"I chickened out." Dani truly hated forcing out those words. "I didn't even get out of my car."

"You know what? I totally understand."

"I'm not sure I do. I'm tougher than this, Allie."

"Give yourself a break. Seriously."

"I will if you just give Kyle the damned hutch and be done with it."

There was a long silence, so long that Dani was about to say, "Allie?" when her sister finally let out a breath and said, "I hate it, but all right. I'll let him know he won. I won't put it in those terms, but it's pretty much what happened."

"Maybe it's the last battle."

"One can only hope. I'll give you a heads-up before he comes to get it."

"Thanks, Al. Is everything else going all right?"

"You know…it is. As good as can be expected anyway, for a nontraditional student still trying to learn the ropes. I have no idea how Mel spent her entire life in school."

"While loving every minute of it. I agree. She's from another planet."

Allie laughed, sounding like her old self for two or three whole seconds and giving Dani a glimmer of hope that maybe she was sorting things out. "If you have any trouble with Kyle, like if he snaps off any standpipes or anything, let me know."

"Will do. And you promise not to worry."

"Fat chance, but I'll do my best."

THAT AFTERNOON AFTER working her last horse, Dani caught Lacy and led her out onto the lawn to eat grass. Gus followed, flopping down under a tree, lifting his head as the landline rang inside the house. Dani pushed herself back to her feet and jogged to the house, leaving the mare to graze under Gus's watchful eye.

Gabe? One of her sisters?

Sister.

"I got an extension on my internship." Jolie's voice vibrated with excitement. "Until next March, which means more money in the pot for the arena and a winter I won't have to spend waiting tables or something. I won't be able to move home until spring, but, hey—more money for the arena."

"That's incredible," Dani said.

"My lease is up next week, so I'm moving in with Shelby. That'll save even more money."

"Both of you in that camp trailer?"

"Just for a couple months."

"Like what? Six months? I guess that'll test the bonds of friendship."

"There's more," Jolie said.

"More?"

"They said this could work into full-time."

"No kidding?" No one got a full-time job in

horse science right out of college. Few people *ever* got a full-time job in the field.

"Yeah. I guess there might be some funding available and…I don't have all the details, but there is a possibility."

"That's…great! Wow. Unexpected, too."

"Yeah. I know. Paycheck! Okay, so anyway, I have to run. I'll talk to you soon!"

"Sure thing."

Dani hung up, wondering just how she felt about this new development. She'd been looking forward to Jolie moving home and now it looked as if she'd spend the winter alone. But as Jolie had said, a longer internship meant more money saved for the arena and year-round training. If it worked into full-time, well, then Jolie had some decisions to make. Would she give that up to come back to the ranch and run clinics? Or would she go with the guaranteed paycheck?

If Jolie's job became permanent and she didn't move back home…well, Dani was going to have to reassess her master plan. Without Jolie, it was going to take double the time to buy the covered arena, so double the time until she could train year-round and thus have an income that didn't depend on a second job. And then there were the ranch repairs that were stacking up. She was applying Band-Aids as quickly as she could, but there was no getting around the fixes that needed to be made before a roof blew off or a fence fell down.

By agreement, the sisters split the cost of repairs, just as they split the ranch income—which at the moment was zero. However, Dani couldn't ask her sisters to pony up money for repairs they got no benefit from. Maybe if they started running cattle again, but right now…

Right now she was wondering if she should start looking for that second job immediately, since Jolie wasn't coming home until the spring— if she came home at all. She'd have to wait until her current contracts were done so that she could arrange her training schedule around whatever job she managed to land, but maybe she needed to start looking.

Was it time to call Gina, see about getting on at the café part-time?

She reached for the phone, but instead of dialing Gina, she called Mel. To her astonishment, her sister picked up.

"You're in cell range and you didn't call?" Dani demanded.

Mel laughed lowly. "Well, honestly, I thought I'd shower first, since I haven't seen water in four days."

"Don't you remember the pact? Sisters first, shower second?"

"You know, I don't remember agreeing to that," Mel said.

"Well, you did. Three glasses of wine in. Have you talked to Jolie?"

"Nope. That shower thing again."

"She got an extension on her internship."

"Get out!"

"Yeah, I know. And it may lead into something permanent."

"You're kidding."

"Nope." She in filled her sister on the few details she knew.

"You sound happy…but not."

Dani sighed as she sank down into her lone chair. "That sums it up perfectly. I'm happy for her, but concerned about how it affects the business and our plans for the Lightning Creek. The place needs work."

"I'm aware," Mel said drily. "I think I made a pretty extensive before-we-can-sell list when I first moved back."

"We got the painting done." Which made the place look better, but there were issues stemming from long-term neglect that were going to take a healthy infusion of cash to solve. "I'd hoped to put my entire severance toward the arena, but I'm going to have to put a roof on the barn, too." She pushed her hair back. "It's kind of an either-or situation that Jolie was going to help alleviate, but now…"

"I told you the ranch was going to be a money

pit if we kept it. A lot of negatives and not many positives, other than the feeling of being home."

"It seems to me that you got something positive from your time on the Lightning Creek." As in a different perspective, and a reunion with her high-school sweetheart—now her husband.

Dani could hear the smile in Mel's voice as she said, "No arguments there."

"Well, that's a first," Dani said. "And speaking of men…." Her mouth tightened briefly before she dove in and brought her sister up to date on the matter of Chad and his new bride.

"Lovely," Mel said flatly. "So how're you doing with that?"

"I'm fine. Mom doesn't know."

"That goes without saying, but she'll find out."

"True." Dani sighed even though she didn't mean to.

"Don't let one jerk ruin your life," Mel said.

"Funny you should mention that, because I, uh, have a hunky neighbor. He lives in the Staley house. He's…attractive," she acknowledged lamely.

"Does Mom know about him?" Mel asked mildly.

Dani laughed. "No. Not yet. Probably not ever. I'm training a horse for him, he's hot and I'm doing my best to not let what happened with Chad color my future activities."

"And…?"

"And, damn it, Mel, I'm not doing all that well." She wanted some advice. Gina was out of the question, since she, too, lusted after Gabe in a spectator-sport type of way, so that left her sisters. Of them, Mel was her best bet, due to the fact that she was rarely in cell phone range, so she wouldn't have an opportunity ask questions too often. Dani needed an ear, but she didn't need monitoring. Allie was protective and Jolie curious. Mel was definitely the sister for this job.

"Enough said," Mel replied on a heartfelt note, reminding Dani of how twisted up her sister had been before she and KC had come to an understanding about what each of them needed in life. "My biggest piece of advice is to move slowly."

"Slowly." She was doing that, but she was feeling the strong urge to stop doing that.

"Decide what it is you want out of this relationship—"

Dani gave a small cough. "I don't think *relationship* is the correct word. He's not here permanently."

"Ah." Mel cleared her throat. "Are you looking for permission to get laid?"

"I'm scared, Mel. Scared I'm going to use him or he's going to use me."

"Easy way around that."

"Yeah?"

"Talk. If you can't talk to the guy, you shouldn't be, you know…" Her voice trailed off.

"Good point," Dani conceded. "Very good point."

After she hung up, Dani paced through the house a couple times, then finally turned on the water for a shower. Okay, so maybe she had been asking Mel for permission to get laid when she'd told her about Gabe. Maybe she'd wanted to hear, "Guys are always okay with sex with no strings. Go for it!" Instead she'd heard, "Communicate."

Communicating meant figuring out exactly what she wanted and she didn't know, which in turn meant she probably shouldn't be moving forward. She didn't want to use Gabe and she didn't want a relationship.

So maybe she'd best just explain that to him.

Far, far easier said than done.

ALMOST A WEEK had passed since Dani had come to dinner at Gabe's place, kissed and ran, and he hadn't heard one word from her. Was it because of that one small kiss? Was she afraid of things getting out of hand?

If so, he had to do something about that. If she retreated too far, it would totally screw up his plans...and besides that, he missed her.

Finally he couldn't take waiting anymore, so he walked across the fields to her house, glad he had a four-legged excuse named Molly.

Dani was in the pen with a horse he didn't recognize, a large black gelding that wasn't showing her a lot of respect. When Dani glanced over to see what had caught the horse's attention and spotted him, she raised a hand, then immediately went back to work, moving the horse around the pen until he started paying attention to the fact that she was directing his movements—that she was the boss. She worked for another half hour and Gabe patiently stood several yards back from the pen, watching and waiting.

When she finally released the horse, she walked toward him coiling the lead rope. "Hi," she said almost too casually. "Are you here to watch Molly?"

"I am. Where's Kelly?" There was no small car in the drive, no music emanating from the partially open living room window.

"Volleyball camp."

Gabe frowned. "Are you okay with that? Working with no one here?"

"I'm fine." She came to lean her arms on the opposite side of the fence from where he stood. "I take precautions." Her mouth moved sideways and then she said, "I'm actually overly cautious because of what happened to my friend."

"I don't think you're overly cautious having someone here while you work."

"It'll be all right once Jolie's home and until then—"

"You'll take your chances?" Gabe lifted a speculative eyebrow.

"Everyone takes chances."

He nodded, staring out over the pastures toward the mountains that rimmed the valley. "I was thinking…maybe I could come by for a couple hours in the afternoons, work on my laptop."

Her expression barely changed, but there was no mistaking her retreat. A few weeks ago Gabe might not have read it, but today it was obvious to him and he needed to do something about it. This was about more than easing himself into her good graces. This was about safety. Dani's safety.

"I don't…"

"This is just common sense. I can work in your living room, like Kelly did." She didn't look convinced—not even close—and he suddenly wished he hadn't told Neal about Jolie's internship. Neal had worked some magic, the internship had been extended and Dani was here alone. The theory had been that if Jolie had a job, then she wouldn't have such a problem selling the ranch. But Gabe hadn't planned on compromising Dani's safety.

"Look, it doesn't matter where I work when I'm on the computer."

"There's no reason for you to do this."

"Yeah. There is. I like you and I don't want to see you get yourself into trouble." He turned toward her, somehow resisting the strong impulse to put his hands on her shoulders, to make that connection he needed right now. When was the last time he'd needed any kind of connection?

"I appreciate the offer." He waited, sensing she

was on the brink of deciding one way or the other. "If I agree to this—" she pointed a finger at him "—and you have something else to do or it's just not working, say so."

"I will."

She continued to regard him through slightly narrowed eyes. "All right, if you're certain you want to do this."

He smiled at her overly serious expression. "I can get my laptop."

"I'm close to done today. Why don't we start tomorrow?"

"When do you want me here?"

"Kelly used to come around ten."

"I should be out of bed by then." She opened her mouth, but he raised his hand, shushing her. "Kidding."

"I bet." But she smiled and the dimple showed and Gabe had to fight not to lift his hand and touch her beautiful face.

"I'll stay out of your space," he added, just in case she needed a final reassurance.

"And I'll try to stay out of yours," she said softly, so softly he thought he might have heard incorrectly, but one look into her serious hazel eyes told him he had not.

"Meaning?"

"I shouldn't have kissed you the other night."

Gabe stilled. "Didn't live up to standards?"

"No…" she said slowly. "It felt like it might surpass standards."

"I see." He put his hands in his back pockets to keep himself from touching her. He didn't know what to say, which was something to think about, since he always knew what to say.

"I don't want to use you."

His eyebrows shot up as he took her meaning. "You mean like a sex object?" Because many parts of him had no problem with that at all.

She smiled wryly. "Well, that wasn't exactly what I was thinking, but it's close."

It was all he could do not to ask how close. Silence hung between them for a moment and Gabe somehow kept his hands firmly jammed into his rear pockets. "Well, if you ever feel in need of a sex object, I'm just a phone call away."

"A phone call?" she said, lifting her eyebrows dubiously.

"And in the meantime, I'm going to stay here while you work your horses and make sure you don't get stomped. I don't want fear of using me to get in the way of your safety."

"I'm not afraid. I'm…uncertain. About a lot of stuff."

And cautious. Very, very cautious. He reached out and tucked a few strands of golden-brown hair behind her ear, then cupped her cheek in his palm when she didn't move away from his touch. "I know the aftermath of getting burned, Dani.

I've been there myself. And I appreciate what you just told me."

"Honesty is important to me." And hearing her say those words again made something shift in him uncomfortably.

"Then I guess I'll fess up and tell you that I'm a great kisser, but for the time being I'm going to make you take my word on it."

She lifted her eyebrows again, challenge lighting her eyes. "Yeah?"

"Yeah, right up until you feel ready to make that phone call. Until then, I'm your safety guy."

GABE SPENT THE next three mornings in Dani's nearly empty house, showing up at ten as she'd asked, and leaving at two. She agreed to work her most challenging horses during that time, including Lacy, and other than pacing to the window every fifteen or twenty minutes to see how things were going, Gabe settled into working with remarkable efficiency in the nearly empty house.

He liked being in her space. Liked knowing she was outside. There was something calming about having her close, which ironically also put him on edge when he thought about it. When had he ever experienced a feeling like that?

Never.

Finally, after the second day, he decided not to

analyze and simply go with the feeling, see what shook out. And then Neal called.

"How has Dad sounded to you during the past few calls?"

"Impatient."

"No. I mean physically."

"The cough?"

"Exactly!"

"I thought he had a cold."

"It's been going on for over a month."

"Have him see a doctor."

"Yeah. His yearly physical isn't for another six months."

Gabe exhaled, putting his fist against his forehead, hoping this wasn't going to turn into something serious.

"I'm just…worried. Okay?" There was definitely a note of quiet anxiety in his friend's voice.

"And I'm working as fast as I can," Gabe said.

"What?"

"I thought you were going to tell me that if he just had this property, he'd feel better," Gabe said.

"He will, but I was going to say something more along the lines of encourage him to see the doctor next time he coughs into the phone."

"I will," Gabe said sincerely. "And I'm about to move forward on the acquisition."

"Excellent."

"Just don't get his hopes up just yet."

"I won't. Thanks in advance."

"No problem." No problem at all, because Stewart was the closest thing to a long-term father that Gabe had ever had.

HAVING GABE ON the property made it difficult for Dani to focus on training, since her mind kept drifting to the man in her house and his assertion that sex was only a phone call away. Maybe they were on the same page, which opened up some interesting possibilities. Today, however, she managed to tear her mind away from Gabe and zero in on the matter at hand—putting her last hours in on the palomino gelding that would get picked up later that afternoon. The big golden horse represented her first finished contract and she was determined that he would be just as perfect as possible. If he wasn't and Marti heard about it... But she wasn't going to go there.

After the round-pen session, she worked on quietly loading the horse in the trailer and then unloading him. After three perfect loads, she called it a day. As she closed the trailer door, she noticed the plume of dust as a familiar white SUV turned into her driveway. Her ex-brother-in-law.

Excellent. Give her head a shake, she took the horse to her pen and released her without grooming. Kyle pulled up beside her trailer and got out of the vehicle, in full official-cop mode, which was bogus, since Dani was fairly certain he was there on a personal mission. Sure enough.

"Have you talked to Allie?" he asked after a quick hello.

"About the armoire? Yes. You can take it—just as soon as the tractor is parked back beside the barn where it belongs."

A corner of his mouth twitched as if he was surprised by her easy acquiescence. Allie had probably fought him long and hard, so he hadn't expected Dani to simply roll over. "I can bring the tractor by tonight."

"Fine."

"You'll be here?"

"I wouldn't dream of not being here." She smiled at him, an anything-to-get-rid-of-you smile. "Could you give me an exact time?"

"Eight."

"That's rather late."

"I'm on duty until six and I have some business to attend to."

Dani shrugged. "Eight, then."

"You know that the armoire was supposed to be mine."

"And that you let Allie have it, only to renege. Yes, I'm more than aware," she said carelessly. "Sometimes things work out that way."

"Yeah," he said abruptly. "No hard feelings, okay?"

"When have you and I ever had hard feelings?"

The question hung in the air for a brief second and then Kyle's chin lifted as his eyes focused sharply on something behind her. Dani didn't have to turn around to know that Gabe had just come out of the house.

Kyle's demeanor shifted and he squared his shoulders as Gabe approached. Dani waited until she heard the crunch of his boots on gravel before she turned around. "Hi, Gabe. You've met Kyle, right?"

The men regarded each other over her head. "Yes," Gabe said slowly. "We've met."

"Yeah." Kyle's eyes remained narrowed, as if he was working extra hard to figure out just what the hell Gabe was doing there, in the house.

Surprise, Kyle. None of your business. If he'd been the one screwing around on her property, then Dani was fairly certain he wouldn't do that when there was an able-bodied guy on the place. And he wouldn't have a legitimate reason to set foot on the property after tonight. Once he had the armoire, there was nothing else for him to take.

Dani smiled sweetly at Kyle as Gabe came to stand beside her, close enough that if she'd leaned a few inches to the left, their arms would have been pressed together. For a moment the three of them stood in charged silence and then Kyle settled a hand on his utility belt.

"I need to get going." His radio came on then, reiterating the point, and he started to the vehicle.

"I'll see you later," he said as he got into the SUV. He gave Gabe a brief salute, then closed the door and started the engine. Gabe stood planted where he was next to Dani as Kyle swung the rig into a neat three-point turn and then drove past them. Dani pushed her hands up into her hair, pulling it away from her face then letting it fall before turning to Gabe.

"Well, you being here certainly messed with his mind."

"Is that a good thing or a bad thing?"

"I'm thinking good."

"What did your sister see in him?"

"They were high-school sweethearts and Allie needed security. Dad's death hit her hard." Dani ran her hands over her upper arms against the chill of the wind that was starting to pick up. "Kyle had his good points. He's easy to talk to. Dependable in some ways."

"Some ways?"

Dani exhaled. "It's hard to explain. He had this idea that he was beyond doing things the way other people did—he wanted to skip a step. The one that involved paying his dues."

"He felt entitled."

"Yeah. He did. He wanted the ranch to be a roaring success, started all these projects then either didn't finish or finished them poorly."

"Like the standpipes."

"For one. And the roof on the shed."

Gabe grimaced as he studied the slipshod job.

"He's a planner, not a doer, and it drove Allie crazy. Eventually she couldn't take it anymore." She glanced down at the gravel. "There were other things, too. Battles of will, basically. All in all, they weren't a good match. Just like me and Chad."

"Your fiancé."

"Ex-fiancé."

"That's right. The cheating asshole."

Dani lifted her eyebrows. "You know him, then."

Gabe smiled, his eyes crinkling at the corners in a way they hadn't when they'd first met. He was relaxing with her as much as she was relaxing with him.

And that meant…? That meant she was more drawn to him than ever. She halfway wanted to ask him to be there with her when Kyle came by that evening, but it was enough that he was coming over on a daily basis and doing her the favor of being there, just in case. She wasn't going to push things. No, she was not.

"I finished my last horse," she finally said to break the unsettling tension that was building between them as they silently regarded one another.

"All right. I'll pack my stuff."

"I'm not kicking you out." The words came out a little too quickly.

"Are you inviting me to stay longer?"

Dani's breath caught a little. "I'm not sure."

Gabe took a few slow steps closer, stopping less than a foot in front of her and, even though he was no longer smiling, there was warmth in his expression that made Dani want to slide her arms up around his neck and pull him closer. "I won't stay until you are sure."

For a brief moment she thought he was going to reach out and draw her close—prove that he was indeed an excellent kisser. And she would have been okay with that.

Who was she kidding? She'd be all over that.

Instead he took a step back and although Dani stayed planted in the same spot, she felt her expression soften. "I appreciate you coming over," she said.

"I've got to go," he said, even though he once again stepped closer.

"I know," Dani murmured as he reached out to gently take her face between his palms, just as she'd done with him a week or so ago. He lowered his head, took her lips in a gentle kiss that deepened almost immediately into something more. Dani slid her hands up his arms, over his surprisingly muscular biceps, to flatten on his hard chest, steadying herself as she leaned into his kiss.

It took her a moment to find words after he lifted his head, and when she did, it was an inadequate "Okay."

"Couldn't help myself," he said.

Dani smiled a little as she stepped back, letting her hands drop to her sides. What could she say? *Stay? Kiss me again?* Both of those sentiments were ready to tumble off her lips, but she needed time more than she needed a hot-and-heavy make-out session.

"I think I'll go now," Gabe said, even though she guessed from the way he was looking at her that it wouldn't take much to get him to stay.

"So, I'll see you tomorrow," she said, her voice a touch huskier than usual.

"Yeah. Tomorrow."

DANI WAS IN the corral working Molly when Gabe arrived the next morning, laptop in hand. He wanted to walk over to the round pen and watch her train, but knew it would be best for his concentration, and probably hers as well, if he went straight into the house and started work.

Straight into the much emptier house.

Gabe paused in the doorway. The giant armoire was gone. What the hell? It'd been there at five o'clock yesterday. There was no way Dani could have hauled it to a different room without help.

There's nothing saying she didn't have help. She had friends, after all, but why move the behemoth?

Whatever. Gabe settled at the kitchen table and brought up a screen on his laptop. Soon he was deep into CAD, designing an ornamental bridge to cross the stream behind Dani's barn. Another design he didn't know if he needed, but it would be useful to have this stuff on hand if he did.

Gabe worked for a while before checking his messages. Neal had called that morning, worried. Stewart was still coughing and his color was getting bad—to the point that he'd finally agreed to move up his yearly physical to the next available appointment. He was now on a cancellation waiting list and the fact that he'd agreed to that concerned Neal as much as the coughing.

After setting the phone back on the table, where he could keep tabs on it, Gabe ran a hand over his face. He and Neal had agreed that stress was no doubt playing a lead role in whatever was wrong with Stewart—stress beyond the normal stress he'd dealt with every day of his long career. The kind of stress brought on by being betrayed by a trusted friend and associate and then needing— really, really *needing*—payback.

Gabe had to broach the subject of a sale with Dani. Soon. He and Neal were in agreement on that, but Gabe was still debating the best way to do that. Broach the sale and not alienate Dani, because it was becoming very important to him that he not alienate her.

And it was also clear that he needed to come through for the man who'd saved his life.

He worked for close to two hours, every now and then crossing the living room to look out the windows and make certain Dani was still where she was supposed to be. She got on a horse at one point and headed out across a field that would one day be a golf course, and Gabe noted the time on his watch. She worked each horse for an hour, so if she wasn't back in an hour, he'd head out after her. Just in case, he set a timer. He did tend to lose himself once he was deep into a design.

When the timer buzzed, he crossed back to the window, frowning as he realized that the yard and corrals seemed still and empty. The horses were standing with their heads down, heels cocked in the heat. He started for the door, then caught sight of the big black-and-white dog trotting along the edge of the barn. A second later Dani appeared carrying a bridle.

He blew out a breath. He'd figured she was just late, but all the same, it was good to see her.

She started toward the house and he logged out of the program and shut his laptop. Time to go. He was so not going to push things, which was difficult, since he was a pusher by nature. *Driven* was a better word. He was driven to succeed, because failure felt too damned bad. Especially when other people were counting on him.

Dani's boots sounded on the porch, then she pulled open the door. "I'm done for the day." Her expression was open, but she folded her arms over her chest, closing herself off.

So he hadn't been the only one who'd done some deep thinking the night before. He wondered if she'd come to a more definitive conclusion than he had, because right now, he had no idea what his next move was.

Gabe smiled at her and headed for the kitchen table, where he packed up his laptop before slinging his jacket over his shoulder. "I'll see you tomorrow."

She walked with him to the door, holding it open as he stepped outside. He paused briefly on the porch to look back at her with an amused smile. "By the way, I thought you were working on getting more furniture, not losing what you do have."

"It couldn't be helped. But the tractor's back."

"Kyle has the armoire?"

She nodded. "But that's all he's getting. There's nothing else here for him to take and he won't dare try for the tractor again after the lawyer threatened him."

"Then he has no reason to come back."

"Not one."

And Gabe felt better for that.

CHAPTER ELEVEN

DANI HAD A decision to make and Gabe was giving her the space she needed to make it. In the days after he'd kissed her in her living room, Gabe showed up almost exactly at ten, waved to her and disappeared into the house. After she finished her last horse, he'd amble down to the corrals and they'd talk about ordinary matters—her progress that day, or his—and all the while sexual undercurrents swirled around them. She'd never been more aware of the nuances of a guy's facial expressions, or the way his muscles flexed when he leaned on the fence next to her while she discussed her equine clients.

And she wasn't ashamed of the fact that she had relived "the kiss" more than once. He hadn't been bragging when he said he kissed well and if she felt it necessary to review the evidence a time or two while debating her next move, so what?

Gabe didn't push things. He was interested. She knew that from the way he'd start to touch her, then think better of it and drop his hand. And that, of course, only made her want to be touched. So what *was* her next move? Things were safe at the moment.

Was she good with safe?

Yes, to a degree, and that disturbed her. Was she going to allow her experience with Chad to screw up her life, her perception of others? Screw up her chance of discovering what else Gabe could do with those clever lips?

That seemed a sad prospect.

Dani always saved Molly for the last session of the day so that she and Gabe had something safe to talk about before he left. He usually waited until she'd untacked and was brushing the horse down before stashing his laptop case into his car and then walking down to join her. It was a surprise, therefore, to return from her hour-long ride on Saturday to find Gabe leaning on the fence, waiting for them.

"If you had to leave, you should have gone."

"Nope. I'm done with my project, waiting for another, so I thought I'd take a breather."

"How long until you get your next project?"

"Until I think of it. I'm doing some spec designs."

"Ah." She got down from Molly and rubbed the horse's neck.

"How's she doing?"

"She's amazing." She couldn't help smiling at Gabe. "Want to try your skills on her?"

"Uh…"

"Just get on. I'll lead her."

"I can ride. It's just been a while."

"Twenty-five years?"

"Twenty-four."

"She's quiet. You won't have any trouble. I wish my novice owner had brought me this horse instead of Lethal."

"Lethal?" Gabe asked as he laid a hand on the mare's neck.

"His real name is *Lieben*, German for 'to love.' It doesn't quite fit him."

"I'll give her a try," Gabe said.

"Great. Give me a second to adjust the stirrups. This saddle might be a little small for you, but it'll do."

DANI ADJUSTED THE STIRRUPS, then walked around to the horse's left side. "All right. We're set." Gabe went to stand beside her, trying to remember something, anything, about riding a horse. "Now you're going to put your foot in the stirrup, grab the mane so you don't pull the saddle off, then shift your weight up over the horse, like this—" Dani demonstrated, then dismounted "—so you don't pull her over."

"Lot of detrimental pulling possibilities," he muttered as he put his hand on the horse's neck.

Gabe followed her directions, grabbing the mane along with the reins in his hand and shifting his weight over the center of the horse as he mounted. Molly swayed a little, but stayed put as he swung his leg over. Automatically he gathered the reins, surprised at how natural it felt. Maybe there was still some of his innocent eight-year-old self somewhere deep inside.

Dani came over and adjusted the slack in the reins, covering his hands with her smaller ones as she pulled the leather through his fingers until she was satisfied. "Yes. Like that. Now give her a very slight nudge with your legs."

He barely moved his heels and the horse calmly moved forward. He resisted the urge to grab the saddle horn, which would have been difficult anyway since he had the reins in both hands. Dani said nothing, but instead retreated to the edge of the pen, where she watched as he rode in a slow circle.

"You have a good seat," she called.

"So do you," he called back.

She laughed. "Probably not talking about the same thing, are we?"

"Maybe not," he agreed, amazed at how right it felt being back on top of a horse. Molly wasn't nearly as tall as Dozer had been—or at least he didn't think she was—but his memory may have been warped by his only being about four feet tall at the time he'd ridden the Thoroughbred. But he felt just as...*free* was the best word he could think of...now as he had then.

"You're either a natural or you had lessons you didn't tell me about."

"Just a few rides on my foster sister's horse."

"She taught you well."

"I was eight."

"You remembered, so she did something right."

"She put up with a needy eight-year-old." Gabe glanced at Dani as he rode by.

"I can't see you as ever being needy."

"I worked hard not to be, but at that age, sometimes you crack." He rode on past, but not before catching the thoughtful look on her face. He didn't like sharing, never had, and now he had her thinking. He didn't want her thinking about his life, feeling sorry for him or anything.

"You want to trot?"

"Not really," he said, recalling Dozer's bone-jarring gait with a mental grimace.

"She's smooth."

"Fine." He nudged and she started to trot. Gabe started to bounce. Oh, yeah, just as he remembered.

"Don't use the reins to balance yourself. Sit back on your seat and let your abs take the shock."

"Trying..." His teeth clacked. Posting. Jenny had taught him to post.

"You need to be supple in the waist, not tight. Let yourself bend."

Uh-huh. Bend...

Molly had a nice slow trot and after a few more teeth-clacking steps he made a serious effort to relax his middle, and follow the movement of the horse. The jarring diminished.

"Don't lean back," Dani called.

"So much for being a natural."

"Don't be so freaking hard on yourself." She folded her arms, watching him with a critical eye. "There, you're sitting better. Feel it?"

"I do. And I'm ready to stop."

"No loping?"

"Not today." He pulled back gently on the reins and the mare obediently dropped to a walk, bobbing her head up and down as she walked.

"Nice. Bring her over and dismount."

He got off a bit more awkwardly than he got on, but he made it to the ground and then as Dani took the reins from him, he found himself smiling down into her face.

"You liked it, didn't you?"

"Felt a bit awkward, but yes. It brought back some pleasant memories."

"You'll have to tell me about those," she said as they started walking together toward the gate."

He shrugged casually. "Not a lot to tell. I was eight. I lived with that family for about a year before my mom decided she wanted to try again. What a cluster-you-know-what that was." He opened the gate and Dani led the mare through, stopping to wait as he closed the latch.

"So," she asked slowly, "it was pleasant because you weren't with your mom?"

He considered for a moment, then said, "Yes. I'd say that sums it up well."

"Sad."

"Yeah. Well, we can't all have a sitcom life."

"I didn't have one of those, either," Dani said as she led Molly to the hitching rail. She hooked a halter around her neck, then took off the bridle and masterfully replaced it with the halter. Gabe automatically reached out for the bridle, taking it from Dani as she shot him a quick look. "But I did love living with my mother…even if times were rocky after Dad died." She started undoing the cinch, focusing on the leather as she said, "What about your dad?"

"Who?"

"I see."

She stilled as he put a hand on her shoulder, then slowly turned toward him, holding the leather strap in one hand, a faint frown on her face as his hand fell away. "Dani, I…" He frowned back at her, then said, "I don't talk about this stuff."

She shrugged to hide her disappointment. She wanted to know more. "I understand," she said as she began to turn away. He stopped her with another gentle touch.

"No, I don't think you do," he said as his hand ran down her arm to gently circle her wrist. "I mean that I've never talked about this with anyone who didn't know me back then."

"Has anyone asked?"

"Maybe in a superficial way." He ran his thumb over the smooth skin of her wrist before letting go. "Then I would use my many talents to redirect the conversation."

"I can believe that," she said as she pulled the saddle off the horse, "even though your childhood isn't your fault."

"I know." At least the early years weren't his fault, but keeping his past a secret was something he did. Logical or not, he didn't like people to know that his mother had valued her messed-up lifestyle more than him.

He took the saddle from Dani and she smiled up at him, albeit a touch wryly. "I'll stop asking questions."

"You don't have to," he said gruffly, surprised that he actually meant it. "I just can't guarantee answers." She opened the tack-room door, he stowed the saddle, then stepped back outside.

"I guess I can say the same," she said as they walked back to where Molly was tied. "Don't mind the questions, can't guarantee the answers."

She untied the mare and together they walked the few yards to the pasture.

"In that case—" Gabe opened the gate and she led the mare through "—I have a question. What was your fiancé thinking when he cheated on you? Is he stupid or something?"

"Yes," she said matter-of-factly as she unfastened the halter buckle. "He was stupid and he thought I was stupid, too." She patted the mare on the butt as she released her. "I was—at first.

Chad was pretty clumsy in his clandestine affairs, but I trusted him. Eventually I caught on, though." Dani sighed as they started back toward her house.

"Clumsy how?" He should probably stop asking questions, because in spite of Dani's detached tone, he could see that this wasn't an easy topic.

"Oh, texts came in at odd hours. He'd read them, smile and delete. He did it right in front of me, told me they were dirty jokes from a friend and that he didn't want them on his phone." She blew out a breath. "He'd 'work late,' then come home missing his vest or something. When I finally confronted him, he denied it at first." She glanced over at him, her expression growing hard as she said, "But after I showed him the panties I found in his car, he confessed and said that the only reason he hadn't broken things off with me sooner was because he knew it would kill me to lose him."

"There's some ego for you." The kind of ego that made him want to smack the guy a good one on general principle.

"I think…" Dani shook her hair back as they crossed the driveway to the walk. "I think that he had every intention of keeping us both hanging on for as long as possible. I think he was into the danger factor."

"I know people like that." They stopped at the end of her walk, under the aspen tree whose roots were buckling the concrete. "How long were you together?"

"We'd gone out for a long time—since high school really. We went to different colleges, but hooked up when we got out and both moved to Missoula. I honestly had thought he was my perfect mate. I mean, we did so well together…"

"Except for that cheating thing." He reached out to lightly put a hand at her waist and she moved toward him, stopping just before her chest came up against him.

"Yeah. That cheating thing." She addressed the middle of his chest before raising her gaze to meet his. "Screws things up every time. And now—" she let out a short breath "—he's back in town. Moved here with his new wife—the other woman, of course—to manage a local branch of a bank." She put her hands on his chest, spreading her fingers over his flannel shirt.

"Sorry to hear that."

"Mmm," she replied absently, her focus still on his shirt. "It does make going to the grocery store more of an adventure."

"Have you guys bumped into each other yet?"

"Nope." She pressed her lips together momentarily, then looked up at him. "I had a chance to a week or so back and chickened out. An Eagle Valley Days planning session. He was there. I didn't go in."

"I don't blame you."

"I blame me. I was a blatant coward."

"Who wants an uncomfortable reunion in front of a crowd?" he asked reasonably.

"Nobody wants that, but I expect more of myself."

"Knock it off," he said huskily, before taking her lips in a long, deep kiss that had her sliding her arms up around his neck and pressing the length of her body against his.

"I don't know what it is about you that has me breaking promises to myself," she said as she stepped back, putting some space between them.

"Hard to resist?" he asked on a wry note. Because that was exactly how he was finding her.

"Obviously."

"I don't want you breaking promises." Doing things before she was ready. He didn't want to screw up whatever was growing between them and that thought gave him pause. His objectives were getting muddled here, which usually didn't happen to him.

"You make me wonder why I'm making them," she said in a low voice. Then she gave her head a small shake as if clearing it. "That said, I'm not quite ready to make that phone call we spoke of."

"Understood." And he also understood that for now that was a good thing. "Eagle Valley Days—what are they?" he asked, grasping at the first safe subject that came to mind. "Is it a reunion or something?"

"Community celebration," she said, her voice a little husky as her eyes dropped briefly from his eyes to his lips—which wasn't doing his self-control a whole lot of good. "There are all kinds of events. Parades, ice-cream socials, a pig roast, carnival booths, a dance with a silent auction—that's what I'm supposed to help with, even though I truly doubt I'll attend the dance. And, yes, come to think of it, there are reunions, because a lot of graduating classes plan their reunions to coincide with Eagle Valley Days."

"Makes sense. And that way you aren't trapped with your graduating class if you didn't particularly like them."

"Did you go to your reunion?" she asked curiously.

"I doubt I would have, had I actually graduated."

"You didn't graduate high school?"

"I took a nontraditional approach to my education," he said with a half smile.

"But you have a college degree."

"Worked my ass off to get into college and then to get through."

"Impressive."

"Someone once hit me upside the head and pointed out the error of my ways. I changed," he said simply.

"Changed from what? Or do I want to know?" she asked as she pushed the door open.

"Changed from the wrong path to the right one."

"Ah," she said as if she understood, when he knew she hadn't a clue as to how close he'd come to being a criminal before Stewart stepped in. There were times even now when he looked back and shuddered at how damned close his life had been to going down the crapper.

Once inside he crossed to the kitchen to retrieve his laptop, his footsteps echoing across the almost empty room.

"You need furniture," he said as he returned to find her waiting for him by the door, an uncertain expression on her face as if she was debating her next move. He knew exactly what he wanted that move to be—and it didn't involve her suddenly offering to sell her ranch.

For a moment their gazes held and even though she said, "I'll eventually get a few things, a sofa and such," he sensed that was not the true direction of her thoughts.

"After you pay for your arena."

"Yes." She forced a smile that Gabe wasn't buying. She was fighting with herself and he could tip the scales. All he had to do was cross that space and take her back into his arms, and she would be his. He had no illusions that it was all about him. She wanted to purge some memories, help herself move on, and he was there. And it bothered him that he wanted it to be more than that. Again, those muddied objectives. How had that happened?

"The arena will ultimately make me money. The furniture will only cost me money."

"Interesting way to look at what some people consider a necessity of life."

"You mean an indoor arena?" she asked innocently.

"Yeah," he agreed. "That's exactly what I meant."

Dani sighed and took a few steps into the room, stopping in the middle with her hands on her hips. The tension between them began to diminish as they edged back into their roles of friendly neighbors. "I have kind of thought about hitting the local thrift stores to see what they have. And Craigslist."

"But you're too busy."

"Not a lot of hours in the day for that kind of stuff. I'll have a little more freedom when Jolie moves home."

Except that he'd seen to it that that wasn't going to happen in the near future and right now hearing Dani talk so confidently about her sister coming home was kind of killing him. Who the hell did he think he was?

Someone who was simply trying to get everything to work out well for everyone involved. Including Dani and her sisters.

Especially Dani and her sisters.

Yeah. That's who he was.

"IT'S HIS HEART," Neal said, making good on his promise to call Gabe after his father's appointment with his physician. "He got called in for a cancellation appointment this morning. As luck would have it, I was with him in the car when he got the call, so I got to go along."

"How bad?" Gabe asked, deducing from Neal's grim tone that the situation wasn't good.

"Potential for heart failure. The cough is from fluid building up in his lungs because his heart isn't doing its job as well as before."

"Shit." Gabe pressed his fingers to the bridge of his nose. "How did Stewart take it?"

"Oh, he was shaken up for a whole minute, maybe two, then went straight into denial—like he can finagle his way around this the way he does a business deal gone wrong."

"So what happens medically?"

"They'll lower his blood pressure with drugs, but there isn't a lot we can control in this situation, including Dad." Neal cursed again, then muttered, "The doctor was clearly worried, Gabe, and so am I." He exhaled deeply. "So is Dad, or he wouldn't have rushed into denial so damned fast."

"I agree."

"His blood pressure has skyrocketed since his last physical." Neal gave a soft snort before asking, "Do you remember how cool he used to be? So confident that he'd figure out a way to come out on top, regardless of how a deal was going down? He never sweated."

"One of the things I've always been in awe of," Gabe stated honestly. If plan A didn't work, Stewart would calmly swing into plan B, followed by plan C if necessary—until last year, when matters had become personal and the cool factor had evaporated. Now plan B was a vendetta and there was nothing cool about Stewart's drive to compete head-to-head with Timberline.

"I'm getting close on this property thing," Gabe said, although he should have been closer. He had reasons for moving slowly in the beginning, but now…now he was allowing personal issues to get in the way of his objective. That damned muddied objective.

"Nailing down the property won't fix everything, but I think it'd help. That last news article about Jeffries's 'unique approach to resort management' almost sent Dad over the edge."

Gabe didn't say anything. He'd read the article and Jeffries's quotes had pissed him off, so he could well imagine how Stewart had taken the implication that Timberline's roaring success was due to the fact that Jeffries had left Widmeyer and followed his own vision. He'd been stifled at Widmeyer, but once he left—success!

Neal sighed into the phone. "So anyway, that's where things are now. He goes back next week

for a blood pressure test to check the effective-
ness of the meds."

"Keep me posted."

"Yeah. Will do. Serena's on the other line. Talk
to you later."

The phone went dead and Gabe let out a curse
of his own as he set the phone on the table.

He needed to do his job and that meant he had
to focus on being Dani's neighbor, not her lover.
He'd do this thing for Stewart and then deal with
his own issues and needs later.

THE HOUSE WAS just too empty without the armoire. It had been stark before, but now it was
pathetically barren. Amazing what a giant-ass
piece of furniture could do for the place. Apparently sensing that Dani wouldn't lend a hand,
Kyle had brought two of his buddies to help him
move and load his new prize. Dani had stood
back and watched, arms crossed, thinking that
the armoire was a small price to pay for Allie's
peace of mind.

Now she stood looking at the faded spot on the
floor where the piece had stood for decades—long
before Allie and Kyle had moved in. The rain beat
on the roof, making it impossible to work outside
for the first time since she'd moved home. She'd
worked on her books, oiled a saddle, made a slow-
cooker dinner that was now simmering away in

the kitchen. She'd spent some time pacing, feeling caged, and couldn't help thinking that she might not have felt so restless if she wasn't trapped in an essentially empty house. It was one thing to sacrifice for financial goals, and another to have a place that was so uncomfortable that she felt trapped when forced to spend time indoors. When she considered heading through the rain to the tack shed, she figured it was time to face facts. She needed to make this place more of a home, as it had been when her family had lived there. Winter was coming and here she'd be, alone in an empty house.

Decision made, Dani grabbed her purse and coat, told Gus to behave and started for the door only to be stop when her phone rang in her pocket. Gabe.

"I just wanted to make sure you weren't going to need me today."

"Not unless my horses grow fins." The corral had a good foot of sand in it, so the footing would be all right, but she didn't fancy getting drowned as she worked. "Thanks for checking."

"Not a problem."

"I'm going furniture shopping." Dani had no idea what made her blurt out the words as if they were a confession.

"You finally broke, eh?" There was a smile in his voice.

"I did. It was the armoire. Now that it's gone, the room is just too empty."

"No, Dani, it was too empty before. Now it's bare."

"I have a chair."

"Almost bare," he amended.

"Would you like to come with me?" This time Dani didn't try to figure her motive for issuing the invitation. It was obvious—she wanted to spend time with him.

There was a brief moment of silence and Dani was about to retract the invitation, when he said in a low voice, "Yeah. I would."

"Shall I pick you up?"

"That depends—which truck are you driving?" She let out a mock sigh. "The good one."

"I'll be ready whenever you get here."

"You caught me going out the door, so how about now?"

"I'll be ready."

Dani hung up with a smile, then went to her bathroom and took a few seconds to put on lipstick and mascara. After all, she was going out in public. With a hot guy she shouldn't have designs on, but did… She was so weak.

Said hot guy came out of his stone-and-glass house as soon as she pulled up to the end of the walkway. He flipped the hood up on his anorak and trotted through the rain to the truck. Once inside he pushed the hood back off, grinning as a few drops of water landed on her face. In the close confines she suddenly became aware of the scent of freshly showered guy. Just exactly what she needed—something to distract her while she tried to focus on driving in the driving rain.

"Do you know how tempting it was to bring the old truck?" she asked as she put the Ford into gear.

"But you didn't because it's not street legal?" he asked.

"Something like that." She shot him a glance. "And I like my passengers to be comfortable."

"Someday I'll take you for a ride in my car and show you comfort."

She liked the idea of that, probably more than she should, but right now—no, for the entire day—she wasn't going to worry about making safe choices. She was going to enjoy her rainy day. He tilted his head back and closed his eyes for a moment.

"Don't go to sleep on me," she said.

"No worries." He spoke easily. "I've adjusted my work schedule. I'm in bed by midnight."

"I know," she said.

"Checking on me again?"

"When I get up during the night, your lights aren't on anymore."

"Still having trouble sleeping?"

"Too much hydration during the day."

"Ah."

She gave a low laugh. "Too much information?"

"Never."

And she had a feeling that was true. He wanted to know about her, but wasn't so comfortable sharing his own life. But he had, and apparently more than was the norm. She wasn't going to ruin her day getting seized up wondering about the implications of that small fact.

"Where are we going?"

She cut him a sideways glance. "Depends on how much time you have."

"All day. I can't face being trapped in that house in the rain." Her lips curved. They were in sync there.

"I thought we'd drive into Missoula and I'd look at new furniture, get disgusted at the prices and then go to the thrift stores."

"Let me buy lunch." It was more of request than a statement and Dani nodded.

"If you want to."

"You gave me a reason to get out of the house on a nasty day. It's the least I can do."

"If you don't like being inside, then Montana winters might be rough on you…although I guess you may not be here for the winter?" He didn't answer immediately, which was in itself an answer.

"Any idea when you're leaving?" she asked.

"I'm taking it day-to-day," he finally said.

"Me, too, I guess."

"Don't get me wrong…" She glanced over when

his voice trailed off. "I like it here. That's why I haven't left."

"But there's no chance you'll stay."

Something shifted in his expression and she had the strong feeling that he was forcing himself to retreat, to keep things from becoming too intimate.

Why? What had changed?

He reached out to put his warm hand over hers where it lay on her thigh, sending her senses into overdrive. He squeezed her fingers before she gently pulled her hand away and put it back on the steering wheel.

"Dani?" She took her eyes off the road for a moment. "I'm just trying to be fair to both of us. Given the circumstances, maybe this isn't the best time to be anything except friends."

"Without benefits," she stated in a remarkably blasé tone, given the way her body was crying out, *No...you want him!*

"Benefits muddy waters."

"Yes, they do," she said. "I understood. I agree. It makes perfect sense."

She kind of hated it.

CHAPTER TWELVE

STICKER SHOCK WAS killing Dani.

Gabe tried not to smile as she flipped over yet another tag and gave yet another small squeak of outrage. He was going to miss the hell out of her when he left, but as soon as he finished doing this job for Stewart, he was going back to Bloomington. As things stood now, his feelings for Dani and his reason for being in Montana in the first place were tied too closely together to not affect one another. He needed to take a step back, review his objectives and get his head on straight, and hanging around Dani made that difficult. He wanted her to be happy. He wanted Stewart to be less stressed. He wanted the world to be logical again.

"Look at this," she hissed. "This dresser is stapled together. Stapled! How can they ask for this amount of money?"

"Because people will pay it?"

"I won't."

They were three stores in and still hunting for a sofa.

"I'm sorry I dragged you along," she said as

they left that store and she consulted her phone to discover their next target.

"I don't mind," he said honestly. Dani shot him a suspicious glance, then, apparently satisfied, went back to her phone.

"You seem preoccupied," she said.

"Look who's talking," he shot back, not liking how easily she'd just read him. "And yeah, I am, I guess. I have a contract and I'm not sure yet how to tackle the job."

"Ah," she said as she pocketed the phone. "More vacation job stress." For the first time since she'd turned over her first price tag, there was true amusement in her eyes.

"Exactly. Now, shall we go find you a sofa?"

"Yes," she said matter-of-factly. "I think we should."

Dani eventually found a sofa marked down to half price that she liked. They'd hit the thrift stores and she found a couple of hardwood end tables that needed to be stripped and refinished and a brand new cedar chest that cost more than she'd intended to spend, but since it was well made and worth the money asked, she'd bought it, too.

He waited until they'd finished lunch at a small Italian restaurant before asking if the furniture shopping was over for the day.

"I need to be careful not to spend too much of my severance pay," she said as she leaned back so that the server could refill her coffee cup.

"Saving for that indoor arena."

"Yes." She smiled softly, making it difficult for him to resist reaching across the table to take her hand in his. Their day was winding down. The rain had stopped, the sofa, chest and tables had been loaded into the back of her truck and were covered with plastic and roped down. Furniture shopping was over and it was time to get down to business.

He took a deep breath and dived in as smoothly as he could. "You know how you mentioned that you and your sisters came close to selling your ranch at one point?"

"Yeah?" Dani said, glancing up cautiously.

"I've been in contact with a friend who's looking to buy a piece of property in the area." He lightly tapped the table with his long fingers. "He's looking for almost exactly what you have in the Lightning Creek and he'd pay top dollar to avoid hassles."

"What kind of hassles?"

"He'd like to do a private sale."

Dani blinked at him. "Sell the Lightning Creek?"

"I'm just passing on information. Since you guys were so close to selling at one point and this could be a done deal with no real-estate-agent commission…" He gave a shrug and reached for his coffee.

Dani frowned, started to speak, then frowned and stopped.

"Sorry. I didn't mean to upset you."

"No. It's just…a surprise. That's all."

"My friend has been looking for a while. His needs are pretty specific. He thought he'd found a place a couple years ago, but that fell through."

"There are a lot of places for sale in Montana."

"I know." Another casual shrug. "He wants something in this area. Lots of acreage, access to skiing, water running through it."

"And you told him about the Lightning Creek?"

"Only that he missed a prime opportunity."

Dani pursed her lips as she focused on her coffee, then her gaze shot up as he reached across the table to cover her hand with his once again. He gave a slight squeeze and she turned her palm up to link their fingers.

"It'd be a bitch setting up my business elsewhere."

"But maybe all your buildings wouldn't need to be roofed."

She cocked her head. "Any idea what his idea of top dollar is?"

"Only ballpark, but I know that if the property suits, he'd pay a fair price. Perhaps a shade more. He's been looking for a long time. Like I said, he had a place he thought was perfect, but lost it. He won't mess around this time."

She frowned down at the table as she slipped her hand out of his grip. When she looked back up at him, she said, "My oldest sister worked in real estate for quite a while. I wonder what she thinks would be a fair price in the current market."

"Ask her."

"I might," she said. "Not to get your friend's hopes up, but, hey, you never know what my sisters would say if a solid offer was put in front of them."

Gabe fought to keep a wide grin from spreading across his face. "I won't say a word to him. Like you say, no sense raising false hope."

SHE HADN'T HATED the idea. Gabe paced through his house, pausing occasionally at his drafting table to stare down at his sketches. He was ridiculously relieved. It was important to him that Dani feel good about that deal. Really good, because that meant at some point in the future, he could reappear in her life, see where this attraction took them. But for now, until the deal was landed, he was keeping his distance. Friendly but not overly friendly. That was what she wanted, too. Or at least what she said she wanted—the way she kissed said otherwise, but he wasn't going to dwell on that.

Things had turned out better than he'd hoped, but Gabe wasn't going to call Neal or Stewart with an update until he was more certain of the outcome. If Dani said no deal, he didn't know what his next move would be, but hopefully he wouldn't have to address that issue.

Say yes, Dani. Convince your sisters. Find a new place to buy.

A simple solution for all involved. The best solution for all involved. Lightning Creek would be in good hands, the sisters that needed money would have it. Dani and Jolie could buy a smaller, more manageable place to build their training facility. Yes. Win, win, win.

Gabe stared at his reflection in the windows. A lanky guy wearing a loose flannel shirt over a T-shirt and jeans stared back. Barefoot, wearing glasses instead of contacts. He didn't look much like his professional self, but he felt a hell of a lot better in a lot of respects. Yeah, he'd gone a bit stir-crazy here in the beginning, but now...now he was getting into working in solitude for a good part of the day, and spending the rest of it with Dani. That left only the lonely nights...

There might be a cure for that, eventually, but not until the deal was settled and he'd had some time to think.

"I'M JUST THROWING it out there for you to think about," Dani said into the phone. She heard Jolie give a low growl on the other end.

"I didn't want to sell before and I don't want to sell now. Why do you?" she challenged.

"Allie and Mel?"

"Mel agreed to go with the majority."

"And Allie? You know how she hates this place

now. Wouldn't it be a lot easier if we sold? She wouldn't have to face it ever again."

"No offense, Dan, but Al needs to man up. She had a rotten time on the ranch, but that's because of Kyle, not the place."

"When I mentioned that, she said Dad died here."

"And I feel like he's there with us."

Dani sighed. She and Jolie were so alike. "Me, too. But Mel and Al don't feel that way. If they had the money from the place, Allie wouldn't have to take out student loans. Mel could pay off her loans and maybe sink some into KC's ranch. We could pool our share and buy another place. One where we aren't playing catch-up with the repairs."

"Is this a for-sure thing?"

"It sounded like it. I mean anything can fall through, but…yeah, it sounded that way."

Jolie went quiet. Dani was about to say her name, when she said, "I'll think about it."

"That's where I am, too. Thinking. I'm not saying a thing to Mel or Al until you make your decision."

"Thank you. I don't feel like being the bad guy again."

"You weren't the bad guy—just the odd man out."

"I love Lightning Creek, Dan."

"I know." Of all of them, Jolie loved the ranch the most. It was as if she came alive when she was there and she was the only one who'd ever planned on moving home permanently—or she had been until Chad revealed himself to be an asshole and SnowFrost went belly up, thus setting the stage for Dani to move home, too.

"I'll think about it. No pressure. Okay?"

"There's not. Gabe just tossed the matter out there. I don't think he's going to bring it up again unless I do."

Jolie blew out an audible breath. "All right." She cleared her throat then said, "And what about this Gabe guy?"

"What about him?"

"You've mentioned him a couple times and I was just wondering…"

"There's nothing to wonder about," Dani said casually, wishing it was so. The truth was she was wondering. Wondering what she was thinking, forging ahead as she was. But just as with the land deal, there was no pressure. Gabe showed up every day to work on his computer while she trained. Sometimes when she worked late, he stayed on for dinner—always a slow-cooker meal—and he always offered to do the dishes. Dani would say no and he would go home, leaving her feeling alone.

Maybe that should be a red flag, but it didn't feel like one. It felt like another step in a natural progression.

"All right," Jolie said in a skeptical tone.

Dani didn't bother protesting. The gist of her stilted response was that she didn't want to talk about it and Jolie was respecting that...for the time being anyway.

"I gotta go," Jolie said. "But I'll think about this."

"Do that."

After Dani hung up she walked to the window and stared across the field at the lone light burning in Gabe's house. Then she turned away and snapped off her own light. "Come on, Gus. Bed."

Did she have any qualms about leaving her childhood home? Yes. Now that she was back, it was hard to think about leaving again, but that offer, if it was legit and if the money was anywhere close to what Gabe had indicated, then... yes, she could let go. Allie could forever wash her hands of the place.

She was happy here, but she could be happy somewhere else, too. Her dad had told her that land was forever, but he didn't say that it had to be this land.

And maybe, after furniture shopping and seeing how many things in life she couldn't afford, she was getting a little tired of being land-rich and cash-poor.

KELLY RETURNED FROM volleyball camp the day after the great furniture expedition and Dani greeted her official babysitter with mixed feelings.

Gabe no longer had a reason to spend the morning and early afternoon at her place and shortly she would no longer have an excuse to see him, since Molly's training time was almost up.

That meant, if he was still in the area, that she was going to have to make a decision. Did she want to see him for real, or say goodbye?

She wanted to see him.

Kind of.

Part of her trusted him implicitly and another part of her still sensed secrets untold. Things she needed to know. She would not be blindsided again—not if she could help it anyway.

The next week was full not only with training, but also with the silent auction work. Dani had solicited all the businesses on the list Gina had given her and had scored pretty well. She had a large stash of items in the back of the community hall that she and Gina and any volunteers they could scare up needed to catalog and display before the official Thursday-evening kickoff of Eagle Valley Days.

"You know you're heading this committee next year," Gina said as she held up a flashy silver belt buckle donated by the local Western store.

"What can I say?" Dani asked. "I'm good at phone solicitation. I had lots of experience at SnowFrost." She pointed across the room at the full-length antique mirror Gina had finagled from a furniture store. "It isn't like you had a massive fail."

Gina laughed. "We did well. Now, let the cataloging begin."

Dani had worked several down days into her training schedule when she'd contracted with her clients, which was a good thing, since it took most of the day to catalog and display the silent auction booty.

"Perfect," Gina said as she stood back and regarded the tables that bordered three sides of the conference room. "We're going to make a lot of money!" She laughed roguishly. "I made a bet that we would make more money than the real auction."

"That might be stretching things," Dani said as she followed Gina out into the bright sunlight.

Gina locked the door and pocketed the key. "Do not underestimate the power of silence," she said archly. "I gotta make tracks. My favorite man is waiting for me," she said. "Thanks for all the help."

"Glad to help." Dani started for her truck, only to stop when Gina called her name.

Gina dug the key back out of her pocket. "I forgot that they need this tonight. Would you please take it to the chamber-of-commerce building so I'm not late for the sitter? I want to keep this one so I don't have to beg my mom."

"Sure." Dani took the key and Gina dashed

to her car, giving Dani the distinct feeling that a good babysitter was hard to find. A few minutes later she parked in front of the chamber-of-commerce building, leaving her truck running as she went inside.

"Hi. I'm returning this key for—" She felt her expression freeze as the woman behind the desk looked up and she found herself face-to-face with Megan Branson, the new Mrs. Chad Anderson.

Dani cleared her throat, raised her chin and said, "Gina wanted me to drop this key off." She carefully set the key on the desk in front of Megan, who was still staring at her with an uncertain expression.

High road. Take the high road. Do not ask her if she got her panties back.

"I see you're settling into the community," Dani murmured instead of saying goodbye, as she probably should have.

"Yes. I was lucky to get this position."

Dani smiled at her. "I've been lucky myself recently."

"Oh?" Megan asked, shooting a look over at a woman who had just walked in, carrying an armload of brochures, as if hoping for rescue. They'd never met face-to-face and Dani imagined that Megan could have happily lived her life having never met her. Well, then Chad shouldn't have brought her to Eagle Valley. "How have you been lucky?"

"I dodged a bullet." She smiled tightly. "Give Chad my best."

"You two weren't right for each other."

Dani was amazed that Megan chose to address the situation—and a touch annoyed that her parting shot had been compromised. "Maybe so, but there are classy ways to handle such situations and trashy ways. Guess which one Chad chose? Like I said. Bullet. Dodged." Dani gave Megan a curt nod, then headed for the door, her heart beating hard and fast. Okay. One first encounter over. One to go.

"YOU'RE GOING TO the dance." Which was obvious, because when Gabe stopped by to see if he could nudge the sale situation forward, Dani answered the door wearing an eye-popping green silk dress.

She lifted her chin. "I am." And he'd thought she'd been very clear about not going just a few days before.

"You'll have friends there."

"Of course."

He waited, but Dani had nothing else to say on the matter. "Will Chad be there?" It wasn't his business, but he couldn't keep from asking the question.

"And his wife." Dani tried to smile, but the expression ended up being more of a forced twist of her beautiful lips. She was putting on a pretty good front, but he read stress not just in her expression, but in the way she held her body.

"Would you like a date?"

Dani blinked at him in surprise. "I can do this by myself."

"I know." He had no doubt that she could do this alone. But he didn't want her to.

She studied him for a moment through slightly narrowed eyes. "You're being honest, aren't you?"

"I believe in your abilities. I'm offering company, not moral support."

"I like you when you lie." The dimple showed next to her mouth. "And that's saying a lot because I don't like liars."

Gabe felt something inside of him go a little cold at her words, but he rallied. "Hey, it's just a matter of you facing your asshole ex and his wife in a crowded public venue. What's the problem?"

She laughed wryly. "When you put it like that, everything falls into perspective." Dani bit the corner of her full lip, then said, "Sure. Why not? Since Gina will be busy, I'll have someone to gossip with."

"Can you be a little late?" He opened his arms and glanced down at his black T-shirt, flannel shirt and jeans. "Or am I okay?"

Dani choked back a laugh. "I can be late."

"Twenty minutes."

"It takes ten minutes to get to your house."

"Pick me up. Bring the good truck so you don't get dirty."

Dani rolled her eyes. "Thanks for the tip."

Gabe put his hand behind her neck, but somehow managed to keep himself from leaning in and kissing her. "If you don't mind, we can take my car."

"I guess," she said as if it was a major concession. "I'll drive over to your place and we can leave from there."

"See you in twenty."

She glanced at her silver watch. "Eighteen. You've wasted two minutes talking."

CHAPTER THIRTEEN

GABE PUT HIS hand on the small of Dani's back as they entered the convention hall, spreading his fingers wide over the soft green silk of her short dress. The woman wasn't very tall, but she was all legs and, as fate would have it, he was a leg man.

As they walked into the dimly lit room, he was instantly reminded of the one prom he'd attended. Thirty or forty round tables with white tablecloths and candles burning in round glass containers filled the areas on either side of the dance floor. Strings of small white lights lit the buffet tables and twinkled from the white spray-painted trees on either side of the bandstand. The only addition, which would have been quite welcome at his prom, was a bar with two bartenders busily seeing to the needs of the people lined up in front of it.

"I'm going to check in with Gina," Dani said, leaning close to him as she spoke. "The auction is in the side alcove there."

"I can get us a drink, meet you over there." He needed a drink. Neal had called him while he was changing clothes half an hour ago to let him know that Stewart had a small tumor on his lung, but it was benign. Good news and good news—first he was going to be fine, and second Gabe didn't need to worry so much about letting down a dying man.

"Bourbon for me," Dani said, glancing casually over at the bar. A split second later her back went stiff.

Gabe followed her gaze, then curved his fingers possessively around the edge of her waist as he bent closer to say, "Your ex?"

"Yes." She tilted her head, her voice casual despite the tension in her body as she said, "And I think he has just spotted me. Us."

"I see that." The tall athletic-looking guy standing behind the bar had indeed zeroed in on Dani before sliding his gaze over to Gabe and then back again to Dani. "Where's the new missus?"

"Not sure." Dani scanned the bar area. "Probably not far away."

Gabe scrutinized Chad for a moment before saying, "He seems rather smug."

She shook her head then put her cheek against his to say, "See how he has his hands in his pockets and is rocking back on his heels as if he's in charge of the world? Sure sign that he's uncomfortable. That's his bluff stance."

"You know him well."

"I was going to marry him."

"I'm glad you didn't."

"So am I," Dani said in a husky voice that did things to him.

"Dani." Dani and Gabe turned together to see Marti approaching.

"I never know whether she's friend or foe," Dani muttered to Gabe before saying in a louder voice, "Marti. How are you?"

"I'm doing all right. I wanted to talk to you about the bar schedule."

"I'm not on the schedule."

Marti sucked air in between her teeth. "That's the problem—Gina's baby is running a fever and she's not coming. She just called."

"All the more reason for me to focus on the silent auction."

"We have volunteers to help in there, but we're short at the bar."

Gabe looked down at Dani and said, "I'll do it."

Marti looked startled at his instant response, then quickly pasted on a bright smile. "Usually we have locals help."

"I live here," he said matter-of-factly.

"Uh…" She shot a quick look at Dani, who merely raised her eyebrows.

"Do you want me to work with Chad?" she asked in a curious voice.

"No!" Marti sputtered and Dani actually believed her. "Chad's shift is almost over. I need someone for the next shift."

"We'll do it together," Dani said, touching Gabe's arm.

He put his hand over hers and said, "Sounds good."

"All right…" Marti cleared her throat. "That would be great. I'll let them know."

After she left, Gabe looked at Dani. "And her objective is?"

"I wish I knew." She slipped her arm out of his. "I need to check the auction, see if there really are volunteers."

"And I need to get us some drinks. I'll meet you over there."

DANI HAD NO idea what Marti was up to. The fact that Chad's shift would end before hers began her made her think that maybe the woman really did need a bartender and not a spectacle.

It wouldn't have really mattered, though, because Dani already felt like a spectacle—the logical result of appearing at the same event as her former fiancé, a hometown hero, who'd dumped her after a year-long engagement and then eloped with his mistress within a matter of weeks.

Of course people were looking at her. And talking.

Well, screw 'em.

She poked her head into the auction room to see two women in their late forties—one was a petite blonde and the other sported an impressive bouffant of flame-red hair—straightening the clipboards in front of the items, while a handful of attendees circled the room, contemplating the offerings.

"Hi," she said to the redhead. "I'm Dani. I helped Gina solicit the gifts."

"And you did a great job," the woman replied. "I'm Elsie and this is Lydia." The blonde woman wiggled her fingers at Dani. "Gina had to cancel, so we're holding down the fort."

"I heard." Dani stood for a moment, feeling a touch awkward. "Well, I hope we make a lot of money."

"I'm certain we will. These things start off slow, then snowball as the alcohol flows."

Dani laughed and then turned to find Gabe standing in the doorway, a drink in each hand.

"I'm not needed," she said to him as she came to take her drink. She held it up to eye level. "Did you order me a double?"

"I did not. The pours are generous. Although your ex was maybe too busy checking me out to keep track of how much was going into the glass."

"He's competitive."

Gabe's smile shifted. "He already lost."

"I agree," Dani said softly.

"It's almost time for me to go on duty."

"I guess if you're on duty, then we can't slip away early." His free hand was once again at her back, his touch firm and warm.

"You wanted to slip away early? We barely got here." The pressure of his fingers increased slightly.

"The thought had crossed my mind," Dani said. She gave him a long look, acting on pure instinct and for once not thinking of six or seven different consequences of her actions. "I've achieved my purpose. I showed up at an event where I would see Chad. The worst is over. Now I can slip away into the night…and so can you—or rather, you could have."

It was rather gratifying to see the dawning understanding in his eyes, followed by an appreciative lift of his lips. "I'd say this time Marti turned out to be a foe."

Dani smiled up at him, then sipped her drink.

"Dani!" She turned to see a tall auburn-haired woman pushing through the crowd, drink held high.

"Jessie?"

Jessie Greenway squealed and gave Dani a big hug before stepping back and chanting, "Who's a Spartan? I'm a Spartan, you're a Spartan, too!" Her drink sloshed in time to the chant, slopping over at the very end.

Gabe's forehead wrinkled as he glanced down at his damp shoes, then back up at Jessie. "It's our cult greeting," Dani explained with a wry smile.

"Cult?"

"Cheer cult," Jessie said, leaning closer to Gabe

and waggling her eyebrows. Jessie had obviously been taking advantage of the generous pours the bar offered. Her head suddenly went up and she vigorously waved her hand at someone across the room. "I'll be back! I want to catch Marco before he gets away."

With a jangle of bracelets she was gone, leaving only a faint hint of Shalimar behind.

Gabe shifted his jaw sideways. "Cheer cult, eh?"

"Three years of rah-rah. Jolie did four. We wanted to be on the rodeo team, but couldn't afford it, so…" She shook imaginary pom-poms.

"Were you good?"

Dani ran her fingers over the thin gold chains she wore. "I was great. And I almost married the school quarterback."

Gabe jerked his head toward the bar. "That quarterback there?"

"That's the one."

Gabe looked down at his watch. "Our shift starts soon, but I was thinking that maybe we could be a few minutes late showing up."

Dani considered for a moment. "Or maybe I can stop pussyfooting around and just go and say hello."

"Is that all you're going to say?" he asked on a wry note, but she caught the protective gleam in his eye. She had backup.

She held his gaze for a moment, then slowly smiled. "I have no idea."

GABE FOLLOWED DANI across the room, glad he was there to have her back and hoping at the same time that there would be no blood. Chad seemed to have disappeared, but Dani did not slow down as she wound her way through the crowd. She strode up to the bar, which was at the moment clear of customers, and stopped directly in front of an older man with a thick head of silver hair.

"Hello, Burt. I'm supposed to work this shift."

"Well," Burt said briskly, folding the towel he held and knocking over a glass, which he quickly righted, "I'll just get out of your way, *Dani*." He spoke her name in a louder tone, giving a quick glance toward the partially closed closet door.

"Is Chad in there?" Dani asked with a frown.

"Chad? No. He's not." Burt shook his head as he set the towel down. Then he let out a breath. "But I wish he was. Megan is in there. She's working the next shift."

"Really? Huh." She cocked her head at Burt. "This is someone's idea of a joke, I guess."

"Or cheap entertainment," Burt agreed in a low voice.

Dani pressed her fingers to her forehead. "I have to live in this community. And apparently so do they." She looked up at Burt then back at Gabe.

"Burt—" All three of them looked around as

Chad strode around the end of the bar, coming from the kitchen. He stopped short at the sight of his former fiancée. Gabe started to put a hand on her shoulder, then thought better of it and dropped it back to his side.

"Hello, Chad," Dani said with a dignified nod. He nodded back without speaking, probably half-afraid of what was going to happen next, then his gaze slid over to Gabe as if gauging his worthiness as an opponent. "Someone has set things up so that Megan and I work the next shift together."

"Uh-uh," Chad said, shooting his attention back to her.

"Then what do you propose?" Gabe asked from behind Dani, just so the asshole would know that Dani wasn't alone. He was surprised at just how badly he wanted to do the guy some bodily harm for what he'd done to Dani—and then he had to remind himself that if Chad hadn't cheated, he and Dani probably wouldn't be together right now.

A tapping of a coin on the bar interrupted them. "Bartender!"

"I'll get them," Burt said, looking happy to escape. Quickly he squeezed past Dani and headed for the small group of customers.

"You and I can work the shift," Chad said to Gabe in a take-command voice. "Who are you anyway?"

"Gabe." He didn't offer either his hand or his last name.

"Maybe we should all work together," Dani offered in a flat voice. "The four of us crammed back here. That could be entertaining." She let out a sigh and then called toward the closet, "You can come out, Megan."

The door opened the rest of the way and Megan stepped out with a stack of clean bar towels, looking sheepish as she walked over and planted herself under Chad's arm. "I didn't want to be in the middle of a scene."

"Oh, that's rich," Dani muttered.

"Hey," Chad said, his arm tightening protectively around Megan.

"Well, we are in the middle of scene," Dani said, cutting her eyes toward the milling crowd, some of whom were watching them surreptitiously, while others were openly staring. "And you had to be well aware that this would happen when you moved back."

"I never thought you and I would be at the same events."

"Why not?" Dani asked, propping her hands on her hips.

"Because you were never interested in being social."

"But I live here," she said on a low note of outrage. "How could you possibly think this wasn't going to happen?" She gave her head a disgusted shake. "You thought I'd stay out of your way."

"I know I was going to stay out of yours. You wouldn't have seen us at any horse shows or rodeos."

"That is ridiculous," Dani said. "And I suppose I was to stay away from what…football games and all community events? Grocery stores? Service stations?"

"Excuse me," an older woman said from the other side of the bar, apparently oblivious to the drama playing out on the other side of the bar. "Can I please have a Coors?"

Gabe reached down into the icy cooler beneath the counter, pulled out a beer and popped the top. "Four dollars."

She counted out the bills, then put a tip in the jar. After a moment's hesitation she put in another.

As soon as the lady was gone, Dani pointed a finger at first Chad and then Megan. "You cheated on me. You get no courtesy. I'll go any damned place I want to go."

"Scotch, please?" A soft male voice came from the other side of the counter. "Oh, Dani. How are you? And…Chad," the guy added on a startled note. "How are you?"

Dani rolled her eyes and reached for the Scotch bottle. "I'm fine, Gerry. How are you?" Gabe took it from her and poured the shot.

"Five dollars."

"I thought we could be civilized…and stay out of each other's way."

"At least until Chad gets promoted to regional manager and then we'll be gone," Megan said as if it was going to happen tomorrow.

"What if he doesn't?" Dani asked.

Megan's mouth fell open as if the possibility had never occurred to her.

"Why don't Gabe and I work this shift," Chad said.

"And Megan and I can go powder our noses?" Megan drew closer to Chad and Dani said, "I'm kidding."

"Easy solution," Gabe said. "Dani and I will tend bar. You guys go and schmooze and everyone can be relieved that the first awkward big moment is over."

"It's true," Dani said lightly. "Now you can go to rodeos and I can go to the grocery store."

Chad lifted his chin in a quick movement of agreement and steered his bride out from behind the bar and into the kitchen.

Once they were gone, Dani pushed her hair back from her forehead with her wrist. "That sucked. But it's over." She stepped toward the bar as a group of people approached, pasting on a smile that didn't reach her eyes, but she was more relaxed than she'd been since walking in the door. And no blood had been spilled. Yet.

"Would you mind taking care of these guys?" Gabe asked, settling his hand on her lower back for a brief moment. "I'll be right back."

"Gabe—"

He smiled reassuringly, then headed out from behind the bar toward the coat check. Once he was out of sight, he doubled back and went into the kitchen, where Chad and Megan stood close to the exit, deep in conversation.

"Would you excuse us?" he said to Megan as he approached.

"I will not," she said, flashing him an indignant look.

"Honey, let us talk," Chad said without taking his eyes off Gabe.

"Sweetheart, I don't think—"

"Please."

"This won't take long," Gabe said before turning his attention back to the hometown hero.

"What the hell do you want?" the hero growled.

"I'll tell you what I want," Gabe said as he moved closer. "I want you to stay the hell away from Dani. If you see her in a store, I want you to go the other way."

"It's a free country."

"Which means I'm free to cause you pain if you mess with her in any way."

"Pain?" Chad sneered.

Gabe said nothing. He just continued to stare the bastard down the same way he'd stared down more than one purported badass who'd lived in his neighborhood during the bad old days. Finally

Chad cleared his throat and Gabe stepped back. "I'm glad we understand each other."

He started to turn, caught movement out of the corner of his eye in time to duck, then righted himself and sank his fist into Chad's gut.

Chad let out a low groan as he doubled over. Gabe stood where he was, hands at the ready, just in case the asshole wanted more. Chad wretched again, as Megan rushed between Gabe and Chad, putting her hands out to push the two of them apart.

"I'll call the police," she said.

"He swung first," Gabe replied coolly, thinking that Stewart was going to kill him.

"No police," Chad said slowly, straightening back up, Megan clinging protectively to his arm.

"So we have an understanding?" Gabe asked.

Chad gave a short nod, then brushed by him. It was then that Gabe noticed Dani standing near the kitchen door leading to the bar, looking none too happy. Gabe idly rubbed his knuckles—Chad had a serious six-pack—then gave a shrug. "Who's minding the bar?"

"We are," she said, giving her head a quick shake before pushing her way back through the swinging door.

The rest of their hour-long shift passed quickly and uneventfully, but Dani spent most of the time seemingly lost in thought. Gabe didn't push. The band started playing just before their shift ended. Chad and Megan danced the first dance and Dani leaned back against the wall, folding her arms over her chest as she watched.

"How're you doing?" Gabe asked, mirroring her position, leaning against the wall next to her.

"I've been better, but I've also been worse." Her shoulders rose, then sank again. "I'm glad it's over." She turned her head to look at him. "I'm glad you were here."

"You didn't need me."

"But you needed to threaten him anyway?"

"Pretty much, yes."

She leaned closer and lightly touched her lips to his. "I don't approve, but I forgive you."

He tilted her chin up and couldn't help lowering his mouth to hers in a light kiss. "Good."

"Our replacements are coming now." She softly nipped his lower lip and Gabe started planning their escape when she said simply, "Let's go."

She didn't have to ask twice. Gabe took her hand and wound his way from behind the bar to the door and blessedly fresh air. Once outside, he pulled her into his arms and kissed her long and hard.

"Let's go home."

Gabe didn't know what she considered home, but had the sudden and disconcerting feeling that it didn't matter as long as he was with her.

DANI OPENED HER eyes when Gabe parked next

to Dani's good truck near his walkway. They hadn't spoken much on the drive to his house, but it hadn't been an uncomfortable silence. If anything she felt better than she'd felt in the past several days and the nerve jangling sexual tension building between herself and Gabe only added to her sense of well-being. Tension and well-being didn't normally go hand in hand in Dani's world, but they seemed to do just that when Gabe was involved.

Only now she wasn't certain what her next move was. Did she go home? Ask to stay?

Gabe did. "Want to come in?"

"Yes."

"Stay put." Surprised, Dani took her hand off the door handle then watched in some amusement as he crossed around the front of the car, opened her door and put out his hand to help her out. He kept her fingers in his as he shut the door, then led her up the walk to the front door, where he stopped to dig out his keys.

He'd barely escorted her inside when she framed his face in her hands and kissed him. She heard the keys drop on the counter behind her, then he wrapped his arms around her, one hand threading through her hair as he kissed her back. Dani started unbuttoning his shirt between kisses, as he brought his hands up to slide over her silk dress, his thumbs brushing against the undersides of her breasts. It felt so good to touch a man. No, it felt good to touch this man. She couldn't think of another guy she'd want to be doing this with.

And, bless him, he didn't ask if she was sure. She wouldn't be doing this if she wasn't. There was a reason she'd only had the one bourbon before shifting to water. She wanted her head clear enough to deal with Chad, if necessary, and to drive home from Gabe's place, if she so chose. She didn't. For the first time ever she wanted to sleep with someone just for the experience. And if the hard length of him pressing against her lower abdomen was any indication, this was going to be an experience to remember.

He pushed the silk straps aside and pressed his lips to her shoulder, sending a shiver through her. Dani drew herself up straighter as her breath caught, then she tilted her head sideways, giving him access as he continued moving his lips along the side of her neck, his hands moving lightly over her breasts then skimming down her sides. Dani leaned against him, again feeling his erection pressing against her. She reached behind her to place her palms on the sides of his lean hips, pulling him even closer as her head came back to lean against his shoulder. He gently squeezed her breasts, then curled his fingertips under the edge of the slippery fabric, caressing her skin.

Dani reached up to release the side zipper and the fabric slid to her waist, allowing him full access. He turned her in his arms, leaned back to take a good look, then smiled. "Oh, yeah," he murmured, gently weighing her breasts in his hands, his thumbs moving over the nipples before he lowered his head and gave them his full attention.

"Don't stop," Dani muttered, her fingers tangling in his dark hair.

He laughed against her skin, and Dani sucked in a sharp breath as his hands slid down over her ass, then lifted her onto the counter behind him. She automatically opened her knees, pulling him forward. He leaned in to claim her mouth, his hands resting on her thighs, his thumbs moving against the sensitive skin close to her core. She inched forward, increasing the delicious contact, until she had his fingers exactly where she wanted them. She knew she was hot and damp against his hand, her breathing became shallow as he moved against her. She was being totally, selfishly hedonistic, but he didn't seem to mind. In fact, he seemed to be getting into it.

"Don't come yet," he murmured against her mouth. "Wait for me if you can."

"No. Promises." Dani let her head fall back against the counter, thinking it was no fair for him to make demands like that when his fingers were clearly on a mission to drive her over the edge.

Suddenly she sat upright and scooted a few inches back, breaking contact. She met his eyes, swallowed and then said, "Let's go to your room."

"Excellent plan." He slid her forward, then swung her into his arms, carrying her across the dim living room to the short hallway that opened into the master bedroom, where a single lamp was lit near the bed. Dani had the impression of dark wood and cream-colored linen, but her focus was on Gabe and getting him out of the confines of his clothing.

He covered her hands as they began working on his remaining shirt buttons and pulled them low to cup against his erection through his pants. He closed his eyes for a moment, then opened them again as Dani started working on his belt. He didn't move as she undid the buckle, then the buttons and zipper beneath it. Seconds later she had the long hard length of him in her hands. She closed her eyes as she caressed, savoring the feel of him.

"I need you inside of me," she murmured. "Now." She stepped backward, sinking down onto the bed, bringing him with her, moving her hips to free the dress fabric that had gotten caught beneath her as he pushed her skirt aside.

Seconds later he pushed into her, hard and deep. Dani gasped, then slowly exhaled as he pulled out, then pushed in again, his movements slow, controlled. She arched her back and pressed against him, needing more. Gabe obliged. Her legs wrapped around him, clutching him against her, and he began to move more rapidly. He was losing control and Dani found herself reveling in it, moving with him, meeting his thrusts. Rising. Falling. She tried to hold off, truly she did, but on one particularly deep thrust, she lost it as she arched hard against him, a silent cry caught in her throat as waves of pleasure crashed over her. Gabe made a sound low in his throat as he felt her response, then thrust one last time, hard and deep, before emptying himself into her.

His damp forehead came down to rest on hers as he fought to catch his breath. Then he rolled off from her, pulling her against his side so that she was half-sprawled over him. Her skirt tangled around her legs.

He let out one last breath, then said, "I never even got my pants off."

Dani laughed, her voice low and husky as she said, "I'll pay for the dry cleaning."

He brought a hand up to smooth her hair. "Oh, no. Etiquette demands that I pay."

"And why is that?"

He gave her a wicked look. "Because I wanted you to keep that dress on. All night I watched you and a good part of that time I was thinking about hauling you off into the backseat of a car and making out—high-school style."

"You should have told me. I would have taken you to the parking spot."

"I think this might have been a touch more comfortable, even with the belt involved."

Dani smoothed her hand over his chest, loving the feel of the flat, hard muscles beneath the curling dark hair. "Maybe next time."

He rolled his head to look down at her. "Next time."

She smiled lazily up at him. "Any idea when that might be?"

"As in how long from right now?" His hand moved over her hip, cupping the curve of her ass.

She laughed. "What are your capabilities?"

Lightly tracing the curve of her breast, he said, "Give me a moment and perhaps we'll find out."

"Perhaps?"

He tipped her chin up to kiss her. The heat was already starting to flare again. "Strike the *perhaps*."

DANI PUSHED HERSELF up on one elbow, smiling at Gabe as he lay sleeping in the tangle of sheets. She ached in places she hadn't ached in a while and she realized that while she wouldn't mind aching there some more, she needed to get back to her place to feed hungry mouths and get ready to meet with the client stopping by to pick up her mare in exactly four hours. She slipped out of bed and found her underwear and dress. She picked up her shoes by their sling-back straps, then walked to Gabe's side of the bed to sit on the edge. Instantly a strong arm came around her, pulling her down.

Dani laughed and pushed herself upright. "I'd love to stay but I have a client coming soon."

He smiled sleepily, but it still managed to look awesomely wicked. "I won't keep you…unless, of course, you want breakfast."

Dani leaned down to touch her forehead against his. "I'd love breakfast, but I do have to go."

He kissed her and it was all Dani could do to pull herself away and not crawl back into the bed and have her way with him.

"See you later?" he called as she approached the door.

"I'm working Molly at three o'clock like usual."

"I'll be there."

She certainly hoped so. One thing she wasn't going to do was to let herself think too much. For once in her life she was going to be more like Jolie, living moment-to-moment, day-to-day, certain that everything will work out. She didn't even know how she wanted this to work out. More data was necessary, so for now she'd follow her gut.

And right now her gut was saying to clear some time in her schedule for Gabe.

CHAPTER FOURTEEN

GABE GOT UP shortly after Dani left, wandering out to living room to stare across the field at her house. He'd known going in that he was complicating his life, compromising his mission, but he'd do it all over again. He reached down to shift himself. Dani knew what made her feel good and she wasn't shy about asking and he loved that. He'd done everything she asked—and more—and he was more than ready to do it again. If and when he had the chance.

But as he turned away from the window and headed to the bathroom, where he cranked on the shower, he knew he'd be spending more time with Dani. She didn't seem to be a hit-and-run kind of girl and all of a sudden he didn't see himself as a hit-and-run guy.

The phone rang as he was gathering up his clothes from where they were scattered across the bedroom floor. Serena.

"What's up?" he asked as he shook out his slacks, then loosely folded them.

"Neal said that you were close to brokering the deal."

"I have some cautious interest," he agreed.

"That's what Neal says."

"And what does he think?"

"He's impatient because Stewart's impatient, but they're more than aware that this is a delicate situation."

More delicate than any of them knew, because now Gabe had to broker this deal without Dani discovering that the deal had been his intention all along. Lying to her didn't sit well with him, but who would have guessed that she would come to mean so much to him in such a short period of time? Not him, that was for sure. Sometimes he felt as if he'd been smacked by a freight train.

Serena was talking again and Gabe had to ask her to repeat herself.

"I said I bought a classic car in Seattle and I'm driving it back to Chicago."

"What kind of classic car?"

She cleared her throat self-consciously. "A... uh...'56 Ford Crown Vic. Impeccably restored."

"Nice find," Gabe said mildly, deciding he didn't need to mention that Neal had long coveted exactly that car.

"Yes."

"Is it for you?"

"For now," Serena said.

"I won't ask your future plans," he said. But part of him hoped that perhaps she and Neal would take another stab at life together. Whatever had driven them apart didn't seem to be affecting their relationship now.

Since when had he become a happily-ever-after guy?

Maybe he'd always been one, but afraid to think it was possible.

"When do you plan to be back in the office?" Serena asked. "I have some projects to go over with you and need a few honest-to-goodness notarized signatures."

"Probably in a couple weeks."

"Probably?"

"I'm kind of taking things day-to-day." His statement was followed by such a long silence that he had to say, "Serena?"

"I'm here," she said. "I'm just working on the idea of you taking things day-to-day. I've seen your planner."

That planner had gotten him through college, grad school, his internships, every day on his job. It had kept a guy who'd never in his life set goals on track, but lately he was following his gut more than his planner. A good thing or bad? He couldn't say for sure, but he felt good.

Dani was responsible for a lot of his recent positive state of mind, but Serena didn't need to know that. Nor did Neal or Stewart. Once this deal was in place he'd figure out a way to straighten out all the loose ends without ruffling feathers.

Or maybe he wouldn't have to. He and Dani

could simply continue as they were now. His "friend" Stewart would turn her land into a golf course. Stewart had no reason to know or care just when exactly Gabe had become involved with Dani.

Walked through like that, in a logical step-by-step manner, he saw nothing to feel guilty about, but he was still aware of a vague nagging guilt that refused to stay tamped down.

"I'll send you a schedule as soon as I work one out."

"You do that," Serena said faintly. He could visualize the perplexed who-the-hell-are-you? frown on her face, and laughed softly.

"A working vacation has been good to me," he said.

"Obviously. You're going to have to tell me the secret to embracing vacation sometime," she said.

"I'll do that," he said, "just as soon as I figure it out." Although honestly he knew the answer. She lived next door.

GABE SHOWED UP at 3:00 p.m., as he'd promised, pulling in just as Dani was saddling Molly for an hour-long outing. He got out of the car and sauntered over to the hitching post, moving with an unconscious athletic grace, making Dani want nothing more than to haul him into her house and have her way with him. Again.

Instead she waved at him and started to slip the bit into Molly's mouth.

"Do you have another horse you could ride?" he asked.

"Yes," Dani said on a note of surprise. "I have four horses that haven't been worked."

He gave her a crooked grin. "I thought I might get some hours in on Molly."

And me? How about an hour or two there?

"Good idea. I'll catch the black gelding."

Gabe moved to Molly's head and took the reins from her, capturing her hand in the process and meeting her eye with a look that made her shiver inside. Oh, yeah. She'd get her hour, if not more…

And so began the routine for the next several days. Gabe showed up at three, they rode out together, returned home, groomed the horses, then adjourned to the house, where they made good use of Dani's twin bed.

Usually he then plugged in his laptop until Dani had finished working her other two horses and then she cooked, as in she threw two frozen dinners into the oven if she didn't have something simmering in the slow cooker. But he didn't spend the night and she never asked him, because, really, how much sleep would they get crammed into her narrow bed? And regardless of how much fun it was not sleeping, she did need *some* sleep and so did he.

As the days passed, Dani refused to let herself

think about anything but the here and now. She enjoyed having him around and if it ended tomorrow, she would survive just fine. He was temporary, she knew he was temporary, and although that caused the odd pang now and then, she wasn't going to push for more. She wasn't ready.

Why aren't you ready?

The question nagged at her occasionally, but she resolutely shoved it out of her mind without dwelling on it or trying to come up with any kind of an answer. Probably because she was enjoying her days and didn't want to jinx them.

Gabe, as it turned out, was a natural horseman. His balance was superb and he stayed alert and aware of his horse, even during the times they were talking, which was for most of their hour-long rides. The one occasion when Molly shied violently at a duck that flew out of the weeds next to the river, he'd stayed in the saddle and been ridiculously proud of himself, which only made Dani find him more adorable. She congratulated him for not hitting the ground and then turned her attention back to the trail; there was no way she was going to tell him he was adorable, because in her experience guys liked to be sexy, strong, masterful—not adorable.

But he was.

GABE LOOKED FORWARD to his daily ride with Dani almost as much as he looked forward to taking her to bed afterward. Neal had called twice, trying to nudge Gabe into quicker action.

Gabe wasn't sure he was interested in quicker action. Yes, he owed Stewart and he'd agreed to be the go-between in this plan, but it no longer felt right. He'd casually mentioned the sale again, and Dani had just as casually said that if the four sisters could ever agree on something it might be possible, but not to hold his breath.

Not the kind of news he wanted to bring back to his mentor, but he was rapidly coming to the conclusion that not all deals panned out. Like this one.

"I have something to show you," Dani said after their fifth ride. She flopped the stirrup over the back of her saddle and began pulling the cinch strap free.

"Can't wait." Gabe felt a pleasant twinge of anticipation as he smiled at her over Molly's back before pulling off the saddle. Molly nudged him with her nose as he walked by, a friendly hey-don't-forget-my-grain nudge. He needed to make a decision as to what to do with the horse. A big part of him said he should keep her. Relocate to the Eagle Valley, buy a place he could afford, set up shop. Serena would have a cow, as would Stewart. Travel would be a lot more expensive, but in terms of peace of mind he'd be miles ahead of where he'd been working out of his offices in the Widmeyer suites.

"Ready?" Dani asked after she'd put away her

tack, brushed down the black gelding and turned him loose. She jerked her head toward the house.

"Always," he said in a low voice.

She laughed and reached out to hook a finger in his belt loop as they walked. He'd never had anyone do that before and he liked it.

"Upstairs," she said after they got inside.

"A nice place for surprises."

"Mmm."

He followed her up the stairs to her bedroom, where she opened the door with a flourish and then stood back so he could see. Inside was a new bed covered in a puffy white comforter. A wide bed. A bed that had room for two to sleep comfortably.

"I thought it was time to get a grown-up bed," she said with a straight face, but her eyes were dancing.

"All the better to do grown-up things," he said with a lift of his eyebrows.

"I—*ooph!*" She started to laugh as he scooped her up into his arms, but the laughter stopped when his mouth found hers in a deep, deep kiss. She wound her arms around his neck, pulling him down with her as he set her on the bed. He went willingly, covering her body with his as the exploration continued.

"Do you want to spend the night?" she finally asked against his mouth.

"I'll even cook breakfast."

GABE DIDN'T STAY every night…but he stayed most. When he wasn't there, Gus seemed to realize that she had a lot more bed than before and would creep up onto the empty side when he thought she was asleep. Amazingly, Dani usually did notice when the ninety-pound dog made the opposite side of the bed dip, but she didn't have the heart to kick him off. He dutifully slept on the rug in the corner when Gabe was there, so Dani saw no reason to. He never disturbed her after he settled…or at least he didn't until the night he let out a booming bark, shaking the bed and scaring the hell out of her.

Gus gave another bark, then jumped to the floor and bounded down the stairs while Dani sat perfectly still in her bed, heart pounding, sheets clutched to her chest, ears straining to hear something in the ensuing silence. If it was an intruder, the barks would have continued. Instead she heard the familiar thump of Gus's big tail on the wood floor.

Someone he knew was coming up the walk, and that had to be Allie, Jolie or Mel. Everyone else, including Kyle—and Gabe—was considered deeply suspicious until Gus decided they weren't. Usually that was about the time they stepped into the door, but Gus didn't let anyone who wasn't family into the house until they passed muster.

Dani got out of bed and tiptoed to the window without turning on the light, getting there just in time to see Jolie disappear from view onto the porch. Figured. If one of her sisters was going to show up without calling first, it would be Jo. A split second later she knocked loudly on the door and Gus gave another bark, a happy bark that said, *Hurry up! Jolie's outside!*

Dani trotted down the stairs, hugging her arms around her in the nippy night air. "Coming," she called.

"It's me," Jolie called from the other side of the locked door.

"I know," Dani said as she unlatched the door and pulled it open. "What are you doing here at…" She glanced over her shoulder at the alarm clock sitting next to her chair.

"Ten o'clock?" Jolie asked with a smile. "What are you doing in bed at this hour?"

"I have to be up early."

"So do I and you don't see me in bed at ten."

"I bet you look like hell in the morning," Dani said, stepping out to take her sister's second bag.

"No." Jolie closed the door and dropped her overnight case. "I do not. Wow." She turned in a circle. "You really did buy furniture."

"I got tired of living like I was in college," Dani said.

Jolie gave a considering nod, then pulled off her knit hat, letting her reddish-blond hair spill out. "I can see that. I can also see that your taste has shifted."

"A little." Dani pushed her own hair back and regarded her sister for a moment as she took in the new chairs she and Gabe had bought. "Not that I'm not thrilled to see you, but is there a reason you're here?" If her sister stayed for any length of time, it might cut down on her extracurricular activities, which in turn might put her in a testy mood. She wasn't yet ready to share her budding relationship with Gabe with her sisters, which meant keeping him at arm's length while Jolie, the most observant of her three sisters, was there. Nothing slipped under Jolie's radar, which made Dani darned glad that nine times out of ten, her sister was on her side.

"I sent you a text," Jolie said as she shrugged out of her coat and stuffed the hat in the pocket. "'Get my bed ready'? 'I'll be there tonight, leaving day after tomorrow'?"

Dani shook her head and then walked over to where her phone was plugged in. "It hasn't come in yet."

"Ah, the wonders of technology."

"It'll probably be here by morning." Dani walked over to flip on the lights. "So you're here why?"

"Loose ends. I have training in Missoula on Monday, so thought I'd spend a couple nights on the ranch so that we could talk business."

"Good idea," Dani said. "I don't have a room ready, but I'll lend you half my bed."

Jolie made a face. "I don't fancy sleeping on half of a twin bed."

"A real bed. Queen-size."

"Does it fit in the room?"

"With room to walk around it. Kind of."

"I bet. Why such a big bed?"

"In case of company," Dani said.

"You're not talking about me, are you?"

Dani just shrugged and led the way upstairs. "If you prefer, your old bed is available. We just need to find the bedding."

"It there any left after Allie and Kyle moved out?"

"Just one set of sheets."

"I'll sleep in my room," Jolie said. "I may not get up at the crack of dawn, since technically tomorrow is my day off."

"How's the internship?" Dani asked as she took her old polka-dot sheets out of the linen closet and handed them to Jolie, who shook them out and then spread the bottom sheet over the small bed.

"I'm so happy it was extended, but to tell you the truth, I'm not sure why it was. The work has dropped off now that the project is winding down, but apparently some last-minute funding came in." Jolie tucked in the corners of the sheets on her side of the bed as she spoke. "Trouble is…it may not work into a permanent job as we'd hoped."

Dani wasn't sure how she felt about that, which made her feel a touch guilty. She was looking forward to not living alone, but she also liked entertaining Gabe anywhere and everywhere, a practice they'd have to seriously curtail once Jolie moved home.

He won't be here then.

Dani fought the sinking feeling in the pit of her stomach. She'd known going in that this was a temporary relationship, she just hadn't expected to enjoy it so much.

Jolie yawned as she flipped one of their childhood quilts over the bed. "Apparently the ranch has an early-to-bed effect, because suddenly I'm beat."

"In that case, I'm going to let you get some sleep. We can talk in the morning."

"Right." Jolie yawned again as Dani turned toward the door. "Get me up at seven, would you?"

Dani shook her head. "You'll have to set an alarm. I'll be long gone by seven on my second ride of the day."

"Fine. Be that way, all workaholic-like." But Jolie smiled as Dani shot her a frowning look. For all of her laid-back appearance, Jolie was as much of a workaholic as the rest of the Brody sisters. If she hadn't been, she wouldn't have had her internship extended when everyone else's had terminated on the last day of August.

Dani went to her room and fired a text off to Gabe that said simply, My sister is here, so I'm not going to work tomorrow.

She figured he could read between the lines and know that meant he didn't need to stop by. If he did, fine. It wasn't as if she had anything to hide, but again, Jolie was scary perceptive and she didn't want her to ask a lot of questions, especially when Gabe was the one who had the friend interested in Montana property. That smacked of conflict of interest and Dani didn't need to defend herself on two fronts. Getting Jolie to think about selling so that they could set themselves up in a better situation was her primary goal now and she didn't need anything mucking with her sales pitch.

"LET'S GO OUT for breakfast," Jolie called across the yard after Dani released her second horse of the day. "Either that or let's starve, because you have no food."

"It's shopping day and I didn't expect company."

"I sent you the text."

"Which I still haven't gotten."

"I have no control over the vagaries of the airwaves," Jolie said, waving a hand.

Dani crossed the drive to where Jolie stood on the porch. "I agree. Let's go out." Today was her half day and since she wouldn't be spending the other half with Gabe, going to breakfast with her sister was the next best thing, and she'd have some help with the shopping.

"This place is a wreck," Jolie said as she followed Dani inside the house. "I walked around while you were out and, son of a gun, but Kyle did some half-ass stuff. Have you taken a close look at the roof on the shed? It'll come off first good wind."

"Yeah. I know."

"And since he was the stay-at-home, why didn't he maintain the corrals?"

"Because talking about it was easier than doing it," Dani said. She peeled out of her light pullover and hung it on the coatrack near the door. "I'll take a quick shower, then we'll go."

"No blow-drying. I'm hungry," Jolie called.

Dani snorted and took her time in the shower.

"SO ANYWAY," JOLIE said an hour later as she pushed what was left of her plate of French toast aside, "we're going to have to sink some money into the ranch."

"Yeah." Dani propped her elbows on the table, holding her cup with both hands. "A lot of money. Kyle really let the place slide."

"Well, if he'd put money into the ranch instead of get-rich-quick schemes…" Jolie let out a breath, apparently realizing that she was preaching to the choir. "Anyway, it may be a while until we can swing the indoor arena."

Dani bit her lip as she studied her cup, then raised her eyes to meet her sister's gaze. "There's that other option."

"Selling?"

"Yeah. I've spent some time online looking at what we could purchase outright with our share of the sale. We won't have as much land, but we could get a nice place with enough land and it won't be all run-down. We'd have our arena. People wouldn't be afraid to let us keep their animals on the property..." Jolie frowned and Dani explained, "I heard via the grapevine that Marti has been using the condition of the property to warn off prospective clients."

"That bitch."

"She wouldn't be able to do that if we had a newer, cleaner, shinier place."

"Dani—"

"Sometimes a person has to go with logic rather than emotions. This would solve a lot of problems, Jo."

She hated that her sister looked as if she was about to cry. Angry tears, mind you, not sad. Angry tears were always more dangerous when Jolie was involved. The café door swung open and Jolie's eyes went wide.

"Speak of the devil," she drawled, her gaze hardening. Dani turned, then groaned inwardly. Kyle and two other deputies were taking seats at a booth near the door. "If that jerk had just done as he'd promised, then we wouldn't be in this mess."

The server breezed up just then and smiled at them. "Anything else, ladies?"

"Do you have a lengthy rubber hose?" Jolie asked. The server blinked as Dani kicked her sister under the table. "Never mind."

The woman set the ticket on the edge of the table and moved off to her next station, a confused expression on her face.

"Let's get out of here," Dani said, gathering her purse. She set a twenty-dollar bill on the ticket and scooted out of the booth. Jolie got up, too, but instead of heading toward the nearest exit, she sauntered over to the door closest to the deputies. Dani debated, then gave in and followed her sister, who paused near the deputies' table.

"Jolie. Dani." Kyle greeted them with exaggerated politeness, a smug expression on his face, although for the life of her, Dani couldn't think of one thing he had to be smug about. Scoring the armoire?

"Kyle," Dani said trying to edge Jolie to the door, but her sister was having none of it.

"Long time," Jolie said sweetly. "How've you been?"

"Can't complain."

"We can."

"What about?" Kyle asked.

"The utter state of disrepair you left that ranch in. Seeing as Allie was the breadwinner for five whole years, that place should be looking a hell of a lot better than it is now. We had to pay a buttload of money to fix the fences you refused to maintain and that's just the tip of the iceberg."

Red started creeping up Kyle's neck, spreading from his collar to his cheekbones. Dani took hold of her sister's arm, but Jolie wasn't budging.

"That's bull," Kyle sputtered and Dani decided to take a swing of her own.

"Then why did all the standpipes you installed break around the same time? *All* I can think of is shoddy workmanship," Dani spoke mildly before giving her sister a serious push toward the door.

Jolie gave in, nodded at the other smiling deputies, pushed the door open and exited, Dani close on her heels.

"I just couldn't let him sit there all smug," she said. "Allie would have wanted us to confront him."

"I just hope no more standpipes break," Dani muttered as she got into the car.

"Meaning?"

"Allie and I think he broke the standpipes because he was pissed at her."

"What?"

"Yeah. And I just kind of had to let him know that I know."

"That's…" Jolie let out a breath and marched back to the café. Dani made no move to stop her. A few seconds later she got back into the truck and said, "Let's go to the hardware store."

"Why?"

"Because I told him we had cameras and if he set a foot on the place we'd know." She folded her hands in her lap. "Therefore, we'd best get at least one camera."

"You just announced that?"

Jolie simply shrugged.

Dani's temples were throbbing as she put the keys in the ignition, but maybe this *was* the way to handle Kyle. Make sure he stayed the hell away. She drove straight to the hardware store.

CHAPTER FIFTEEN

BUYING A CAMERA and installing a camera were two different things, but with Dani reading the instructions and Jolie manning the tools, they got the job done. Dani firmly believed that they'd just spent money that could have been used elsewhere, but Jolie had pointed out that they could write it off their taxes and it was a selling point when they kept other people's horses.

"So would bringing those horses to a ranch in better repair. Like, say, a new ranch…"

Jolie leaned back against her car, studying the ground for a moment. "Let me think about it, all right?"

"No pressure." Dani meant it.

"Mel and Allie would be in favor if they knew."

"They would."

"So even if I held out, the majority rules."

"I won't do that to you," Dani said. "It's all or nothing."

Jolie smiled. "No pressure."

Dani reached out to take her sister by the upper arm. "We all agreed to all or nothing. Even Allie."

"I'll give you a call later in the week."

"No hurry." Although Dani had a feeling that

this offer wouldn't last forever, she really wasn't going to pressure Jolie. As it was, they had a lot of land that would only increase in value. It was just that they had so much to do to get it back into proper shape, and now that she'd been spending time with Gabe and wasn't totally focused on the ranch, she found that she could probably be happy anywhere. All she needed was to feel at peace with herself and the world.

And that was the way Gabe made her feel.

GABE PACED TO the window and stared out across the field toward the Lightning Creek. So how much longer was Dani's sister going to stay? If he went up to the loft, he could see her red pickup truck parked in front of the house and he seemed to be making the trip up the stairs several times a day.

He didn't think Dani was in any way ashamed of him or their relationship—he thought that she didn't want to answer pressing questions about a situation they were both figuring out. This was totally new territory for him, this feeling of wanting to protect and care for someone. He'd cared for women before, deeply, but he didn't tell them all his secrets. It was almost as if he'd feared judgment. Yes, he'd feared judgment from Dani, too, but he'd risked it, because he knew deep down that if she didn't know everything about him, they wouldn't be able to have the type of relationship he wanted.

There was only one secret he was carrying now and it was eating at him, no matter how many times he talked himself down. Logically, his big crime was not telling Dani who his "friend" was before the papers were signed. He wasn't lying. He wasn't dealing under the table, but he still felt dishonest.

There was really only one solution. He was going to have to tell her the truth. The whole truth. Risk the word getting out to Jeffries. He owed Stewart, but he loved Dani.

He loved her.

The realization struck him hard.

He loved her, and that was why he had to tell the truth. All of it. They couldn't move forward in an honest way until he did.

Gabe rubbed a hand over the tight muscles at the back of his neck, then let it drop loosely to his side.

Life had just gotten more complex.

Gabe spent the next hour trying to draft, but couldn't focus. Finally he gave up and threw a hamburger on the grill. He wasn't hungry, but he hadn't eaten since breakfast and it was now approaching dinnertime.

He'd just sat down with the burger and a glass of merlot when the sound of an engine caught his attention. It was just gnarly enough to be Dani's truck and he was aware of the fact that his heart had started to thump just a little faster when he pulled the door open and saw Serena getting out of a '56 Ford that was going to give Neal a hard-on.

"Surprise," Serena said as Gabe started down the walk. "I was passing through Missoula and decided to detour south and see you. Neal can wait a couple more days for his surprise."

"He's going to love it," Gabe said, running a hand over the shiny hood. He glanced over at her and she smiled as she brushed her silvery blond bangs out of her eyes.

"I hope so," Serena said, focusing back on the car.

Gabe wanted to ask what was going on, but since he never asked those kind of questions, he didn't. He just hoped that it worked out, since he liked both Serena and Neal very much. Or maybe because for once in his life he was feeling some contentment, he wanted everyone else to feel that way, too.

When in the hell had he gotten so sappy?

Easy answer there, but he wasn't going to dwell on it.

"I just cooked. You want half my burger?"

Serena laughed. "I just ate. I know better than to show up at a bachelor pad hungry. But I wouldn't mind a bed for the night."

"There are quite a few empty bedrooms," Gabe said with a smile. "You've arrived during the off season."

"Will there be an on season?" Serena asked as she pulled her bag out of the backseat.

"It's looking hopeful," he said, reaching out to take the bag from her.

"And that's it?" Serena asked after a brief pause. "No details?"

Gabe shook his head and gestured toward the walk. None that he wanted to share, although he was probably going to admit at some point that he and Dani were seeing each other. But not now. He didn't want to share just yet—not when everything was still so new and...hopeful.

"Did you have trouble finding the place?" he asked as Serena stopped just inside the door and surveyed the interior with a critical eye.

"GPS," she said absently. "Good bones," she added, referring to the house.

"I like it here."

"Even though it's isolated?" she asked, obviously remembering one of their earlier conversations.

"I've found ways to spend my time."

"Working your ass off?' she asked, stepping over to his drafting table.

"No. I've actually slowed down, started doing other stuff."

"Yeah?" she asked, turning and leaning back against the table. "Like what?"

"Well, I'm horseback riding."

"Neal said you'd gone through with buying a horse."

"And, really, it was for you...or at least that was the story when I began, but now I'm kind of thinking about keeping her."

Serena gave a soft laugh. "And here I was looking forward to stabling a horse in a high-rent area. If you want to keep her, she's all yours. The question is, where's a guy like you going to keep a horse?"

"Here."

"You won't be involved with this project once it's online." She tilted her head as if trying to get a better look at him. "Will you?"

He shook his head. "Once the Brodys have made a decision, my work here is done. But that doesn't mean I can't visit."

"Why do I have a feeling it's more than the scenery bringing you back?"

Gabe shrugged. "No idea."

Serena gave a tiny smirk, then pushed off the table. "I'd love a glass of wine."

"You're in luck. I have half a bottle left."

Gabe and Serena talked for over an hour before she finally found her way to a guest bedroom. He kept the conversation focused on her—the so-called vacation, possible new projects, her ideas on the possibility of providing some decent competition for Timberline—despite her attempts to steer it back to him. She gave him a wry smile as she said good-night, along with a look that clearly said, "You aren't fooling me. I know something is up."

Gabe sat up for another half hour, sipping what was left of their second bottle of wine and staring across the room, debating about what he was going to do if Dani and her sisters sold, what he was going to do if they didn't. Either way, he was going to come up with a way to keep close contact with Dani—at least until he had a clearer idea just what their relationship was going to be. He wasn't ready for a huge commitment, but he was ready to cautiously trek along the outskirts of the territory.

Serena was up well before him the next morning. He looked through the packet she'd brought, signed a few papers, then helped her load her bag in the car.

"You want a tour before you go?" he asked, running his hand over the top of the car.

"Want to drive?"

He grinned. "I thought you'd never ask."

For the next hour Gabe showed Serena the sights. She was familiar with the opposite side of the valley, where Timberline was located, having worked on the initial building project, so Gabe concentrated on what would be Widmeyer's side of the valley, driving up the road to the closed ski lodge, where they had an excellent view of the valley below.

"Perfect for a golf course," Serena murmured as she studied the fields of the Lightning Creek Ranch. "That house will have to go."

"I'd like to move it, actually. It's got some nice features."

"You've been inside?"

"Dani and I are neighborly."

Serena merely nodded, her gaze lost in the distance. "This really could shape up into a better place than Timberline."

"Competition, anyway. All Stewart wants is a piece of their pie."

"Bull. He wants to crush Jeffries."

"That, too."

Serena turned to give him a long speculative look. "Damn, but you're mellow. What's the deal? You seem, I don't know—relaxed."

Gabe shrugged. "Must be the air."

"The air, my ass." She twisted her mouth sideways. "You're getting laid."

His eyebrows rose slightly. "None of your business, Serena," he said mildly. And there was the problem with your assistant being a friend in addition to an employee.

She leaned her elbows on the fence and stared out over the valley again. "No. It's not. But I might be just a little jealous."

"You'll get yours," Gabe said, then laughed as she gave him the evil eye.

"Pun intended?"

He wasn't touching that one again. "You want to get some breakfast before you hit the road?"

"Sure." She pushed off from the fence and tidied the long scarf wrapped loosely around her neck. "I have a long drive ahead of me. Sustenance would be a good start to the day."

Gabe drove to the café, the one place he knew they'd have some quiet since it was after the breakfast hour. Sure enough, the lot was empty except for two sheriff's office vehicles, and as he and Serena crossed the lot, the deputies came out the front door—two guys he'd never met before and Kyle. Always Kyle. He was just glad that Dani wasn't there.

He nodded pleasantly as they walked by, knowing that Kyle's double take probably meant he was going to tattle to Dani that he'd seen Gabe out and about with an attractive blonde.

"Have you had a run-in with the law lately?" Serena asked in an amused voice. "Because that guy gave us one long hard stare."

"We've had a chat. He's the ex-husband of the oldest Brody sister."

"Ah." Serena slid into the booth just as Gina approached with the coffeepot and menus. She, too, was giving Serena a questioning once-over and

Gabe decided it was time to clear the air before Dani's phone started ringing full-time.

"Hi, Gina. This is Serena. She works with me."

"I'm his long-suffering assistant." Serena held out a hand, which Gina stared at in surprise before taking it in a brief handshake. "I was on my way across the country and thought I'd stop and see if my boss was really taking a vacation."

"And is he?" Gina asked with a hint of a smile.

"As near as I can tell, no." Serena turned her attention to the menu in front of her. "I'm starving. What's the best thing you offer? And no fair saying everything."

"Well," Gina said, cocking a hip. "That depends on whether you eat like a rancher or an urbanite."

"I see…well, if I said urbanite, what would you recommend?"

"We have an egg-white omelet or fresh melon, berry and yogurt parfait."

"Rancher?"

"Steak and eggs, or hash and eggs."

"Steak and eggs," Serena said, slapping the menu shut. "Any chance of getting a Bloody Mary to go with that?"

Gina laughed. "We can't serve alcohol."

"And you're driving," Gabe muttered.

"It was a hypothetical question."

Gina turned to Gabe, still smiling. "The usual?" she asked and he nodded.

"Which is?" Serena asked once Gina had gathered the menus and left.

"Fresh melon, berry and yogurt parfait."

"You weenie."

"You're talking to your boss."

Serena blew out a breath, then reached across the table to pat his hand. "And my friend, whom I might come to for advice someday."

"Please tell me it won't be about your love life."

She lifted one shoulder in an eloquent shrug. "No promises."

Gabe simply shook his head. "Really?"

"I can't help it. I love him."

"Take it slowly," he said. It was the only thing he could think of to say that didn't sound like a platitude.

"I'm not going to ask you if Neal has ever talked to you…"

"Neal doesn't talk."

She let out a short breath. "I know."

And that, Gabe suspected, had been part of the problem in their relationship. Neal appeared to be a wide-open guy, but the things that mattered most to him, he kept to himself. Serena needed to know those things, share those things. Perceived secrets didn't do well in a relationship.

When Gina arrived with their breakfasts five minutes later, they'd hammered out a tentative work schedule. Gabe intended to bid on two projects and wanted to do site visits and there were several client meetings that couldn't be pushed back. Plus, he needed an answer on the Lightning Creek.

"Here's the deal," Serena said as they walked back to the car. "Neal is worried about Stewart's health."

"I know."

"He thinks this will take his blood pressure down a few notches."

"No guarantees there."

"Agreed." Gabe opened the door for her and she slid in the passenger side. "I think we're getting close." Dani had mentioned talking to her sisters again the last time he'd seen her. He'd smiled and told her no pressure. Yeah. No pressure.

Damn. He hated the feeling he was working her. It honestly was time to come clean. He just couldn't tell Neal.

So GABE HAD had breakfast with a blonde. Good-looking one, too, according to Gina, who'd called to warn her that Kyle might be getting hold of her to spread rumors, but there was nothing to worry about because the woman was Gabe's assistant. Kyle hadn't called and Dani wasn't quite sure how she felt about Gina—and Kyle—assuming that Gabe having breakfast with another woman might concern her. Especially Kyle.

Was she really that transparent?

Dani coiled the lead rope she carried and hung

it in the tack room. Did it even matter if she was transparent? Other than her own feelings of caution, which were rapidly evaporating, she had no reason not to be open about her relationship with Gabe.

Except that they hadn't exactly defined their relationship. The one thing Dani did know was that when she was with him, she was totally content to live in the moment, focus on her time with him. She didn't need anything else.

With that thought, she grabbed a smaller halter and headed back to the horse pens. Two horses down, two to go before lunch. The Thoroughbred's owner was picking up today and since Gabe was riding Molly exclusively, she had room for two more clients. Better yet, she had four on a waiting list. Marti had finally backed off—probably because she and Paul had a waiting list six times as long as Dani's.

A shadow fell over her as she opened the gate and she swung around to see Gabe standing there. A goofy smile spread across her face before she caught herself.

"So…out with a blonde, I hear?"

"Did you hear that from Kyle?"

"Gina." For a moment she simply stared at him, feeling the sexual eddies start to swirl around them. "Not that I cared," she said lightly as he took a step forward. "Much." She inhaled as he brought his hands up to slowly caress the sides of her neck. "You have your friends and I have mine."

"She's my assistant."

"I know."

He leaned down to take her lips. "I figured you would by now."

"I wouldn't have cared."

"Much."

"Much," she echoed as his tongue started a slow exploration of her mouth. She pulled back after a long moment and said, "I have to keep schedule."

He let go of her and stepped back. "I know. I thought maybe I could see you tonight."

A rush of anticipation shot through her as it always did at the prospect of getting naked with him. "Seven?"

"Six. I'll bring steaks over and cook for you. We can eat at seven."

"Or maybe eight?" she asked with an innocent bat of her eyes.

"Or nine," he said, meeting her look with a wicked smile.

"Nine it is," she said as a truck pulling a horse trailer turned into the driveway. "I guess my new client is a little early—by the way, how'd you get here?"

"I walked."

"Burning energy?"

"Not the way I want to, but yes…"

Again the warmth spread through her as she

met his hungry look. Oh, yes. Tonight was going to be...memorable. But until then, she had work to do.

"If you want to, you can borrow the old truck to go home. Bring it back tonight."

"Why then I'd be stranded for the evening."

"Oh, darn," she said before moving forward to greet the woman getting out of her truck. "The keys are in it."

"Thanks," Gabe said in a low voice. "I'll see you tonight."

Dani smiled at him, then called out a hello to her new client as Gabe headed off to where the old truck was parked next to the barn.

Tonight couldn't come fast enough.

AFTER RETURNING HOME, Gabe walked straight to his fridge and dug out a beer, popping the top before the fridge door was all the way shut. He drank deeply, then wandered over to his drafting table. He'd tell her the truth tonight. It wasn't that bad. Stewart Widmeyer honestly was his friend and he honestly wanted the property.

So why did he feel so freaking guilty about not telling Dani the truth in the first place—especially when he really couldn't have, for fear that Jeffries would get wind of it.

He'd been cautious, but not dishonest. He hadn't told any lies—he just hadn't been totally forthright and that would be rectified.

His only real concern was how Dani would take her family ranch being turned into a golf course. Once she sold, she had to realize that things could change. The place could be subdivided or resold at any time. She had a deep connection to the ranch, but not so deep that she hadn't been unwilling to sell after the divorce.

He pressed the cold can to his forehead. This was going to be fine. He and Dani understood each other and she'd understand why he had to proceed as he did. He finished the beer, then sat down for a few hours' work on the proposal package he was putting together.

Sometime in the early afternoon, the sound of tires on gravel brought his head up. Craning his neck from where he sat at the drafting table, he could just see the front of a white SUV—the sheriff's office?

Pushing back the chair, he got to his feet and headed for the door, wondering just what good old Kyle wanted now. And he wanted something—that much was evident from the cat-with-the-canary smile he wore.

"Deputy," Gabe said after opening the door to find Kyle already standing on his porch, ready to ring the bell. "What can I do for you?"

"It's more like what I can do for you," he said.

Gabe leaned his shoulder against the doorjamb. "I wasn't aware that I needed anything that I don't already have."

"I don't think that's true."

"I don't follow you," Gabe said, allowing himself a perplexed frown, all the while thinking, what the hell does this guy know?

Kyle pressed his lips together as if carefully choosing his words. Then he looked up, his gaze sharp as he said, "I think you want the Lightning Creek Ranch and I can help you get it."

CHAPTER SIXTEEN

GABE MADE A conscious effort to relax the muscles in his hand before he said, "What are you talking about?"

Kyle rocked back on his heels. "You want the Lightning Creek," he repeated. "I imagine you want it for some kind of development."

Gabe's insides went cold. "I'm on vacation."

"You have a connection to the Widmeyers."

What a great time to find out that old Kyle wasn't as stupid as Gabe had thought he was. Gabe was no slouch at thinking on his feet, and the first thing he needed to do was to figure out how to play this to gain more information and a bit of time. Calmly he said, "Maybe you could tell me just how you came to this conclusion."

Kyle smiled as if Gabe had just said, "You got me. I'm working for Widmeyer."

"Well," he said, "it's pretty obvious, what with you being out with that Widmeyer lady this morning and telling Gina she's your assistant."

Now it was getting weird. How in the hell did Kyle know who Serena was? He'd seen her for all of ten or twenty seconds this morning. The smug smile grew wider. "Surprised?" he asked softly.

Gabe didn't answer. Instead he waited for Kyle's
ego to take over, give him a bit more information,
so that he had something to work with. He didn't
have to wait long.

"I know Ms. Widmeyer, you see, because I
pulled her over for speeding about a year ago.
She's very memorable."

That she was, but Gabe had no idea that Serena had even been in the area back when Timberline was still in Widmeyer hands. But he'd been
working solely on independent projects back then.

"I didn't think Montana was strict about speed."

"She was going really fast," Kyle said with a
smirk. "But she was good—very matter-of-fact.
She didn't try to talk me out of the ticket. She
just made small talk while I wrote her up. Told
me how good the resort was going to be for the
community." Kyle nodded a little. "She was right.
It was."

"I heard it provided a nice shot in the economic
arm," Gabe allowed.

"So imagine what two resorts will do for the
area." Gabe gave him a polite look, because all he
could do at this point was bluff. "I've been thinking about this ever since I saw her—Widmeyer
lost that place. Now she's back and meeting with
you. You're leasing this house that costs a shit-
load of money, when there are a dozen cheaper
almost-as-nice places to rent. You've been being
really *nice* to Dani… Well, I figure something's

cooking and I think you're looking at buying the Lightning Creek, expanding your holdings."

"You're real good at deduction, Kyle."

"I have my moments. Also—" he smiled with a touch of false humility "—Allie said something about cutting all ties with the place last time we talked."

"She's still talking to you?"

"Which is good for you," Kyle said flatly.

"I'm not saying you're right," Gabe said, "but given the relationship you have with the Brody sisters, I'm kind of wondering just how you think you can help a person who wanted to buy the place."

"Allie and I have had our differences, but I know the Brodys and I know how to work them. Pretty much, I know how to work one sister against the other. Right now you have two that want to sell, one that's probably ambivalent and one that'll fight to keep the place. They made an all-or-nothing pact. I think I can change your situation to all. Right now, the way things stand, it's nothing."

Gabe took a step closer. "If I accepted help, then what do you get?"

"Finder's fee."

"How much?"

"I'm not greedy. Five percent of the sale."

"Very reasonable…if I were in the market for help. Which I am not."

"You'll need it. These ladies are stubborn."

"I'm still working on how you would sway them. Is Dani going to start experiencing a lot of strange occurrences? Horses released in the night and broken water pipes?"

Kyle's eyes narrowed. "I don't know what you're talking about." But his face started to go red—the curse of bad liars and the fair-skinned. Kyle was both. "And no, I wouldn't do shit like that."

"What would you do?" Gabe asked softly.

Kyle shook his head. "Waste my time, it looks like."

"My reasons for being here are none of your business," Gabe said. "And if you harass Dani or her sisters in any way, I'll have to do something about it."

Kyle took a half step forward, his hand on his utility belt. "Yeah? Like what?"

"To begin with, I'd contact your boss."

"You have nothing to report to him."

"Nothing I can prove anyway, right?"

"Look. I came here to do you a favor. Plain and simple. No skin off my nose if you don't want my help."

"No skin except for not getting the finder's fee."

"Look, asshole—"

Gabe took a quick step forward before he could stop himself, but then he unclenched his fists, flexed his fingers, reminded himself that while he could still mop up the porch with the guy, he was no longer the kid that settled things with his fists. Or he wouldn't be unless Kyle messed with Dani.

"For the record," he told Kyle, "Serena is no longer a Widmeyer. She's now my assistant. I work for myself."

"Yeah? Well, I don't notice you saying you're not interested in the Lightning Creek."

Gabe folded his arms over his chest and gave the guy a stony stare. He wasn't going to lie, but he wasn't going to help him out, either. "I'm saying my business is none of yours and that you'd damn well better leave Dani and her sisters alone."

"Or what?" Kyle asked quietly. He shoved his jaw sideways as he regarded Gabe, then with a curt nod, turned and headed for his SUV.

Gabe stood where he was until Kyle turned the vehicle around and roared down the driveway, turning to go toward town rather than Dani's.

Well, at least there was that, though Gabe didn't doubt for one second that Kyle was going to continue to stir the pot. Who would have thought that breakfast out with his assistant would create such a shit storm?

Gabe went back inside, tried to work, but couldn't settle. Instead he paced. Dani was busy with horses and clients. Kelly would be there by now…and if he raced over to head off a possible move by Kyle, it would only make him look as if he had something to hide. Which he didn't.

He had no doubt that if he could, though, Kyle would twist things around, but he was equally certain that Dani wasn't going to believe anything her ex-brother-in-law told her without first looking into matters. The best way to deal with this was to simply go over this afternoon as usual, tell her everything and hope for the best.

DANI HAD JUST stripped down to get into the shower when her phone rang. She debated, then cranked off the water and crossed the hall to her bedroom to scoop the phone up off the dresser.

Allie.

"Hey, what's up?" she asked, walking back into the bathroom.

"Kyle called."

"Yeah?" Dani asked in a cautious voice. "What's he want now? My new furniture?"

"What do you know about this Gabe guy?"

There was a note in her sister's voice that put Dani on full alert. "Why?"

"Kyle thinks that he's there to buy the ranch. That he's been there the entire time to buy the ranch. That he's been hanging out, biding his time, manipulating things so that you trusted him before he made the sales pitch."

Dani went cold inside.

"Since when does Kyle know jack?" she asked.

"Yeah. I know, but this time he sounds like he's actually concerned. I mean…I can't think of any way that telling us helps him."

"He's Kyle. There's a way." Which was exactly what Dani had to believe. The guy who'd smashed her standpipes was mad at Gabe for some perceived slight and was getting his revenge.

"What is it?"

"I don't know." Dani sat on the edge of the tub, staring at the floor tiles between her feet. "You sound like you honestly believe him."

"I guess that Gabe had a visitor recently."

"His assistant. Yes."

"And apparently that assistant also works for the Widmeyers—or did when they were hammering out the Timberline deal."

"Maybe she changed jobs," Dani said. That wasn't unheard of, although having her work for first the Widmeyers and then someone who also happened to be spending time in Eagle Valley—that was kind of pushing the coincidence boundaries.

"Her last name is Widmeyer. Kyle stopped her last year for speeding."

Dani's stomach felt like a rock, but she battled on. "He's sure it's the same woman."

"I guess she's pretty distinctive."

Which was exactly what Dani had heard from Gina. "Damn," she muttered. Gabe never mentioned a connection with the Widmeyers, even when they'd discussed Timberline. He'd had every opportunity and hadn't.

He was going to give Molly to his best friend's wife. What if that best friend was a Widmeyer?

"I talked to Mel, Dani. She thinks it's totally possible that Widmeyer plans to make another resort in this valley. She says that the Staley property combined with ours would be a prime locale, and get this—the Staley property was purchased through an LLC registered in Nevada, so no one knows who the true owner is. It could well be Widmeyer Enterprises."

"Speculation."

"I agree, Dan. That's all it is, but what if this guy has been working you? You need to think about this—especially, if, well…"

"Right." Dani lifted her chin, thinking she was already beyond the *if-well* stage. "I'll talk to him tonight. I'll ask him if what Kyle says is true."

"What if he lies to you? I mean, liars tend to do that."

"I guess I'll have to see what my gut says."

And right now her gut was screaming, "No fair!" She finds a guy she really connects with and…this? It couldn't be true.

But what if it was?

TROUBLE. THAT WAS what her gut said an hour later when Gabe parked the truck in its place near the barn and started for the house. There was an aura of tension around him that, if anything, became more pronounced when he walked into the house.

"Hey," she said, not moving toward him as she would have done if Allie hadn't called.

He studied her for a long moment and her stomach tightened to the point that she thought she might be sick.

Give him a chance.

Fine. She'd do that, but everything in her shouted that something was so very wrong.

"Hi." He held up the bag he carried. "The steaks."

Food was about the last thing she wanted to think about, but Dani went through the motions, for the moment anyway. "Let's lay them out to season."

She turned and walked toward the kitchen and he followed, as did the dark cloud that seemed to surround them.

"Kyle called Allie," she said as she took the bag from him.

"I figured."

She turned then to face him. His expression was tight. Grim. "What's going on, Gabe? Who do you work for?"

He wasn't stupid enough to try to touch her. She'd give him that. "I work for myself."

"Are you contracted by the Widmeyers by any chance?"

"We're friends."

"Ah," she said as if he'd commented on the weather, while her insides were beginning to churn. "I guess it's not too hard to guess who your 'friend' is who'll pay a decent price for the ranch."

"It's Stewart Widmeyer."

Okay. One point taken care of.

"Did you come here expressly to buy the Lightning Creek?" she asked quietly.

"I did."

"You son of a bitch."

"Wait—"

"No. I won't wait," Dani said, taking a couple of paces toward him, her hands clenched into fists by her side. "You came here to manipulate me—us—into selling our ranch."

"I came here to get the lay of the land, to see if it was possible to buy the ranch. I didn't come here to manipulate you into selling it."

"Then why do I feel manipulated? Why do I feel like I've been used?" She practically spit the words at him.

"I haven't used you."

"Bull. Shit. You set out to get close to me from day one. You bought a freaking horse even though you didn't ride." She put her hand to her head and shoved her hair back. "You bought a horse to get to know me and you don't call that manipulation." Her eyes went wide. "It was no accident that you were at Lacy's pen, was it?"

Gabe's lips were pressed tightly together, the line of his mouth nearly white as he shook his head.

"You son of a bitch," she repeated. Dani bit her lip and turned away, having a sudden, almost uncontrollable urge to throw something, anything, and see it smash against the wall. Or better yet, against Gabe's head.

"It wasn't like that."

"Oh, yeah?" she asked coldly. "Then how was it?" She folded her arms over her chest and waited for him to try to put a spin on it, as Chad had tried to put a spin on his activities.

"First of all, I was going to tell you everything tonight."

"How convenient. You're forgiven," she said acidly.

"Dani…"

Now she was the one pressing her lips together, trying so damned hard to keep it together until she got this bastard out of her house. At least she wasn't crying. Yet.

Tears of anger, she told herself, resisting the urge to brush the back of her hand under her eyes. She wouldn't give him the satisfaction. "You bought a horse under false pretenses. You hired me to train said horse under false pretenses—all so you could get your grimy hands on my ranch."

"All right. The horse part wasn't totally above-board, but the rest of it was."

"If it was, then why didn't you tell me the truth

when you brought up your friend who wanted to buy the ranch? Why didn't you say, 'My friend Mr. Widmeyer wants to buy your ranch because it adjoins this other property and then he can—'" she waved her hands in the air "—do whatever it is he wants to do?"

"Because I couldn't risk people knowing that. If that happened, the land prices would skyrocket and we'd have one hell of a time getting the acreage we needed at an acceptable price. Jeffries would have made certain that happened."

Dani didn't know who Jefferies was and she didn't care. "But if you strung me along, you could get the land quietly and for an acceptable price." She curled her lip up and asked, "How do you look at yourself in the mirror?"

"Dani…I didn't want this to play out this way."

"Oh. How did you want it to play out? In the way where you banged me a few more times, then disappeared back to wherever it is you live?"

"I didn't plan on falling in love with you."

For a moment she simply stared at him, too damned angry to find the words she needed. "You fell in love with me."

"Yeah." He shoved his hands into his back pockets in an uncomfortable gesture.

"You don't treat people you love the way you treated me."

"I was going to tell you. I was going to lay out everything. Ask you to understand that I started off the wrong way, but ended up…ended up caring more for you than I've ever cared for anyone else."

"If this is the person you are—the kind that slides into situations and looks for ways to take advantage so that you can achieve your goal—well, you can just go to hell."

He shifted his weight again, his troubled gaze still drilling into her. "There's more."

"How can there be more?" she asked him incredulously.

"Stewart arranged to have Jolie's internship extended."

Dani's mouth fell open, then she snapped it shut again. "And did you arrange for Kelly to go to volleyball camp, too?"

He shook his head.

"Leave." Dani pointed to the door, needing to get him out of there, because if he stayed much longer the angry tears were going to flow and she didn't need that particular humiliation on top of everything else. "And take that horse with you." Having Molly around was only going to remind her of what this guy had done to her.

Two liars in a row. How could she be so stupid? "Go."

The word dropped out of her mouth like a stone. Gabe drew in a breath, then turned and walked out of the kitchen. A few seconds later the front door opened and closed. Dani turned to lean on the countertop, her forehead pressed against the old cabinets as she pulled in a choked breath. She let it out again, and then the tears starting hitting her hands and the counter beneath them like raindrops.

Son of a bitch.

Taken again.

GABE TOOK DANI at her word, borrowing a halter from the tack room and using it to lead Molly back to his place. He'd send the halter back. Somehow. Right now he needed to figure out what he was going to tell Stewart and Neal. Not only that he'd lost the deal, but that it was also highly probable that word would soon be out about what they had planned, and once again Jeffries would win.

As he walked through the clear evening, following the deer trail across the fields to the Staley house, Molly walking placidly behind him, he tried to come up with alternative plans—for both the Widmeyer deal and Dani. Especially Dani.

Was there any chance that once she'd had time to cool off that they could talk?

It sure as hell hadn't looked that way when he'd left her kitchen.

He was in deep shit and he couldn't see any way out of it. His only choice was to plow through it and see if he could salvage anything—on either front.

Maybe there were other suitable properties they could find in the area—if Dani didn't instantly tell the world about what he'd done. She might not. She might not want the world to know that the guy she'd been dating had been, in her eyes, stringing her along. That Brody pride.

If she didn't tell, then Kyle would.

He was well and truly screwed. What killed him was that if Kyle hadn't recognized Serena, then all would have been well. He could have secured the ranch, continued his relationship with Dani, told her the truth…or most of it. He didn't see where he would have ever told her about arranging that first meeting at Lacy's stall, but everything else.

Stewart was going to be livid, but that wasn't ruining him nearly as much as recalling the look of utter betrayal Dani had worn after she'd demanded the truth of him.

When he got home, he put Molly in the pasture next to the house, removing the halter as Dani had taught him. Once she realized she was free, that she wasn't going back to the Lightning Creek to be with her buddies, she raised her head and let out a long series of whinnies, her ears perked forward to hear any distant answers.

Nothing.

Which was how it was probably going to be with him and Dani.

CHAPTER SEVENTEEN

DANI COULD HAVE called a sister. It wasn't as if she didn't have a lot to choose from, but instead she paced the house—the house now filled with furniture she'd bought while with Gabe the Liar, which was getting in the way of her stalking path.

How could she have been so manipulated and not seen what was happening? How could she have accepted that he was buying a horse for his best friend's wife? And paying to have it trained? People didn't do things like that. She was an idiot.

Although who would have thought that someone would go to such lengths to get to know someone? And Jolie's internship! What kind of power did Gabe have?

Widmeyer power. The power of money.

Well, they were not buying her. Now it was a matter of principle. She'd been made a fool of twice, once by Chad and again by Gabe, and she wasn't going to do either of them any favors.

Stupid, stupid, stupid!

And what really killed her was that she'd liked him—pretend Gabe had been a good guy. Funny, sexy, caring, intelligent. She had no idea what real Gabe—if that was indeed his name—was like and she wasn't going to find out. *Fool me once, and all that crap...*

Argh.

Dani finally stomped upstairs. She felt as if she'd been crying for days instead of for an hour. She stalked by the window, refusing to look out of it and see Gabe's lights burning. How much longer would he be in the Staley house, now that he'd failed to get the ranch for his rich friend?

Not long, she bet. He'd be on his way. Off to fleece other trusting souls on the behalf of Widmeyer Enterprises.

Dani sank down on her bad and clasped her hands loosely between her thighs, staring at the floor. Her face felt raw from tears. Tears of anger, she reminded herself. Not tears of gut-wrenching loss. She hadn't lost anything real. It had all been pretend, all in her mind. She'd been manipulated and used. Slowly she toppled sideways onto the bed, pressing her cheek against the fluffy white bedspread.

He'd been so perfect for her. Why couldn't he be real?

"IT'S VERY UNLIKELY I can finesse this situation." Gabe leaned his forehead against the refrigerator. It was the third call from Stewart in less than twelve hours—this time a conference call with Neal on the third line. The first two had been a confession followed by a this-is-unacceptable return call.

"Do you have any idea where it got away from you?" Stewart asked yet again. "Can we back-track at all?"

Backtrack? How?

"No. I'm not quite sure when it got away from me." Maybe it had been the minute he'd staked himself out at Lacy's pen as a way to meet Dani Brody. Or maybe it had been when he'd realized they had something between them and he hadn't come instantly clean, because he'd hoped he could confess half the lie and not the really sleazy stuff, like pretending to need a horse trained when that was maybe the last thing on this planet that he needed.

"We need to act fast before word gets out that Widmeyers own the Staley property," Neal said, stating the obvious. "You're certain that Danica Brody will mouth off about this?"

"She's pretty damned pissed at me," Gabe said, "but I don't know how she's going to handle it. The brother-in-law will. I have no illusions about that."

"*Why* is she so pissed?" Neal asked.

Because it's personal. Because she feels be-trayed yet again.

"All that matters is that she is," Gabe said.

"No," Stewart replied irritably. "If we know the why, we can work from that angle."

There'd be no working from that angle. "She feels manipulated," Gabe said. "She's angry that I didn't tell her why I was getting to know her before I made the offer."

There was a second of silence and Gabe knew that both Stewart and Neal were thinking that Gabe had followed the only reasonable course of action.

"Maybe she just needs some time to get over the feeling that she was manipulated," Neal said. "Give it a few days."

"You want me to give her a few days, then try again?"

"Let her cool off," Neal said.

Gabe ran a hand over his face. He wasn't going to tell Neal exactly why that was highly unlikely, as in he'd been sleeping with Dani, which made his betrayal doubly painful to her—probably to the point that she was feeling vengeful—so he settled for, "When I last saw her, she gave no indication that she would cool off."

"We have to salvage before word gets out and prices get out of hand. Go with plan B," Stewart barked.

"Plan B?" Neal asked. There was no plan B and Stewart knew that, but he was so damned insistent on showing up Jeffries that he didn't appear to be thinking much better than Gabe was.

"Come up with a plan B," he amended. "Gabe—

be here in the offices on Monday and lay it out for me."

"What about the other sister—the one who was married to the deputy?" Neal asked. "Have you tried negotiating with her? She seems like the weak link."

"There are no weak links, Neal."

"There is always a weak link," Stewart said. "We need to figure out how to work one sister against another. That's our plan B."

GABE FLEW OUT of the Missoula airport late Sunday afternoon. Molly was at a horse-boarding facility—he'd had to rent a truck and trailer to get her there—and he told the owner that he was thinking of selling, so if she knew of any potential buyers, to let him know. The prospect of selling her bothered him, but he had to do what was best for the horse and if things continued as they were now, he wouldn't be back to the Staley place except to pick up his belongings.

Was he giving up that easily?

He stared out over the wing of the 737. Maybe he was. He didn't want to continue hassling Dani, had given up on the fairy tale that while it might hurt her to have been manipulated by someone she'd come to trust, she'd be happier on another property with more modern facilities.

No matter what happened, she was going to harbor bitterness against him.

He felt as if a hole was being eaten in his gut.

When he got to his Bloomington apartment close to midnight, he was overwhelmed by how stuffy and almost claustrophobic it seemed after he'd kicked around in that giant-ass house for over a month. He opened windows rather than turning on the air, then closed them again as the muggy heat rolled in.

Okay. Trapped in what had once seemed like a luxurious space with fake air and a giant load of anxiety. Oh, yeah. This was the life.

After a grand total of maybe two hours' sleep, he was up again, showering and shaving. He forced himself to stop for coffee and a bagel before heading to the Widmeyer offices. His space, which he leased on a yearly basis from Stewart, was on the same floor as corporate, so it was just a quick walk down the hall to the boardroom after dumping a few things in his office.

Stewart was already there, seated at the head of the table, his computer set up in front of him. Gabe paused in the doorway, drawing a breath. This guy had saved his life.

"You're early."

"Yeah." He walked forward and set the case containing his laptop on the table.

"Neal will be here in a few minutes." Stewart typed a few words then looked up. "He moved back in with Serena."

"How do you feel about that?" Gabe asked,

surprised that the Crown Vic magic had worked so well. If only he could figure out a way to straighten things out with Dani so fast.

"They don't seem to be able to let go of one another, so it's just as well they work it out. Serena's an asset to the team."

"She's joining the team?" Gabe asked.

Stewart looked up. "She's only your part-time assistant, correct?"

"You pay most of her salary," Gabe said, wondering if this was a nudge toward the Widmeyer door. "She's whatever you want her to be."

Stewart focused again on the screen in front of him, his body posture tense. He hated losing and most of all he hated losing twice to someone who'd betrayed him. And Gabe didn't know how he could help him.

"Hey," Neal said as he walked into the room. "Back from the Wild West." His voice was friendly, but there was a reticence in his expression.

"Not with the outcome I envisioned."

"We all knew that this approach was speculative," Neal said smoothly.

"It's a situation we need to rectify. Fast." Stewart placed his palms flat on either side of his computer as he spoke, emphasizing the point. "Plan B?" he asked with a pointed look at both men.

"I'm not in for pitting one sister against the other," Gabe said, making himself clear on that matter before taking his chair after Neal had closed the door. "There's got to be another way."

"Like showing up with a truck of money fast?" Neal asked with a smile as he took his seat.

"We'll make another offer. Soon," Stewart agreed.

Gabe gave a slow nod. It might work—but he sincerely doubted it would. Stewart was once again giving him the long hard stare and he felt a bit like he had that night he'd been bailed out of jail, which in turn made him feel like one hell of a failure. "I don't yet have a viable plan B, other than looking elsewhere for property we can develop."

"Next to skiing and water? Good luck."

"Here's my plan B," Neal said. "We make another offer to the Brodys and also make it clear that whether they sell or not, the Staley property will be developed into a resort."

"It can't compete with Timberline."

"We'll get to that. If the Brodys choose not to sell, they need to understand the impact this will have on their lives. Traffic across their property, close to their house, will increase exponentially. I foresee developing the acreage where the two properties adjoin—also close to their house— into an area where we can hold weddings and other large-scale affairs. Privacy fences, landscaping, will keep out guests from being troubled by the view of their property, however, the noise…

Sometimes the noise can get out of hand. Parties late into the night. That kind of thing."

"Your plan is to convince them we're going to be a nuisance?" Gabe asked.

"I plan to convince them that their lives on the ranch will not be as private or as quiet as they were before." Neal tapped a finger on the table. "They are used to isolation."

"Dani lived in the city."

"Then why isn't she still there?"

Stewart cleared his throat. "I think we need to start building a structure—"

"A water slide!" Neal interrupted. Stewart frowned and Neal continued, "An *adult* water slide." He leaned his head back and laughed. "We could make an adults-only playground out of the place."

Stewart actually smiled a little. "I'd prefer a resort with a golf course, but if push came to shove…"

Gabe rolled his eyes. This was turning into a bona fide nightmare.

"I NEED TO talk to you."

Maybe Gabe needed to talk to her, and he seemed convinced that he did, since this was his fourth message in a day and a half, but she didn't need to talk to him. Dani pushed Delete on her answering machine, wondering how much longer this would persist. She'd already blocked him on her cell phone, but this was her business phone and she couldn't block calls on the landline. All she could do was screen via the answering machine.

She had new clients and two of her previous clients were so pleased with the first thirty days that they'd asked for another stint. She'd explained to Jolie that her extended internship was the result of pulled strings and likely to evaporate at any time, so soon her sister would return home and they'd continue with their plans to build the Lightning Creek Training Facility.

No matter what, they would not sell to Widmeyer Enterprises. She'd rather burn the place to the ground.

It was close to ten o'clock when the phone rang again. Dani jerked awake, the book she'd been reading when she fell asleep slipping to the floor. Gabe. Again. Only this time it took over a minute for the message light to start blinking.

Leaning her head back against the chair cushions, she closed her eyes, debated. What could he possibly have to say to her that mattered? Or would change how she felt about him?

Nothing. She didn't care if he crawled across the state on his belly, she was done.

If you're done, they you should have no problem listening to the message.

Okay, maybe she wasn't so much done, as she was wishing she was done.

She inhaled deeply, then exhaled as she acknowledged the truth. It ripped her up to hear his voice—and not only because the guy had lied to her, betrayed her. But part of her was also still grappling with the fact that he wasn't who he said he was. Part of her was in mourning.

Listen to whatever it is he has to say. Hopefully it would outrage her, give her the kick in the ass she needed to wipe him out of her mind.

Yeah. Good plan.

But her hand was shaking as she pushed the play button and gingerly put the phone to her ear.

"Dani, hear me out before you hang up." The words came out rapidly and then his voice slowed to its normal cadence. "Widmeyer is going to send someone else to talk to you about selling, and now that word of the proposed resort is out, I wouldn't be surprised if other people contact you to buy, with the hope that Widmeyer might need the property someday. Just a heads-up. And, Dani—they probably aren't going to play nice."

Just a heads-up that you're about to be further harassed. Dani pushed her hair back from her forehead, determined to stay on the line until she heard the message end.

"I wish I hadn't helped bring this into your life. I didn't expect…" Dani sat up a little straighter, dropping her hand as the utter sincerity of his words stabbed at her.

This is what he does. He's very, very good.

He cleared his throat. "That's no excuse. Anyway, if you ever want to talk about this, you have my number."

That was when Dani hung up. As if she would ever call him.

DANI WAS SWEEPING the porch when a car pulled into the drive—a Lexus she'd never seen before. She leaned her broom against the wall and headed down the walk, expecting to give directions or greet a potential client, until the woman got out of the car. Tall with angular features and her silvery hair pulled into a chignon, she fit the description of Gabe's assistant—the woman whose appearance had tipped off Kyle as to Gabe's duplicity.

If this woman hadn't visited Gabe, if Kyle hadn't recognized her, would Dani have ever known how she'd been played? Would Gabe have really told her the truth as he'd said he'd planned to?

She didn't believe so.

And then the bigger question—would she have been happy not knowing? Blithely unaware that the man she thought she'd loved had manipulated her? It smacked too much of trusting Chad while he was screwing Megan on the side. She hadn't known. She'd been happy—but once she'd discovered the truth, the memory of those happy, oblivious days made her feel humiliated and stupid.

Dani stayed where she was on the porch as the

woman opened the gate and strode up the walk, moving pretty damned well considering both the state of the sidewalk and the height of her heels. The muscles in Dani's jaw tightened as she prepared for whatever she was about to face.

"Hello," the woman called politely as she approached.

Dani gave a cool nod and waited, marveling at the chutzpah of these people.

"I'm Serena Widmeyer."

"I figured."

Serena stopped at the bottom step, lifted her chin and then smiled a little. "You know who I am."

"Gabe's assistant. Or pretend assistant. He told me so many lies, I'm not certain what to believe."

"I'm his assistant—or I was. I've since moved to another part of the company."

"And you're here because…?"

"I'd like to make an offer on the ranch."

Dani tried to stifle a startled laugh and it came out as a choking sound. "And I'd like you to get in your car and leave." Gabe's warning had proved to be true, although her cynical side now wondered if maybe he was now sliding into the good-cop role in a good cop/bad cop scenario. Before her stood the bad cop.

"Will you at least hear the offer?"

"No." Dani folded her arms over her chest and set her jaw. "Any more questions before you go?"

"No, but I have something to tell you."

"Which is?"

"If you don't sell, we'll be moving forward with a new project on the Staley property."

"It's yours. Do as you like."

"You understand that there will be radical change in the amount of traffic and noise you experience here."

"Not much I can do about that but endure."

"Or you could swallow your pride and take a very generous offer."

"I don't think so."

"What do your sisters think?"

"We're in agreement.

"I've been in contact with Allison."

"If you have, she would have contacted me."

Serena merely raised an eyebrow, making Dani wonder if perhaps she was telling the truth. Just because Gabe was a liar, it didn't mean everyone associated with the corporation was. If Allie had been tempted by an offer, she might not tell immediately.

"We'll need an answer in ten business days," Serena continued as if Dani had not made it clear they weren't selling.

"What happens if you don't hear in ten days?"

"Construction of the water park begins." She turned and walked back to the gate. Once there she pulled a card out of her jacket pocket and slipped it into the hinge. "Just in case," she said.

Dani jerked her chin up in a fat-chance gesture, but other than that stayed stock-still as she
waited for Serena Widmeyer to drive away. Once
the dust had settled and she could no longer hear
the distant sound of the engine, Dani picked up
the broom again and began sweeping vigorously.

Water park? She didn't want to live next to a
water park. Who above the age of eighteen did?

Plus, the roof on the barn was leaking and as
things stood right now, she and her sisters couldn't
afford any more new fencing to replace the sag-
ging stuff that Kyle was supposed to have replaced
five years ago. The posts he'd bought at that wonderful price hadn't been pressure-treated and they
were all rotting off at ground level. Yes, they'd
replaced the worst sections this past spring, but
there was so much more to do. And they needed
that indoor arena in order to work year-round.

She wasn't selling to the Widmeyers.

Both Jolie and Allie called that afternoon before
she could call them. Jolie wanted reassurance that
they wouldn't sell and Allie cursed the fates because they hadn't before they'd known what was
going on, because now she was in agreement with
Dani. She wasn't going to sell to the Widmeyers.

Serena had indeed contacted her, offering a
good deal, but Allie wasn't going to get pushed
around or seduced by a corporation with under-
handed tactics.

"Besides," she'd said before ending the call, "we

can always sell to someone else eventually. Or put in a pig farm next to their water park. Screw them up that way."

Dani smiled in spite of herself as she hung up. Sometimes she liked the way Allie thought.

CHAPTER EIGHTEEN

On exactly the eleventh day after Serena had showed up on the ranch, giving Dani the ten-day deadline, the surveyors arrived, setting up their equipment and staking out an area of Staley ground adjacent to the Lightning Creek's north boundary—about a hundred yards from the house. Dani's great-grandfather had designed the ranch so that the house would be buffered from neighbors by the fields spreading out into the valley. The land behind them had been owned by his brother and it had seemed unreasonable at the time to think that his brother would sell. He hadn't, but his son had. So now Dani could well have close neighbors to the north…unless this was all a bluff.

Dani ignored the orange-helmeted men as they strode around, calling directions to one another, planting stakes and running lines. It could be a bluff. It was one thing to stake out a project, another to actually build it.

The Widmeyers were trying to force her into a decision by building close.

"Shut the old gate across the road," Jolie said when Dani had called to tell her what was going on. "Keep them from driving across the place."

"One—its hinges are rusted. Two—we can't do that legally and I have a feeling that Widmeyer is just waiting to jump on something like that."

"No doubt. Well, when I get home, we'll see what we can do to cause them some pain."

"We can't do anything, Jo. They have all the power here."

"Maybe they are just bluffing, like you said. Trying to force our hand."

"That's my hope."

A hope that was shattered the next week when the heavy equipment arrived and the gravel trucks started to roll. The ripping and tearing of the earth and the rumble of the trucks had the horses severely on edge—to the point that Dani got dumped by a new horse on her daily ride and had to walk back to the ranch, hoping that the horse was there waiting for her.

It was and so was her sister. Jolie had tied up the mare and was just starting out to look for her when Dani walked into the yard, pissed beyond measure.

"You're all right, I see."

"Physically." She waved at the construction site on the other side of their back fence. "Mentally, not so much so."

"We can't even put pigs there," Jolie said. "Unless we want them in our own backyard."

A low rumble shook the ground as a front-end loader dug into a pile of gravel. "This is no environment for horse training," Dani said, planting her hands on her hips in disgust. "Those assholes."

And Gabe was the king asshole.

"They won't be doing this forever," Jolie said. "Construction has to stop sometime."

"No. Then the loud people come."

"If they really build a waterslide."

"I think they're going to. This is too much equipment for a bluff and I checked with planning and zoning. They can do it."

"Damn. Well, at least I'll be here to share the pain." She gestured at her overloaded truck. "This is the second-to-last load of my stuff. One more load tomorrow and then I can turn in my key to the landlord *and* start work at the café." Which was how she was going to support herself until the spring when her clinic schedule began.

Another rumble shook the earth beneath their feet and Dani shook her head. "I hate these guys."

A WEEK LATER, the construction stopped almost as abruptly as it began, making Dani think that, yeah, it had all been a ploy. Right up until she spoke with Mike Culver, the owner of the local feed store.

"According to what I hear, they'll be building. A few minor approvals and they're good to go. And while they wait, the earth beneath the pad has time to settle."

"Good to know," Dani murmured ironically.

"There'll be a lot of activity on your end of the valley when they get that thing finished. All the kids are real excited and they're talking about putting an old-fashioned drive-in there, as well. Kind of a retro thing."

Dani somehow managed not to smack her forehead. "Again—good to know. Well, I'll see you," she said brightly, her smile evaporating the instant she turned around.

She wasn't giving in and she wasn't going to think about what this might do to her property value. It was just possible that people with the money to buy her place didn't want to live next to a water park and drive-in theater any more than she did.

"THEY AREN'T BUDGING," Serena told Gabe as they shared a drink after he'd finished up his last official Widmeyer contract. He was now his own boss again and frankly, he wished he'd never gone back to consulting for Widmeyer, no matter how lucrative it had been.

"*They*, meaning...?"

"The Brody sisters." Her eyes narrowed slightly as she said the name, as if gauging his reaction.

"I didn't think they would."

"They won't take my calls," she said conversationally.

He knew the feeling. He'd tried to call Dani another time but she still refused to pick up.

"Stewart's starting to get a little weird about the situation."

Gabe snorted. "He's been weird about it since day one."

"I guess. But I understood why he was so angry and it seemed like a reasonable face-saving response to what Jeffries had done to him."

"I thought the same way," Gabe said. It had seemed reasonable. He would have been tempted to employ a similar tactic had he been betrayed by a longtime friend and partner. But he'd also like to think that he would have seen when his behavior had started to get obsessive.

"Even Neal has noticed, and you know how blindly he follows Stewart."

"Yeah."

Serena lifted her glass. "Here's to Stewart's great white whale. Let's hope it doesn't kill him."

"Amen to that." Gabe drank deeply. When he put his glass down, Serena was studying him with an expression that made him decidedly uneasy. "What?"

"You look like hell."

"I need a haircut."

"You need some sleep."

"Yeah. Well." He ran a hand over his chin. The stubble was thick and apparently not doing too good of a job of drawing attention away from the circles under his eyes.

"Did you and that Dani person have some kind of a thing going on?"

"Why?"

"Because you're acting like a guy who has a problem and no idea how to solve it, so he's all cranky and snarly and hard to deal with."

"What if I did?"

She exhaled deeply and then drew a squiggly line in the condensation on her glass. "Having met her, I'd say you're screwed if you intended to pursue something there."

"I agree."

"So you're not going to do anything?"

"I didn't say that."

"You don't know what to do?"

"Yeah, I do. I can change the subject to something that is your business rather than leave it on something that isn't."

Serena let out a soft sigh. "Whatever. Just trying to help."

ALMOST A MONTH after Gabe had finished his last Widmeyer contract, Stewart got the official okay from the Eagle Valley planning commission to commence construction on his water park. The only problem was that Gabe knew as well as Stewart did that he didn't want to build a water park— he wanted a resort with a golf course to compete with Timberline. He was still hoping the Brodys would change their minds.

And Gabe was starting to worry about his former mentor and his pursuit of his great white whale.

Stewart didn't have much to say to him, but Gabe had a couple months left on his office lease, so he continued to work out of the Widmeyer offices, continued to see Stewart every day or so. He did not look good. He was scheduled to have the tumor removed from his lung, but the doctors had postponed surgery, telling him that his blood pressure was too high.

That was telling, according to Neal, since high blood pressure had never before been a problem. Timberline's much-lauded grand opening, after a summer-long soft opening, hadn't helped. The resort got rave reviews, had been featured in two travel magazines and on a Travel Channel Best New Places to Explore segment.

Finally one night, when both he and Stewart were working late, Gabe approached Stewart's office and knocked on the door. When there was no answer, he opened it a crack to see the older man sitting at his desk totally focused on the screen in front of him.

"Can we talk?" Gabe asked.

For a moment he thought Stewart was going to say no, but instead he gave a grudging nod.

"You're making yourself sick," Gabe said as he walked into the room and approached Stewart's desk.

"*I'm* making myself sick?" He let out a scoffing snort.

"I'm going to say what Neal won't. You've got to let this go."

Stewart didn't ask what *this* was. He knew.

"I'm going to give that bastard some competition."

"With a water park and a possible drive-in theater?"

Stewart's mouth tightened. "You know as well as I do that I'm only doing those things if I have no other choice."

"You don't. The Brodys aren't going to sell." Gabe gestured at the chair across from Stewart's desk and the older man nodded. Gabe sat, leaning his forearms on his thighs. "They won't sell and you're going to end up with a revenge water park."

"It'll serve them right and should make some decent money."

Gabe looked down at the parquet squares beneath his feet, considered his words for a moment before he looked up and said, "So you punish the Brody women for not selling to you and Jeffries sits across the valley, laughing because he has a world-class resort and you have a water park."

Instead of going red as Gabe had expected, Stewart went a little white around the mouth.

"I'll have my resort."

"Not if you build the water park."

"I'll get the additional land."

"You won't. I know these women." Gabe tapped his fingers together between his knees. "We can start fresh somewhere else. Somewhere where you're building because you believe in the project, because it's something you want to build, and not because it's part of a vendetta." Gabe stopped talking, waited for a response—any kind of response. But Stewart remained stubbornly silent. "Vendettas are unhealthy," he said softly.

"So is betrayal," Stewart said grimly. "It eats at you—especially when you've trusted someone as deeply as I trusted Jeffries."

Oh, yeah, Gabe thought. There was karma taking a nip at him. Dani had trusted him.

"Believe it or not, I'm aware."

"Who betrayed you?" Stewart asked in a curious tone.

"It's more like who did *I* betray," Gabe said.

"Who?" Stewart frowned deeply, as if surprised there was something about Gabe's life he didn't know.

"Dani Brody."

"How?"

"I lied to her. For our gain."

"A betrayal involves a personal relationship," Stewart said.

"Exactly," Gabe said.

"You and—" Stewart waved a finger back and forth in front of him "—her?"

"I love her," he said simply. "And because of what I did, she hates me."

Stewart made a disparaging noise. "So you want me to back off. Because you *love* her."

"No," Gabe said slowly. "I want more than that."

"What exactly do you want?"

"I want you to sell me the Staley place."

MOLLY WAS BACK. For a moment Dani simply stared at the mare when the excited fifteen-year-old girl with the swinging ponytail unloaded her from the horse trailer and led her proudly forward.

"I know you've already worked with her, but that the previous owner stopped short of sixty days," the girl's father said.

"He did," Dani said vaguely.

"I'm kind of new at riding," the girl said, "and I thought that you could work with both of us, if I could come after school."

Dani smiled, bringing her attention back to her livelihood. "That's the deal I worked out with your mom," she said. She glanced at the dad, who walked around the new truck after closing the door on the new horse trailer. These guys were new to horse life in every respect. "I just didn't realize that I'd already worked with the horse."

"Does that make a difference?" the father asked.

"No," Dani replied brightly. "It makes things easier. I know Molly and Molly knows me." She smiled again at the girl, who was now petting Molly's neck as if still trying to believe she owned a real live horse. "She's a nice mare."

"I just love her." The girl beamed. "Mom thought I might want to barrel-race, but I just want to trail-ride with my friends."

"Good plan," Dani said. "Molly's not built for barrels, but if you're interested in trying it out, my sister has just moved in and she'll start running barrel-racing clinics in the spring." Despite water parks and drive-in theaters and whatever else Widmeyer might throw their way.

"We'll keep that in mind," the father said, settling a hand on his daughter's shoulder.

"Follow me." Dani gestured toward the pens with her head. "We'll let her settle in, then start the first lesson tomorrow."

"I can't wait."

Well, at least Gabe had found Molly a good home. She'd give him credit for that. Found the horse a home and left town shortly thereafter. All in all about as perfect of an ending to this chapter in her life as she was going to get.

And it still sucked.

THAT NIGHT THERE were lights on in the Staley house. Dani stood at her bedroom window, toweling her damp hair as she peered out across the dark fields that separated the two houses. What now?

A new tenant? Another aggravation to deal with? Or was Gabe back?

Dani wadded up the towel and headed back to the bathroom. There was nothing she could do about what happened on the Staley place. For the moment, she and Jolie had some peace. The construction had stopped, but everyone in town who knew anything—and that was almost everyone—told her that this was because they were transitioning between phase one and phase two.

Meanwhile Dani was transitioning between aggravation and extreme aggravation. She and her sisters hadn't done one thing except refuse to sell their property and now they were being made miserable by a rich guy who didn't like to hear *no*.

Dani dropped the curtain and sank down on her bed. The rich guy may be over at the house right now. Or it could be that Serena character, or a project manager, or any number of people, but she was pretty damned certain that the current resident was not Gabe Matthews. Because he had no reason to be there…and because she really, really didn't want him to be.

Jolie gave a knock on her door and came in to sit beside her.

"Long shift," she said, rubbing her neck. She pointed to the window, where lights were now shining where they hadn't shone in well over a month. "New resident?"

"Apparently."

"I wonder what this means."

"I was just wondering the same."

"Can't be good," Jolie said.

"I think not."

"We'll get through this."

"Pig farm," Dani said with a smile.

"Pig farm," Jolie agreed, standing up again. "And a shower for me. I'll see you in the morning."

"Yeah," Dani said, once again focused on the lights. She couldn't help but recall how comforting she used to find those lights not that long ago. And now... Now they mocked her and her penchant for trusting the wrong people.

Later that night, when she woke after a whopping three hours of sleep, she got out of bed and crossed the hall to the bathroom, where Gus was taking up most of the floor. On her way back to bed she stopped as the light across the field caught her eye.

Someone was still up at 3:00 a.m... .just like Gabe.

She let out a shaky breath, blinking rapidly at tears that shouldn't be forming, and got back into bed, giving her pillow a couple of healthy punches to knock it back into shape before falling back against it.

What in the hell was wrong with her? Why could she not accept that she'd fallen in love with a lie? Why did she keep wanting something that didn't exist—had never existed?

But it had felt so very real...

CHAPTER NINETEEN

THE STALEY HOUSE was dark the next night. Dani pulled the curtains over her bedroom window anyway, as she had the night before, but she couldn't help peeking out in the wee hours of the morning when she couldn't sleep. No light. The next afternoon the heavy equipment disappeared. After that all was quiet, but Dani knew something was coming, construction would continue. After all, they'd gotten the go-ahead from the county and there was no way that the Widmeyers would cause such a stink, then simply back off.

Not knowing was almost worse than listening to the equipment work.

Molly's new owners showed up two weeks after they'd dropped her off so that Dani could demonstrate Molly's capabilities and evaluate their daughter's, Amber's, riding ability. The demonstration and the lesson went well; Amber was eager to learn and Molly was on her best behavior. By the time Dani put the mare away, Amber's mother, Ginny, was discussing the possibility of buying a horse for herself and the father was laughingly saying that he'd prefer a motorcycle.

"It's quieter than it was the last time we were

here," Ginny said as they walked to the car. "I imagine you're relieved that the place sold."

Dani stopped abruptly. "Sold? Are you sure?"

"I just got my real estate license," Ginny said. "The people in my office are sick about it being a private sale, but apparently it changed hands between friends."

"I see." An awful possibility began taking shape in Dani's mind.

"The new owner used to live there."

Dani forced a smile after a few seconds of stunned silence when she realized that the family was giving her odd looks. "A new neighbor. That'll be nice."

"As long as he doesn't build a water park, eh?" Amber's father chuckled.

"Right." Somehow she continued walking with the family to their car, making inane small talk, barely aware of what she was saying. She smiled and said goodbye, waved as they left. Once they were gone, she put a hand to her stomach and sank down to sit on the mounting block next to the hitching rail.

Gabe had bought the property.

This was worse than living next to a water park. Now she had to live next to the guy who'd screwed with her head, made her think she loved him.

Instead of the annoying trucks and heavy equipment rumbling nearby, Gabe would once again be driving across her property to reach his house…except that he wasn't. Yet.

That didn't mean he wouldn't be in short order.

As soon as Jolie pulled into the yard, Dani met her at her car. "Gabe Matthews bought the Staley place."

Jolie's chin jerked up. "What does that mean for us?" she asked slowly.

"Nothing, I hope."

"I don't believe that for a minute," Jolie said. Neither did Dani.

Two edgy weeks passed and there was still no sign of Gabe.

Where was he and why had he bought the property? Those were the two questions that Dani managed to keep at bay during the day, but they cycled viciously through her mind during mostly sleepless nights.

Why did she feel so unsettled not knowing where he was?

For the same reason she wanted to know where a snake was, even though she had no intention of making contact. Self-preservation.

Every now and again, Dani caught herself staring out across the emptiness between the Lightning Creek Ranch and the Staley house, wondering when she would ever feel as if she'd truly healed, truly moved on, while Gabe owned the place.

Not while she was waiting for that inevitable encounter...

Not until she had some closure of some kind.

"You can stop being so jumpy. He isn't coming back," Jolie said one Saturday morning.

Dani turned on her. "I'm not jumpy."

"Are you kidding? You practically have whiplash from swinging your head around every time a car drives up the road."

"Fine. Well, you know what? I'm going to contact him, find out what his plans are, because until I know, I'm going to be on edge."

"What happens once you do know?"

"I'll be unhappy, but not on edge." She'd know where the snake was.

Jolie snorted. "We'll see."

Dani waited another two days before she brought up an old voice message on her cell phone, and pushed the call-back button before she had time to talk herself out of it. Gabe answered so quickly that for a moment she couldn't find her voice.

"It's Dani," she finally said.

He appeared to be just as stunned because it took him a moment to say, "Yeah, I know. It's good to hear from you."

"I'm calling because, well, I wanted to know what your plans are for the property. The Staley property." She pushed her fist against her forehead. As if there was another property he owned that she would need to know about.

"Nothing."

"What do you mean, nothing?"

"I have no plans for the place."

Dani frowned deeply. "You aren't going to make it into a resort?"

"No."

"Or live there?"

"Not permanently."

"You're going to sell, then?"

"No." His voice was clipped, impersonal.

"That makes no sense, Gabe."

"Maybe not."

"You aren't the kind of guy who does things that make no sense."

"Maybe I've changed."

"I'll have to take your word for it," Dani said darkly. "Because I'm not going to find out firsthand."

"I guess you will."

"Why'd you buy the Staley house?" Because she simply needed to know. No answer she came up with made sense.

There was the briefest of hesitations before he said, "I did it for you, all right?"

"For me?"

"For you and your sisters. So that things would be the way they were before I made the proposal to Stewart. I'm trying to put things back."

It took her a moment to say, "Why?"

"Why do you think, Dani?" He practically growled the words. "I have to go. There's a call on my other line."

He hung up without a goodbye, leaving Dani staring at her phone and wondering what had just happened.

GABE LEANED BACK in his chair and pressed his fingers to his tired eyes. Two days, max, and he'd be done with this project and then on with the next. He needed all the work he could get, since his retirement fund was officially tied up in a property that he wasn't going to personally use—at least not in the near future. So he'd be paying land taxes and bare-bones utilities to keep the place from freezing and being foreclosed on. He'd have to have people take care of the inside and out and hope word didn't get out that he was never there to avoid having the place gutted by opportunistic thieves.

Or he could rent the place. At least temporarily.

The one thing he wasn't going to do was sell… or contact Dani.

Just hearing her voice had been hell. She hadn't forgiven him, that much was obvious from her icy tone. And what did he want with a woman who wanted nothing to do with him?

At least Neal and Serena seemed to be working things out, although Gabe had to admit to feeling a touch of jealousy. Having screwed up his own love life made witnessing their happy moments difficult. He wasn't a sour-grapes kind of guy— or at least he hadn't been prior to messing things up with Dani.

He pulled his laptop closer, took a look at the CAD drawing, then hit Save. Enough for tonight. He was supposed to go out to dinner with Neal and Serena as the proverbial third wheel. They were going to a place where they parked your car, took your coat, made you smell a cork, perhaps forced fancy snails upon you. All he wanted was a nice steak in an unpretentious restaurant, alone…with Dani.

Wasn't going to happen.

At least he wouldn't have to talk about his new purchase tonight, or his motivation for buying, since they'd already gone over all that a few nights before during happy hour at the local pub.

Upon hearing what Gabe had done, Neal had been first stunned and then appreciative. Serena had only smiled in her enigmatic way, which seemed to indicate approval, and Gabe figured she was probably glad she wasn't going to have to make another trip to Montana to try and strongarm Dani into selling.

After agreeing to sell, Stewart had shifted gears. He already looked healthier and less stressed and was now going balls to the wall with another project in the southwest corner of Montana, closer to Yellowstone and the money to be made there. He wasn't as enthusiastic; neither Neal nor Gabe knew whether or not he would ever get over his former partner's betrayal, but at least he'd given up on the great white whale.

Everyone was grateful for that.

Now all Gabe had to do was to figure out what to do with his house. He might rent it, but for the time being, he was not going to sell.

DANI USUALLY DISCUSSED everything under the sun with Jolie, no matter how personal, but she couldn't quite bring herself to confess that Gabe had told her he'd bought the house for her. Well, for her *and* her sisters, but she knew it was mainly for her.

And despite that, he'd made no attempt to make contact with her. Was that because of guilt? Because he thought he owed her?

Or was it a new type of manipulation? He'd hang back, let her come to him?

She was thinking too much, analyzing too much. It was driving her crazy, so when Mac called to tell her he was back in town and would be hanging at his brother's bar, Dani had told him she'd meet him there at nine, even though it was a Monday and she had a superfull schedule the next day. She needed to talk to someone who wasn't involved in this mess she'd gotten herself into. More than that, she needed an objective opinion.

If anyone would give it to her, it was Mac. He'd helped her buy a horse, so maybe he could help her out with this, too. A guy's point of view—someone to tell her, yes, what Gabe did was a standard manipulative man ploy.

She spotted him the instant she walked into the bar, which wasn't hard to do since he was a head taller than almost everyone there. He stood as she approached his table and enveloped her in a mighty hug. "I missed you," he said after releasing her and waving her to a chair.

"I missed you, too," she said as he lifted the pitcher and poured her a glass of Budweiser. He topped off his own, then raised his glass. "Salute."

Dani smiled and drank. "So how's life on the other side of the state?" she asked, wiping foam off her upper lip with the back of her hand.

"Lonely."

"Awww…" Dani reached out to pat his upper arm in mock sympathy.

"I had a visitor, though."

There was something in his tone… "Yeah?"

He nodded. "It was Gina."

Dani's mouth dropped open. "She traveled across the state to see you?"

"She did. Brought the little guy and everything."

Dani had wondered why Gina asked about Mac every now and again in that almost too-casual voice and, looking back, her friend had perked up whenever his name had been mentioned. But she'd

never considered the possibility of vivacious Gina
hooking up with someone as steady and, well, almost boring, as Mac. Gina had always gone for
the wilder guys, but now she had her son to think
about.

"And how do you feel about that?"

From the way the color was creeping up his
face, Dani got the feeling he felt pretty good about
it.

"She's been going through a lot—needed some
time away from her mom." Mac tightened a corner
of his mouth. "We've been talking on the phone
for a while, and then, well…she asked if she could
come see me."

"So are you going to keep seeing her?"

"I'd like to. I'm kind of scared of screwing up.
I mean…this is two lives, here, Dan, what with
her having a kid."

"Yes, it's different when there's a child involved," she agreed, even though she had no personal experience in that regard. And she hoped,
really hoped, that Gina wasn't just looking for a
guy to be a decent father to her son. Gina was her
friend, but so was Mac.

"Take it slow," Dani said, thinking of Mel's advice to her.

"I will. It may go nowhere, but…" He shrugged
his big shoulders.

Dani lifted her glass in a salute and the mood
between them began to edge back to comfort-

able—although it was going to take a while for her to get used to this whole Gina-Mac hookup. Talk about opposites attracting.

"So what's going on with you?" he asked as he scooted his chair a little closer to the table, setting his elbows on either side of his glass.

"It's been one strange summer, Mac."

"I heard there's going to be a water park next to your place?"

"I don't know. The equipment is gone and… someone else bought the property." She pushed her glass from one hand to the next as she debated how to dive into this getting-man-advice thing. "The, uh, guy who was supposed to get us to sell the Lightning Creek to Widmeyer Enterprises bought the property."

"*He* wants to build the water park?"

"Not according to him."

"Then…" he asked, obviously confused. "What's going on, Dani?" She shook her head, still trying to come up with words. Mac waited almost a full minute before asking gently, "Why the sudden inability to articulate? What's that about?"

"It's about my own stupidity," she blurted. "I liked this guy—Gabe. Really liked him. We got to know each other—I thought—but I didn't get to know the real him. I got to know the him he wanted me to get to know." Mac looked no less confused, quite possibly because she was rambling.

"Start at the beginning and go slow, okay?"

So Dani did, from the moment Gabe had engineered the meeting at Lacy's pen right up to where he'd bought the Staley property and now had no intention of doing anything with it.

Mac was quiet for a long moment, then he said, "I get why you're angry."

After a few long seconds, Dani cocked her head. "But…?" she prompted, waiting for Mac to present another take on the situation, something she hadn't considered, as he always did when they discussed life. He was a natural devil's advocate.

"No buts. I get it."

Great. The one time she was hoping for devil's advocacy, she hears, "I get it."

"So I should be outraged and angry."

"I would be."

Why did she feel deflated by his agreement? How sick was that? Dani took a bracing swallow of her beer, thought about ordering a shot. "Why do you think he bought the property next door only to have it lie fallow?"

"Maybe he cares about you."

Dani's chin lifted at the expected response, then she dropped her frowning gaze to stare at her glass. Gabe was a player. He had an angle.

"Why don't you believe him?"

Dani glanced up again, her expression dark. "Gee. I don't know. Maybe the fact that he spent two months working me?"

Mac gave a soft grunt of acknowledgement.

"So…he was employed by Widmeyer, a friend, and came here on a professional mission."

"Yes."

"To make an offer on the property."

"Yes."

"If he'd come right out and offered on it when you first met him, what would you have done?"

"Turned him down."

"Any chance he knew this?"

"Of course he knew it. That's why he worked me," Dani said impatiently.

"Just checking the facts. And now he's failed on his mission, he quits Widmeyer's and buys the property, which he has no plans for." Mac raised his eyebrows as he met Dani's gaze. "It wasn't a cheap purchase, was it?"

She slowly shook her head, afraid to acknowledge the logical path Mac was laying forth. "So what's in it for him?"

"That," he said, lifting his glass, "is the question."

Dani exhaled heavily. "Yeah…" She gave Mac a weary half smile. "You were supposed to have answers. Something brilliant that made everything clear."

"You want things to be clear, you'll have to talk to him."

"I'd be afraid to believe him."

"Why afraid?" Mac asked.

Dani closed her eyes. "Because he can hurt

me." *Still.* A truth she hadn't wanted to face. "I don't know if I can trust him. Or myself."

"So, no matter what he does, he's screwed… even if he cares for you."

Dani didn't want to think about him caring for her. "All I want is to have him out of my life, so I can re—"

She stopped abruptly, but Mac merely lifted his eyebrows and said, "Re*cover*?"

"Re*coup*—recoup my lost time."

Mac lifted his bottle. "Here's to recouping lost time." He spoke the words in a way that told Dani he was talking as much about himself as her. He and Gina—go figure. Well, at least Gina was an open book. No secrets there. If she liked you, you knew it, and the same if she didn't.

"Indeed." She touched her glass to his, then once again took a long drink.

CHAPTER TWENTY

"YOU SHOULD GO see her." Serena tipped her martini glass toward Gabe as she spoke, then lifted the olive out and popped it in her mouth, setting the toothpick aside.

"Not a good idea."

"Kind of like dinner last night?" she asked archly.

"No. I liked meeting Lauren." His date, an old friend of Serena's, newly returned to the States from a stint in London, was attractive, articulate, warm and funny. Gabe had enjoyed her company, but when the evening ended, they'd parted ways with no intention of seeing one another again.

"Go settle things with Montana." Serena's nickname for Dani, since she couldn't keep the sisters straight.

"Leave it," he said seriously. She'd already drilled him about buying the place, then continuing to work from his apartment instead of from his new home.

"Fine. *I'll* go see her," Serena said. "Straighten matters out."

Gabe gave a disparaging snort. "You do that."

She arched an eyebrow at him in a way that was pure Serena. "I would if I wasn't so busy keeping Neal...busy."

"I'm happy for you." Gabe took a long sip of whiskey. He *was* happy for them, glad that his friends had patched things up, but that didn't mean he didn't feel a twinge—no, make that a wallop—of jealousy. "I don't think I can patch my troubles up with a Crown Vic."

"It took more than the Vic," she said, swirling the remnants of her drink slowly. "It took a major attitude adjustment...on both our parts." She gave a small sigh. "Mainly mine." Then she leaned back in her chair. "I'm going back to Spokane to pick up another car from the Crown Vic guy. A perfect '57 Chevy for me. Want to come? Road trip? Take your mind off things?"

"Is Neal coming?"

"Yes."

Gabe laughed. "I don't think Neal is going to want to have me along...but thanks for the invite."

Neal eventually joined them and confirmed Gabe's suspicions.

"No offense, love, but the backseat is not big enough for three."

Serena blew out an impatient breath, then covered Neal's hand with her own.

Gabe smiled with a touch of acid and signaled to the bartender to bring him another drink.

IT WASN'T THAT Gabe didn't trust Serena…it was just that Gabe didn't trust Serena when she had it in her head that she needed to help him fix his life. His drawings, his books, his rough-draft proposals—yes, she could have a hand in fixing those. His life? No.

After she and Neal set out on their weeklong road trip to pick up the new addition to their classic car family, Gabe found it even more impossible to focus than usual. What if she took him at his word and stopped to hash things out with "Montana"?

That was the very last thing he needed.

He needed to hash those things out himself. The sane way of doing that seemed to be to give her space. Help her believe that he wanted nothing tangible from her—that he respected her anger, understood her lack of trust. Hell, she was reacting just as he had in his untrusting days, after being burned a few times, so he honestly understood.

He hadn't been forgiving or quick to trust, either. It'd taken years for him to control his defensiveness and even then he hadn't been able to fully open up to anyone…until he'd met Dani. He trusted her.

She didn't trust him.

He needed to do something about that and like Serena had so sweetly mentioned the night before, what would keep Dani from moving on with her life with someone else while he was so gallantly giving her time to stop being angry at him?

Later that day, he called his three clients, told them he'd be working from Montana the next few weeks, but everything would proceed on schedule. The next morning he flew out of Chicago into Missoula…in the midst of one of the earliest snowstorms in recent history.

"I'M GLAD YOU decided not to travel today," Dani said to Jolie, cupping the phone against her shoulder as she stared out into the solid mass of white filling her window. "It's practically a whiteout."

"Equally nasty here," her sister said. "But Allie is making hot toddies, so all is well." There was a voice in the background and then Jolie said, "Allie wants to know if you've heard anything new about Kyle's rumored transfer."

"Gina said it was a done deal," Dani said. "And since the café is cop central, she probably knows."

"I hope he goes soon."

So did Dani. That would be one hurdle cleared as far as Allie putting her life on track. With Kyle on the other side of the state, he'd hopefully leave her alone. She was about to say so when a low mechanical groan from the furnace made her jump, then the lights went out.

"Just lost power," she said to Jolie. "I'd better go."

"Hey," Jolie said, "stay in the house."

"No kidding? And here I was going to go make a snowman." She smiled and said, "Goodbye. Enjoy your furnace and electric lights."

She hung up and turned to face her house. Empty. Silent. Lonely.

Kind of like certain aspects of her life.

She walked to the door to call Gus, whom she'd let out just before Jolie called. Dry snow swirled around her when she stepped out onto the porch, stinging her skin as she pulled the door shut behind her.

"Gus!" She hugged her arms around her middle, hunching over as the wind smacked into her. "Gus!" she yelled again, thinking that he couldn't hear her over the wind, but he never strayed too far unless he was hot on the trail of a rabbit. Or deer. She'd seen a few does in the field with the cows when she'd fed them that morning.

The snow pelted against her face as she started toward the gate, calling Gus's name. He had to be in the barn. A deep shiver ran through her and she reversed course, heading back to the house to get her coat and boots. A few minutes later she emerged from the house and headed toward the barn, following Gus's tracks, which were rapidly being obliterated by the snow. She followed them around the barn toward the field where the deer had been pushing snow aside to graze earlier that morning.

Great. Just great.

She checked the barn, in case he'd come back from his adventure and sought shelter. No Gus.

And no Lacy.

The other horses had taken advantage of the windbreak between the barn and the field and were huddled together, but not Lacy.

Dani's temples started to throb. No dog. No horse. Snowstorm.

Squinting against the snow, she could make out a trail leading across the pasture toward the steep part of the creek bank near the road. This couldn't be good. She called the dog one more time, then pulled her knitted cap down lower over her ears and followed the trail across the rapidly drifting snow.

GABE WAS NO slouch at driving in the snow, but when he started bucking some serious drifts on the way to the Staley house, he was glad that he'd ponied up the outrageous extra fee for the last four-wheel-drive vehicle on the rental lot. Even with the four-wheel drive, he wondered if he was going to make it to his house, which was going to be seriously cold and dark.

Cold and dark he could deal with. Dani, on the other hand…

A drift caught his front wheel, pulling the SUV sideways and jerking his attention back to the road. The snow had let up, but the wind was still blowing, whipping snow across the hood of the vehicle, making it difficult to see. The wheels bumped hollowly as he crossed the bridge over Lightning Creek and in the distance he could make out the dark shapes of Dani's barns. Only about a mile to go—

A flash of movement near the creek caught his eye and he slowed. A deer? One of the elusive coyotes?

If so, it was wearing red. He stopped the car and got out, hunching his shoulders against the flurries as he moved around the front of the car. He could no longer see any movement, but he'd definitely seen a flash of red. "Hello?" he shouted into the wind.

There was no response, so he waded through the snow to get closer to the fence, called again as the wind suddenly stopped. The snow settled to the ground in the eerie silence as he strained his ears for a sound, then a blast of wind hit his back, lifting the snow and swirling it around him again with a vengeance. He heard nothing, but during the moment of stillness he'd caught sight of a distinctive black-and-white horse standing near the willows that edged the creek. What was Lacy doing so far from the barn in a blizzard?

He plunged through the snow in the direction of the horse, only to run into the half-buried pasture fence. He struggled through the wire strands, snagging his coat before finally wrenching his way through. Lacy started to move away.

"Lacy!" He wasn't certain why he'd called out. It wasn't as if the horse would stop at his command, but she did. And then he heard Dani yell something indistinguishable.

"Dani?" He started toward the horse and the creek bank.

"Mac?" He could just make out the name before the wind blasted into him.

"Where are you?" He burst out of a drift onto a patch of almost barren ground. Once again the wind relented and he saw Dani hunched in the willows near the creek, Lacy standing close by. And then came the plaintive canine whine. Gus, too.

"Here!" she yelled, looking over her shoulder. Her chin lifted as she recognized him, then she turned back to what had to be Gus. Within a few seconds Gabe was beside her, bending down to help her free her dog from the tangle of branches that had him trapped on the steep overgrown bank.

"I just found him," Dani said through gritted teeth. She held tight to his collar, trying to keep him from sliding farther down the bank and into the water. Gabe threw himself onto his belly at the edge of the six-foot embankment and attempted to wrap his arms around the dog's middle only to find himself sliding toward the rushing waters of the creek himself. Too late to save himself, so he twisted, crashing through the brush and land-ing on his knees with an icy splash. Frigid water blasted through his clothing, filling his low boots, making his breath catch in his lungs. But he managed to keep Gus from sliding in after him.

"Gabe!"

"Hang on," he muttered, adjusting his grip so that he could give a mighty shove. His feet slipped and he went down again, his knees splashing into the freezing water, but he'd managed to push the heavy dog up high enough for Dani to drag him over the edge of the bank. A split second later she reappeared, leaning down to take his hand, but he managed to pull himself up the bank using the broken willow branches. The last thing he was going to do was to pull Dani down into the icy flow.

When he reached the top, she took hold of his arm, steadying as he got his balance on his rapidly numbing feet. And then for a long moment she stared up at him as if trying to make sense of everything—why he was here, how he'd managed to appear out of nowhere.

"Dani…" He reached up to touch her frozen hair but she shook her head, took hold of the arm of his coat and started toward the fence, following the trail he'd broken through the drift, dragging him along behind her.

"Got to get you out of the weather," she muttered.

Gabe's teeth were rattling by the time they

reached the car. The wind cut through his soaked pants, making it difficult to walk on numbing legs. He didn't argue when Dani opened the passenger door and pushed him inside. The blast of heat that met him sent an uncontrollable shudder through his body.

A moment later Gus hefted himself into the backseat and Dani got behind the wheel. She put the SUV in gear and slowly eased it forward. Gabe forced himself to keep his mouth shut and not tell Dani how to get them both safely back to the ranch—as if he could with his teeth chattering against his skull.

THE POWER WAS still off when they got to the house, but there was enough water in the hot-water tank to fill the tub. Dani practically shoved Gabe into the guest bathroom before tossing his small suitcase in after him. She didn't want to talk. Not yet, but he stopped her before she closed the door.

"Are you going out after Lacy?" He was shivering again, but his expression was serious as he added, "Don't go out there alone."

"Lacy's fine. She'll get back on her own." The only reason the mare had been in the field, instead of behind the windbreak with the other horses, was because of Gus, and Dani had seen her heading back across the drifted pasture toward the barn as they'd climbed through the fence. "I'll check her in a bit."

"Not without me."

"Fine."

Gabe studied her for a moment as if ascertaining whether or not she was humoring him, so she put a hand on his chest and pushed him into the room, pulling the door shut behind him.

And then she paced. Through the living room, over to the window, then back to the hall leading to the bathroom and the staircase. Gus was lying on his rug, damp but not injured, his heavy head on his paws, looking as shaken and exhausted as Dani felt. She closed her eyes, holding back tears of relief, anger, frustration...especially frustration.

Gabe wasn't supposed to be back.

She didn't know how to handle him being back.

Once he warmed up, once she was certain he wasn't going to keel over from hypothermia, he was getting into his rental and bucking drifts to his house. His cold house with no electrical power to run the furnace.

She didn't care. Once he warmed up, it was not her affair. She owed him for saving Gus, and saving her from a dunk in the icy creek, yes. But she couldn't have him here. Not now. Not until she got her sense of emotional equilibrium back. Chad had hurt her, but Gabe had crushed her. A knockout punch skillfully delivered after Chad's quick jab.

Dani shrugged off the thought and stoked the fire. The wood was low so she went out for more, dropping a load into the wrought-iron log rest next to the fire. Gabe was here. In her house. He'd appeared out of nowhere, helped her save Gus.

Too. Much.

She pressed her fingers to her forehead just as the bathroom door opened. She looked up to see him appear at the end of the hall, hair damp, glasses on, carrying his suitcase in one hand, his wet clothing in the other.

"Are you warm?" There was a sharp edge to her voice.

"Warm enough." His teeth didn't rattle, so maybe he was telling the truth.

Dani nodded, telling herself that it didn't matter if his face seemed more gaunt, or that his expression seemed almost haunted.

"I should go."

She didn't argue with him, even though part of her wanted to—the part that wanted to lambaste him for not being the man she'd thought he was.

"I see that Gus is okay. Is Lacy back?"

"She is." She'd checked when she'd gone for wood.

He gave a slow nod, then started toward the door, putting down his suitcase just long enough to shrug into his damp coat that had been spread over Dani's chair. He had his hand on the doorknob when she blurted out, "Your tactics suck."

Had she really said that? Had she really just stopped him when he was on the way out her door? Having him there, so close, so damned close…she wanted to rage at him, beat on him, but instead, to her horror, she felt the angry tears coming.

She dropped her gaze, turned away from him, hugging her arms around herself as she fought for control in a way she'd never fought before. Son of a bitch. She would not cry.

"They did."

Past tense? She jerked her gaze up. "*Why* are you back?"

"Why do you think I've come back, Dani? In a snowstorm? To lie to you some more?"

"I thought you didn't lie to me," she said, hating the tone of her voice, but needing to say the words.

"I lied through omission. I'm not going to argue that point. I came here on a mission, to help a guy who'd helped me…a guy who helped me stop destroying my life." He cleared his throat. "As you know, that didn't work out."

What didn't work out? The job or the destroying-his-life part?

Let him go.

"Destroy your life how?" she asked in a low voice.

"A long story, Dani. One I should have told you long ago." He exhaled deeply, his hand still on the doorknob. "I need to go." He meant it. She could see it in the set of his features, the finality in his voice. He needed to get out of there. And she wanted him gone, but…

"You show up out of nowhere, rescue my dog, then disappear into the night." It was both an accusation and a statement of fact, as if she needed to get a handle on everything that had just happened in too short of a period of time.

"Would you have it any other way?"

"I don't know."

His hand fell away from the doorknob, but he stayed where he was, waiting for her to make a final decision.

She swallowed hard, then forced a few more words out. "Did you come back here because of me?"

"Yes."

She took a few paces away from him, toward the stove, feeling the need for warmth, comfort. "I want to hear your story." When he didn't move, she gave him a sharp look over her shoulder. "I think you owe me that. I want to know the motivation behind your actions."

"Would it matter?"

She looked back at the stove, afraid to answer. Afraid the truth might pop out—yes, it might matter. Her heart gave a few quick, stuttering beats when he started walking slowly toward her, his steps echoing on the old flooring. His hand settled on her shoulder and although she stiffened, she didn't shake it off as she might have done only a few minutes before. If anything, she savored the contact for a moment, hating that it felt so right. "I want you to have a reason for what you did, Gabe. A good one."

"I had a reason." She turned to look at him then, drawn by the intensity in his voice. "I thought it was a good one. I thought I was creating a win-win situation for everyone. Or rather, I was doing my best to convince myself of that." Dani had no words; they'd been over this ground. "Stewart Widmeyer kind of saved my life," he said abruptly.

That caught her off guard. "Kind of?" she asked with a frown.

"I'd probably still be alive," he admitted, "but… my life wouldn't be anything like it is today." He let his hand fall away from her shoulder, breaking the connection, making her feel as if he'd just put a couple of miles between them. "I definitely would have spent time in jail."

Dani just barely kept from gaping at his admission. "Jail?"

"I'd dropped out of school, my foster family had kicked me out and I was supporting myself selling weed. Small-time stuff, but I got caught with enough to get me into some serious trouble. Neal Widmeyer was a friend, so I called him for bail money. Stewart came instead."

"You were a small-time hood?" Dani could see it. He had a tough edge under the buttoned-up, logical front he put forth to the world. She walked over to her new sofa and slowly sat down, staring across the room.

"I'm not proud of what I did."

"I'm not judging you." But she was working over this new information, making sense of it.

He looked less than convinced. "Stewart laid things out clearly. He'd bail me out. Hire a lawyer to plead down the offense and eventually get it expunged from my record."

"Generous."

"Yeah."

"Why did he do that? Because you were friends with his son?"

"I don't think so… I don't know." The look on his face, the intensity of his voice as he spoke, ripped at her. She could see that he honestly didn't understand the whys of the situation, didn't know why Widmeyer had helped him. "And there was more to the deal…"

He went on to explain that Stewart had offered to pay tuition for two years of technical school if Gabe managed to finish his GED, and in return, Gabe had to clean up his act. See a counselor. Attend AA. And not associate with Neal until he was clean.

"That part was easy since Neal was starting school at Cornell, but the rest… I had a hell of a time getting myself straight. But I did it because I thought Stewart expected me to fail. Twice I tried to back out of the deal. He called me ball-less. Goaded me into forging on."

"He was playing you?" Dani asked softly.

Gabe gave a slow nod. "I'd say yes to that. So I finished my two-year degree, went on to get a degree in landscape architecture and then an MBA."

"You're a success today because of Widmeyer."

His mouth tightened. "Yes."

"This is a lot to process," she said. And she wished she'd known this earlier. It might have helped her piece things together.

Gabe seemed to follow the direction of her thoughts. "I have a hard time—"

"Talking about your past. I know." She shook her hair back as she looked up at him. "But your past is not you."

"It is now," he said simply and she understood it was because she wasn't going to let go of what he had done in the recent past. "I bought the Staley place to square things with you," he continued. "I thought I could do that and then let things be, but I can't. I miss you in my life. I screwed up the best thing I've ever had by trying not to screw up the other best thing I ever had." He turned his palms out in a resigned gesture. "I don't know what else to say."

Neither did Dani.

Gabe picked up his suitcase, tucked the wet clothing under his arm. "I have to get to my house before it gets dark," he said. "No power, you know."

Dani rose to her feet. "Why didn't you tell me about Widmeyer earlier? After I found out about the land deal?"

"Would you have believed me at that point?" he asked grimly.

"I don't know," Dani said in a low voice.

"Yes, you do."

For one long moment, their gazes held, as if he was waiting for Dani to deny his claim, then when she said nothing—what could she say when he'd spoken the utter truth?—he opened the door and disappeared out into the winter twilight. And all Dani could think as she stared at the beat-up oak door was that it didn't matter if he'd retreated, it didn't matter if she'd been burned—like it or not, this was not over yet.

The big question was how would they find a middle ground? A place of trust after everything that had happened?

CHAPTER TWENTY-ONE

GABE'S SUV DIDN'T make it to his house, but Dani didn't know that until the next morning when she stopped in front of her bedroom window and stared out across the snowy landscape toward the Staley house. When she saw the bright blue vehicle sitting catawampus in the ditch, midway between his place and hers, her heart all but stopped.

If that damned man had frozen to death...

She raced downstairs and found her phone, which was nearly dead thanks to the power outage. Praying that she had enough juice to make a connection, she searched through her previous calls for Gabe's cell number, then tapped the screen. It rang four times and she was already shoving her feet into her boots when he answered.

"You're alive," she blurted.

"What?"

"Your SUV—it's in the ditch."

"Yeah. One drift too many." He sounded drained—like a guy who'd flown from Chicago, driven through a blizzard, rescued a dog from icy waters, then spilled his guts to a woman he professed to care about.

"So...you're okay."

"Pretty much."

Dani exhaled deeply and sank down into a kitchen chair, one boot on, one off, resting her forehead against her palm. "You are ripping me apart," she muttered.

"Dani…"

"I'm coming over." She hung up before he could answer and when her phone rang, she ignored it.

The overhead light came on as she started up the staircase and after a deep groan the furnace roared to life. A sign?

Maybe.

She dressed in jeans and a sweater, jammed her feet back into her snow boots. She started to braid her hair, then abandoned the process after screwing it up twice.

Damn it, her hands were shaking. And she felt close to tears. *If he had frozen to death…*

She pulled her wool cap on, grabbed her gloves and headed out the door. It took a few tries to get the tractor started, and then she let it warm up for several minutes before putting it in gear and driving it out of the barn. She got off to close the door, then once again started chugging toward the Staley house and…she didn't know what.

The only plus was she was remarkably well rested—after resigning herself to a long night staring at the ceiling and thinking deep thoughts, she'd fallen into an exhausted sleep almost as soon as she'd crawled into her chilly bed. The knowl-

edge that Gabe had had a reason for his actions
had given her a sense of peace she hadn't expected. A sense of hope. He'd had a reason that
went deeper than simply doing his job. A reason
that had probably tied him in knots as his relationship with her had progressed.

Yes, he could have told her, but he hadn't and
she understood him well enough now to know it
was more than because she wouldn't have believed
him. He was still ashamed of his life before Stewart Widmeyer had thrown him a lifeline, despite
being the guy he was now—the guy she'd fallen
in love with. They'd work on that.

As she approached his vehicle, she saw him
heading down the road toward her, hands shoved
deeply into his pockets, head down against the
cold. He looked up as she maneuvered the tractor
around the Toyota and stopped in front of it and
she thought she may have caught a hint of a smile.

She wasn't certain, though.

And, yes, her hands were still shaking a little.

She climbed down off the tractor and started
toward him through the snow, stopping when he
was still a few feet away. She must have imagined the smile, because he was once again walled
off.

"You are not going to rest until you pull a bum-
per off one of my vehicles, are you?" He spoke
matter-of-factly, but she could read the uncertainty

in his eyes. He was playing this cool, as was she, neither certain of the other.

She shrugged. "I was thinking more like the axle."

"I bought the insurance," he said. "It seemed like a good move with the blizzard and all, but again, I don't think I'm covered for this."

"You might have a little faith in me," she said, waiting a beat before she added, "Just as I'm going to have some faith in you."

"Dani…"

"I never properly thanked you for saving Gus."

"No need." He shoved his hands more deeply in his pockets, but his eyes never left her face.

Silence fell between them, making Dani all the more aware of the bitter cold biting at her cheeks. Finally she said, "I'm scared to death, Gabe."

"You, too?" She nodded. "What are you afraid of?" His voice was low, almost a growl.

"Losing a chance to start over. With you."

He frowned at her, as if wondering if he'd heard her correctly. She tilted her chin sideways as a look of dawning hope flashed in his gray eyes. And then he was moving toward her. Dani did not hesitate, did not analyze, did not fear. Her guy was alive. He was with her. She threw herself into his embrace and he closed his arms around her, holding her tightly against his chest, pressing his cheek against the top of her head as she inhaled deeply, drawing in his scent. Home. She was home.

"I just want a chance to be the guy you thought I was." He murmured the words against her temple, his breath warm on her face, and Dani realized she was still shaking and it wasn't from cold. He held her for a few more seconds, then leaned back to tip up her chin to take her lips in a heartbreakingly sweet kiss.

Dani slid her hands up around his neck, pushing aside the thick collar of his coat, needing to be closer to him. This was the guy she loved. This was the real Gabe.

When he finally lifted his head, he took her face between his gloved palms and said, "No more secrets, Dani. No more omissions. Ever. We start fresh here. Now. And we will build something strong between us."

Dani raised her lips to touch his once again.

She believed him.

Five months later

"I DON'T KNOW that breeding Lacy makes sense." Gabe put down the pen he'd been holding and settled his forearms on the kitchen table.

"There are a lot of things in this life that don't make sense," Dani replied with a half smile, "but we do them anyway." She leaned across the table toward him, watched the shift in his expression as his gaze dropped to her lips. "But in this case, it makes sense. She has excellent breeding. She shouldn't pass her issues along to her get…she had a sweet personality before Len Olsen had his way with her."

"Are you going to be able to sell a baby after what happened to Lacy?"

"You can't let one incident color your life," she said. "I'd have concerns, but there are lots of people out there who give their horses wonderful lives. Look at how well Molly landed."

"I have to admit that was the first time I've ever received holiday greetings from a horse." The Christmas card was still attached to his refrigerator with a magnet three months later.

Dani reached for his hand. He threaded his fingers through hers. "I think it's a good idea."

She smiled and squeezed his fingers. It was her decision, but she liked bouncing things off him, talking through her concerns and he had started doing the same, albeit slowly. He'd even asked for her input on making a final decision before taking a bury-the-hatchet contract from Stewart, wanting to make certain it didn't bother her if he worked for the guy who'd threatened her with a water park. Dani didn't know that she would ever warm up to Stewart and Serena, but she loved Neal and understood that Stewart was the closest thing to a father that Gabe had ever had.

He'd therefore be the closest thing to a father-in-law that she would have.

Dani could live with that.

Gabe's thumb moved over her wrist, sending a tingle of anticipation shooting through her, and she fought a smile as she met his eyes. "Are we done?" she asked, indicating the business plan they'd been working through prior to the Lacy discussion.

"For now." There was a wealth of promise in those spoken words.

Dani stood and Gabe followed, his hand sliding up her arm as he leaned in to kiss her. "My place or yours?" Dani asked against his lips. Dani had continued to live at the Lightning Creek with Jolie while Gabe traveled back and forth to Chicago, finishing his contract with Widmeyer Enterprises. "Jolie isn't due home for at least an hour."

"Mine," Gabe said, touching her forehead with his. "We'll take the business plan with us."

"The plan?" Dani asked with a lift of her eyebrows.

"Well…we'll need something to do."

Dani laughed and pulled him closer, showing him exactly what they would be doing. "Gabe," she said in a patient tone. "There's a time for plans and there's a time for action. At this particular point in time…I vote for action."

* * * * *

Look out for the next
BRODYS OF LIGHTNING CREEK *book,*
Jolie's story, coming later this year from
Jeannie Watt and Harlequin Superromance!